A Woman Walking

NANCY KING

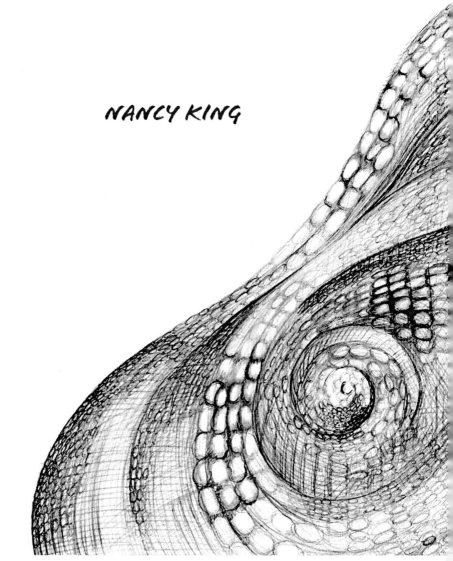

First Edition.

Editing by Cinny Green, THEMA, Ideas in Print.
Cover Illustration, Interior Illustration, and Book Design
by Maureen Burdock, THEMA, Ideas in Print.

Printed by Lightning Source, International, St. Louis, MO, USA

www.nancykingstories.com

10 9 8 7 6 5 4 3 2 1

TABLE OF CONTENTS

INTRODUCTION

"Something weird is happening," I told the man sitting behind the desk.

"How is it weird?" he asked.

"I can't explain. It's a kind of pressure in my head but it's not a headache."

"Something wants to get out. Go home. Go to your desk. Write whatever comes to your fingers. Don't worry about making sense. Just let it come."

I was too afraid of what might come out to act on his suggestion until one day, after a painful phone call, instead of hiding under the covers, I sat down and wrote the title, "The Birth of the Storyteller." About twelve pages materialized. None of what I wrote had anything to do with the phone call, yet afterward I felt exhausted and peaceful.

About a week later, after a fierce argument with my mother, I felt the same curious sensation in my head. I sat down and wrote the title, "The Well," and wrote about fifteen pages. This time the young woman in the story had a name. I showed the material to a friend while I was in London, and she asked, "What happens next?"

I had no idea.

The next five episodes also popped out without conscious thought or planning, a process I didn't understand until I began to explore the idea of "popping out stories" in my book, *Dancing With Wonder: Self-Discovery Through Stories*, published in 2005 (www.nancykingstories.com).

Eventually I came to a critical place. Without knowing it, I had worked the character, Ninan, into an inward spiral where there was increasingly less space in which she could travel. The man behind the desk suggested I think of a way to move the spiral up and out, to give Ninan new possibilities. At this point I did not know how to consciously start a story but a painful encounter with a person I thought was my friend sent me reeling to my desk. The title, "Gathering Strength" spurred me to move in a new direction.

What astonished me was that none of the writing or the stories Ninan told related to what I was experiencing in my life, yet each bit of writing eased my mental anguish. Initially, the novel ended with Ninan ready to reclaim her grandfather's book and her grandmother's shawl. However, my editor said she found the ending, "unsatisfying," which somehow made me laugh. When she suggested I write a new chapter, I worried that after so much time between the original ending and a possible new ending, I wouldn't be able to write another "popping out" story. She shook her head and said, "Of course you can."

She was right.

ONE
BIRTH OF THE STORYTELLER

In a time long ago, in a place far away, in a small village near the edge of a large lake, there lived a husband and wife who spent their days caring for their seven sons, farming the land, milking the few cows that managed to survive the barren hillsides, and collecting scraps of wood to burn for cooking and warmth.

When soldiers came, ransacking the village for food and young men to serve in the army, the couple hid their children, keeping them safe from the marauders. Despite the parent's care, when sickness ran as rampant through the village as a river rushes towards the sea, all of the couple's seven sons died. In time, a daughter was born, small and weak, yet she lived. Growing up, the girl felt the sorrow and despair of her parents, the loss of their sons, the burden of being their only surviving child.

For many years, the small family lived their lives, each day much like the next. One night, as they gathered for their evening meal, the old parents seemed more fragile and troubled than usual. At last their daughter broke the thick silence. "Why did you tell the butcher I could not marry him?" The parents turned away from her and from each other. She waited for them to speak; the stillness felt unbearable.

"It is not possible," replied her father.

"We have tried to find another way. There is none," responded her mother.

"What is wrong? Surely you can tell me what is bothering you. We have been through many difficult times together," urged their daughter.

"These troubles are not to be shared with a young girl," said her father.

"Girls my age and younger are married, with children of their own," she said bitterly. "I want to marry the butcher."

"We do not need to talk about this."

"Yes, Papa, we do."

"The matter is closed," he said sharply. Looking at his wife, his eyes silently pleaded for her help.

Her mother spoke with difficulty. "Perhaps the time has come to talk. Our sons, your brothers, are dead. Only you, our daughter, lives to do what must be done." Once again there was a long, heavy silence. Tears filled the old woman's eyes. She opened her mouth to speak but no words came. Her husband's eyes were full of pain.

The young woman looked at her parents, who seemed to be slipping away from her even as she watched. "Please," she begged, "let me ease your burdens."

Her father stood up, quietly crying, looking at the woman who had been his wife and companion for more years than he could remember. He turned to his daughter. "You do not know what you ask."

"I will never know unless you tell me."

"She is right, husband, it is time. We can wait no longer."

With difficulty, the old man walked to the far corner of the room where he opened a small door in a cupboard, removing a piece of dark red cloth, the remnant of an old dress. Slowly, he made his way to the table where his wife and daughter sat. Carefully spreading out the cloth, he hesitated for a moment, as if to gather strength. Before moving, he took a deep breath and then returned to the corner, pried up two loose floorboards and took out a dark wooden box that he put on the cloth. Struggling to keep going, his heart as heavy as his legs were old, he walked back to the corner and removed a large brown sack of loosely woven material and an old book. He handled them reverently, as if they were too valuable to touch, gently placing them on the red cloth. Lost in time, he stood staring at them, as if remembering when he first saw them.

A sudden noise made him jump. Moving as fast as he could, he put the loose boards back in place, then picked up the book and hid it under his shirt. Holding it to his chest, he watched the door, ready to defend his treasures against all odds. "Do not open the door!" he whispered.

Despite her father's protest, his daughter opened it, looked out, and then closed the door gently. "It is the wind, Papa. The wind blew down a branch." The old man went to the door and listened until he was satisfied all was well.

Only then did he move to the table cradling the objects, reluctant to put them down. He looked at them for a long time, not ready to face his daughter.

"Speak, Papa, please," she urged.

"Husband, she is right. We must tell her everything, now, before it is too late."

The old man cleared his throat, and even then there was an agonizing silence before he spoke. "My father was a storyteller. My mother told me about his life, how he walked from village to village, telling stories of what was, what had been, and what might yet be. People looked forward to his storytelling because he was so full of joy and life. Yet even his goodness could not protect him." The old man hesitated. "Perhaps there is no need to tell this story."

"You must, husband. She needs to know what happened."

The old man nodded, still reluctant to speak. "One night, as he was walking past a small stream, my father heard cries for help and rushed to where the sounds were coming from. A group of young men were battering a woman, trying to force her to the ground. My father yelled at them to stop, but when they saw him, they attacked, beating him savagely. The young woman tried to help fend off the attackers but the men knocked her down. My father kept fighting though there were too many against him. Soon, he felt nothing. A deep, thick, blackness descended upon him.

"When my father awoke, the bright sun hurt his eyes. His body ached. His tongue felt thick and useless. He tried to sit up but collapsed. He tried to call out, but made no sound. Helpless, he lay waiting to die, hoping the end would soon come.

"Yet this was not to be. The woman, who had survived the attack by hiding in the bushes until the men had gone, stayed to help the man who had saved her life. She wiped his forehead with cool wet cloths, fed him the small amounts of food he could swallow. She cared for him, tenderly putting drops of water on his lips, bathing his wounds, healing his injuries. She would not help him lose his unwilling battle with life and death. For many days he lay by the side of the stream, hidden in the bushes.

"Although he could feel his strength return as the pain lessened, no matter how he tried, he could make no sound. The words in his head refused to live in the world. The young woman comforted him. 'I can see you are growing stronger. You will soon be walking.'

"This was no comfort. Without the ability to speak, he could not tell stories. The pain in his body was nothing compared to the pain in his heart. Despair washed over him like a river overflowing its banks. One day, when the woman went to gather food, my father tied heavy rocks around his waist and threw himself into the deepest part of the stream.

"As she was picking berries nearby, the woman sensed something was wrong and rushed back in time to jump in the water to save him. My father cursed her with his soundless words, fighting against her help, silently screaming to let him die, but his silence sent no message and her will that he should live was stronger than his despair. She loosened the rope that held the rocks and he floated, unable to sink back into the depths. Struggling with his weight, she brought him to the edge of the stream and held him close. Lovingly, she embraced him, forcing the water from his body, out of his mouth. When the breath of life filled him, she half carried, half dragged him from the stream and gently sat him in the sun so he could feel its warmth.

"She gave him food to eat and water to drink, cradling him at night when terror struck his body, offering comfort as she sang him songs she had learned as a child. Time passed.

"One day, the woman decided it was time to leave. 'You are strong enough to walk. Let us go to the nearest village and look for work and a place to stay.' Without waiting for him to respond, the woman picked up their few possessions, took his cold hand in her warm hand, and led him safely past the stones and ruts that lay on their path. When they came to the village, people greeted him, remembering his wonderful stories. They did not understand why he turned his head in shame. 'We need a place to say for the night,' said the woman. 'My husband has been ill.' The villagers led them to a small hut and bid them welcome.

"When the woman heard he was a storyteller, she could think of nothing else as she watched him, tossing and turning, too angry to look at her. Quietly, with more calm than she felt, she said, 'I will soon return. Have a good sleep.'

"To my father, it seemed as if he had been abandoned, that he had nothing left to live for. He closed his eyes and waited for death. When he woke and felt her loving hand caress his cheek, he realized she had returned to him. He felt a faint stirring of life.

"She spoke so softly he could barely hear her. 'It is likely you will never again

tell stories as you have done in the past, but still, the stories are inside you. You have eyes with which to see, and ears with which to hear. Teach me your stories. I will learn to tell them for you.'

"The pain of never telling another story was so great my father turned his back on the woman who had nursed him back to life. He refused to think about this new and unbearable form of storytelling, but she knew he had lost his gift fighting to save her and refused to allow him to give up. Her eyes followed his turned back. Her heart met his hostile eyes with loving looks. Her spirit refused to hear his wordless *no* and *not* and *never*, insisting on *yes* and *can* and *will*. The time came when he had no more energy to fight her. He stopped turning away. Fury gave way to resignation and wonder. With eyes full of questions, his wild gesticulation confronted her. How was he going to teach her stories if he could not talk? Triumphantly, she put into his hand a small stick that she had sharpened and burned into a fine point. Suddenly she wondered what she would do if he did not know how to write what he had only spoken. She dared not breathe; she was afraid the slightest movement would disrupt her plan. Then slowly, painfully slowly, the man put the point into the earth, and when he stopped, too weary to continue, my mother read what he had written.

"Her intonation was flat. The words, carefully sounded out, were separate, like beads of water with no relationship, one to the other. He groaned, angry that he had let himself be drawn into her hope and dream. Yet she persisted, finding rhythm, making sense of what was there, adding words when she lost his. Her actions infuriated him. He was afraid that soon she would not need his words.

"He stormed out of the hut and hurled his wordless rage to the wind. She watched, her heart heavy, knowing this was a battle only he could fight. Only he could win. In the early hours of the new day, with the dew soothing his parched soul, he made his way back to her. The two of them wept until he fell asleep dreaming of stories.

"He woke to find the woman had once again disappeared. Feeling a terrible sense of loss, my father wrote feverishly, making marks in the earth knowing only the words could keep him sane. He was sleeping when she returned and she did not wake him. When he awoke and saw her watching him, he waited, staring at her. She took an old book out of a brown sack. 'I found this book of empty pages. We will use it for your stories.' My father often wondered how she came upon it

because books were rare and valuable, but he dared not inquire and she offered no explanation. They kept the book in the brown sack and never let anyone else ever see it.

"Although he was afraid she might say no, one night by the light of the campfire, he wrote in the sand, 'Will you marry me?' When she said yes, with no hesitation, a heavy weight lifted from his heart. The ceremony was simple, with just a few villagers and the rabbi present, yet it was enough to give him hope that he could still be a storyteller, though not as he used to be. Never again as he used to be.

"Using the burnt end of the stick to write, my father wrote for many days in the book of empty pages, barely able to sleep or eat. The torrent of words turned to a trickle then stopped. Then, he gave her the book with his stories and began to teach them to her. His wife, my mother, watched carefully as he showed her how to use her eyes and hands, when to pause to let a thought sink deeper into the hearts of those who listened, and when to speak quickly, urging the audience to keep pace with the action. She was a good student, learning faster than he could have imagined. And, when the time came, when she told him his stories, one by one, as if she had known them forever, he was unable to restrain his pleasure.

"That evening, they joined a group of villagers resting in the market place after the long day's work. When the man beckoned the villagers to sit, to listen, the woman began, carefully forming her words until the power of the story overwhelmed her hesitation. The villagers listened with rapt attention, absorbed by the intensity of the woman's telling. When the story ended, there was a joyful response and they begged for another, but the woman was tired. 'We will return,' she promised, 'but now we must rest.'

"As my father and mother made their way back to the hut, an old woman hobbled up to my mother, holding a dark wooden box in her hands. Opening it, she took out an exquisitely embroidered shawl made of fine wool. 'Please, it is cold. Your clothes are thin. Take this shawl for your own. It will keep you warm.'

"'It is very beautiful but we have no money to pay you for it,' protested my mother.

"'Hearing your story is payment enough.' The old woman held out the box until my father accepted it. She draped the shawl around my mother's shoulders. Holding one hand of my father and one hand of my mother, the old woman spoke. 'You must tell your stories wherever you go for you have a great gift. Do not stop.

We need to hear your stories. Promise me you will never stop telling your stories.' She squeezed their hands hard as they stood before her, giving her the promise she demanded. Satisfied, the old woman disappeared into the darkness.

"My father saved a woman's life, and she in turn saved my father's life. Their love grew as their lives entwined. They spent their days traveling from village to village, he writing down what he saw, she telling what he could not speak. I was their only child and learned the story I have told you when I was a boy. When they grew old and tired, I took them into my home, knowing it was my turn to care for them."

"What does all this mean? Why tell me this story now?" asked his daughter.

Her mother answered. "Most young women your age marry and have children, families to tend and care for. This is what they know and this is what is right. We used to dream that one day all our children would marry and we would have grandchildren, but your brothers died. Only you can honor the tradition of your ancestors. It is your duty to take this book, given to you from your grandmother and grandfather. It is your inheritance. Keep their knowledge and memory alive. Walk from village to village telling their stories. Our people need to remember what happened in the past. So many of our elders and storytellers died in the years of sickness and in the times when soldiers came and destroyed our villages. If the living do not hear the stories, they will forget where they came from. How will they know who they are?"

Her mother spoke softly for her sadness was almost too much to bear. "It is a hard life, being a storyteller, one we hoped you would not have to live. Your oldest brother told stories when he was a young child, just as you did when you were his age. We put our trust in him to carry on the tradition, to tell our people the stories of our ancestors, but this was not to be."

Her father continued in a voice wracked with grief. "This is why we kept you from visiting with young people in the village. This is why we have prevented you from marrying. There is no one else to tell the stories. I had no gift for storytelling although I tried. In shame and sorrow I have kept this book all these years, not knowing what to do. Now it is you who must walk in the steps of your grandparents. Your mother and I know you have inherited my parents' gift. We have heard you talk with villagers who come to visit. We have seen how they listen. You understand their pain and suffering. The spirit in your words helps give them

the courage to hope. It is true that this is not a life we would have wished for you, my daughter, but it is what must be."

"Am I never to have a husband of my own? No man to love and cherish? Will I never cradle my own child?" asked their daughter.

Her mother glanced quickly at her father. "Men do not follow women. A husband does not willingly sit in the shadow while his wife sits in the light, attentive eyes upon her, grateful for her words and wisdom."

"Perhaps I will be lucky and meet such a man."

"Perhaps," replied her mother sadly, knowing in her heart this was unlikely.

The daughter closed her eyes and thought of the young people in the village, remembering times when she heard their laughter and songs, felt the strong arms of the butcher as he held her high in the air when they danced to celebrate the harvest. She tried to see herself walking alone, down endless roads, always sitting at the hearths of strangers, calling no bed her own. Shivering, though she was not cold, she spoke in anger. "Who will *make* me do this?" she snapped, rebellion pushing out her words.

Her father opened the dark box and took out the shawl, threadbare and faded, yet still beautiful. "Wear this when you tell your stories. It will keep you warm when you are cold and comfort you when you feel lonely. When you tell the stories in this book, know that you are helping our people to remember our past, the wisdom of our sages. This is why we taught you to read and write, to make stories of what you see and hear."

"You have always been a child with questions," said her mother. "You will start with your grandfather's stories and you will always tell them, but I know there will come a time when they will not be completely satisfying. To keep your spirit free and vital, you will have to discover your own stories, using your senses, your eyes and ears and tongue, just as your grandfather and grandmother used theirs."

"It is your burden and your privilege," said her father.

"And if I choose not to do this?" challenged their daughter. "What if I run away? What if I find a husband? Who will make me tell these stories?"

"If you attempt such foolishness, your husband will die. Your children will not flourish. You cannot escape your fate," said her mother in a harsh tone of voice, sharper than her daughter had ever heard.

"Who says this is my fate? Who says this must be?" the daughter cried out.

"You alone of all our children have survived. You, the smallest and weakest,

are the only one left to tell the stories. You are the only one who remembers."

"I remember nothing. Reading words in an old book does not make me a storyteller. I want a husband and children, just as you have had. Do not curse me. Give me your blessing," she pleaded. Her parents wept with her but said nothing.

She thought to stand up, to leave the table and their cottage, but her feet would not move. Her mother put the book of stories into her hands. Her father gently draped the shawl around her shoulders. Together they placed the wooden box in front of her, helping her up, giving her the little strength they had, quietly feeling the power of her struggle rise and fall, then disappear. Her parents' looks, full of love and anguish and care moved her. She heard herself agree to do as they said she must.

Her mother brought hot tea. The three drank in silence. When their cups were empty, the parents kissed their daughter lovingly and went to bed. She watched them, despair and fear mingling with pride and anger.

In the morning, she brought their breakfast tea, as usual, but dropped the tray when she saw them nestled in each other's arms, dead. Tenderly she laid them out, covering their bodies with plain white cloth. For several hours she sat by their bodies, singing the songs and psalms for the dead, reluctant to take the next step, knowing she could not delay much longer. With a heavy heart, she forced herself to walk to the rabbi and told him of her need. When he arrived at dusk, he found the old husband and wife carefully wrapped in mourning cloth, in an empty cottage, with no sign of their daughter, their only living child.

The villagers buried the couple according to their custom. The women of the village prepared a small supper, waiting until dark for the daughter to return. For seven days and seven nights the villagers sat in the cottage, grieving the death of their neighbors. For days afterward they watched, waiting for the young woman to return to her birthplace. Wondering where she was. Questioning whether they would ever see her again.

In time the villagers went back to their homes and their lives and found new events to think about. But they never had cause to talk about the daughter for no one from the village ever saw her again. It was rumored that a young woman had been seen wandering from place to place, telling stories of the old times and the new, but no one from her village, not even the butcher, knew if she was Aryeh, daughter of the old couple who lived by the lake.

Waiting until sundown so that she would not be seen, the young woman debated whether to stay and marry the butcher or leave and tell stories as she had promised her parents. Her mother and father were dead, she told herself, they would never know, no matter what she chose to do. But she would know she had broken her promise, and she sensed this could haunt her the rest of her life. So even as Aryeh yearned to lie in the butcher's arms, she forced herself not to think of his strong body twined with hers as they stood in the sunlight on the top of the mountain. Wrapping the book in her father's shirt, she packed a sack with the book, the shawl, and food. Before trudging up the dusty path that led out of the village, she took one last grief-filled look at what had been her home and family. Unable to comprehend the sudden changes in her life, she walked slowly, filled with the pain of leaving, mourning the loss of the only life she had known, feeling the anguish of not being present for the burial of her parents. She stared at the road in front of her, wondering where to go. How to begin? What to say?

After she started walking, Aryeh's sorrow made stopping impossible. She walked all night into the next morning. At last, too tired to go further, she sank into the cool grass by the side of the road, carefully put down the sack, and leaned her back against the trunk of a huge old tree. She slept for many hours until evening dew wet her face, waking her up, reminding her of her need for shelter. Not wanting to talk to anyone, she picked up her possessions and looked for an abandoned hut or cave in which she might find refuge from animals and people who roamed in the night.

Aryeh walked for almost an hour in the growing darkness. The sun had just gone down behind the furthest mountain when she came to a farm that looked abandoned. She imagined wild beasts or dangerous men. The closer she came, the stronger was her fear. Although she mocked her worries and called herself foolish, she could not bring herself to stop at the hut's promised shelter, and continued to walk until it was so dark she was grateful for the light of the moon. The road suddenly dipped and led to a curve near the bend of a river. Just off the road she saw a cluster of bushes that looked as if they could provide a bit of shelter. Relieved, she walked to them and nestled among the leafy limbs where she ate her last piece of bread and cheese. Tomorrow, she would have to find work. Too tired to make a fire, she covered herself with the threadbare shawl and slowly fell into an uneasy sleep.

Aryeh dreamed she was standing in front of her grandfather, in a large room full of people. He was trying to speak to her but there was so much noise she could not hear what he was saying. She kept asking him to tell her what it was he wanted her to know, but no matter how he shouted, the sounds of people talking deafened her and his words remained unheard. She started to cry and tried to pull him out of the room, but he would not move. He kept repeating his message as the noise increased and the room grew more crowded.

She woke up sobbing, "Please, Grandfather, come out of this room with me. I want to hear what you are saying." She looked around and saw no one. She sensed the spirit of her grandfather had been trying to tell her something important, information she needed to know. Lying back down, Aryeh closed her eyes, hoping her vision might continue, but the dream had stopped. Finally, she picked herself up, gathered her things, and made her way back to the road.

Tired and upset by the dream, she paid little attention to where she was going. One road was as good as another; all roads must lead somewhere, she thought. As the sun rose, Aryeh noticed she was no longer alone. The road was slowly filling with people, all bringing goods to a market near a village nestled at the foot of a large mountain. No one paid any attention to her nor did she ask anything of those passing by, yet she was filled with an unknown sense of excitement. Following the increasing flow of villagers, she was content to be one among many. For the first time since the loss of the butcher and the death of her parents she found herself curious about the lives of the people who were walking on the road with her. She wondered what stories they might want to hear.

It was not until Aryeh reached the market and smelled freshly baked breads, savory meats broiling over fires, and roasting corn, that she realized how hungry she was. She dared not spend the few coins she had so she walked around, looking for a way to earn money or food. When she passed an old woman who was struggling to put up a bright cloth, she spoke with more cheer than she felt. "Good morning, madam."

"Be on your way, miss. I have work to do."

Aryeh tried again and again but no one needed help for coins or food. She sat by the edge of the road, listening to her stomach growl, wondering what to do next. Perhaps there is a well nearby, she thought. She was thirsty as well as hungry and at least the water would be free. The thought cheered her, and she began looking for it, walking down muddy lanes and well-worn paths, hesitant to ask and call attention to herself. At last, unable to find the well, she forced herself to speak to a shoemaker resting from his labors, smoking a pipe. "Good day, sir. I am hungry and thirsty. Might you know of someone needing work in exchange for food, and would you be so kind as to tell me where the town well is?"

"I can give you work and water to drink, but finding the town well, that is a different matter," he said, puffing on his pipe.

"Why is that?" Aryeh asked.

"There is no town well."

"No town well?" repeated the young woman. "How is this possible?"

"A long time ago, a band of soldiers attacked the village, demanding food and shelter. They ate everything in sight, taking their pleasures where they found them. When the townspeople protested and rebelled, as punishment, the soldiers filled the well with garbage and rocks and covered it over with dirt. The townspeople were too frightened to uncover the well and repair the damage until the soldiers left the next spring. By that time, it was too late; the well water smelled of garbage. No one could stand the taste."

"Did they never dig another well?"

"Oh yes," responded the old man, "but they never found water as clear and cool as the water in the first well. And they dug small wells, never another well big

enough for the whole town to use. Now, when soldiers come, there is no village well for them to destroy."

"But has no one looked at the old well since then?" asked the young woman. "Perhaps the water is clear now. Perhaps it could be used again."

"It is no use," said the old man. "The devastation happened so long ago no one remembers where it was. Those who knew have long since died or forgotten all about it." He tamped down the tobacco in his pipe, looking thoughtful.

"But if someone did remember where it was, would this help to find it?"

"It might," he admitted, "but there is little point in looking for something that was destroyed so many years ago. Here," he said, giving her a slice of thick dark bread and a piece of cheese, "have something to eat while I finish putting the heel on this shoe."

As she ate, forcing herself to eat slowly so he would not see how hungry she was, she watched the old man work. On the top of the shoe, she noticed an unusual design in the leather. The pattern looked familiar. "I have never seen such wonderful carving on shoes," admired the young woman.

"It is nice, if I do say so myself," admitted the old man modestly. "I learned to do this from my father who learned it from his father. I believe there have been shoemakers in my family as far back as memory."

Aryeh kept staring at the shoe. She knew she had seen the design before but could not remember where. "What you have carved reminds me of dancing flowers."

The old man laughed with pleasure. "And you remind me of a young man who used to come here a very long time ago, when I was first beginning to make shoes. He would sit, just as you are sitting now, and watch me work for as long as I would let him. Never had money to buy any goods but he liked to sit and watch. After awhile he would tell me a story. Before I knew it, there would be a whole crowd of people listening to him while I worked. We finally convinced him to tell his stories in the evening, when everyone could listen. Then people fed him, gave him a place to sleep, and, once in a while, a coin or two."

"What did he look like, this storyteller?" asked Aryeh. "Did he travel alone or did he have a wife? Did he have children?"

"Not that I remember. He was a young fellow, tall, with reddish blonde hair and dark brown eyes, friendly, though they were always watching. Taking everything in like whatever he saw or heard would become part of a new story. He kept all he owned in a sack that he threw over his shoulders when he was ready to leave. Whistled real pretty."

"What happened to him?"

"No one knows," answered the old man. "He used to appear, regularly, like the birds in spring, but then he stopped coming. We never saw him again. Pity. He was a fine storyteller, told stories like no one else. Couldn't stop listening if you tried."

"My grandfather was a storyteller," said the young woman shyly.

"And you? Do you tell stories?"

Aryeh blushed, unable to say no, embarrassed and uncomfortable.

"Well now," said the old man, "it has been a long time since I heard a story. It would please me greatly if you told me one while I work, just as the storyteller used to do. I have sorely missed his stories." The old man settled down waiting for the young woman to begin.

As she started to speak, Aryeh remembered where she had seen the design on the shoes. It was in the book of stories. Her grandfather had drawn the pattern on a page. She quickly took the book out of the sack and found the drawing.

"Look," she said, excitedly pointing. "Just like your shoes."

"So they are," replied the old man, intrigued. "How do you come to have this book?"

"It was my grandfather's book," she answered. "The storyteller you described must have been my grandfather." She stared at the old man, amazed. "You knew my grandfather."

"What is written near the drawing?" asked the old man. "I cannot read."

She read the words next to the design, and then said, "My grandfather tells of meeting a wonderful shoemaker who carves a design which looks like dancing flowers on the tops of the shoes he makes."

"Does he say more?"

"He writes about the sparkling water which bubbled out of the town well, so cool and refreshing it could quench the thirst of a person most parched." The two fell silent.

The old man remembered the young man's joy and charm. Aryeh thought about the story her father had told her about how her grandfather met her grandmother. Remembered her dream. She looked at the book and continued to read until she stopped, gasping for breath.

"What is the matter?" asked the old man, startled.

"It is here, in the book."

"What is in the book?"

"The place where the well was. I know we can find the well if we follow the writings of my grandfather." She stared at the pages.

"It is no use. The water would not be good," said the old shoemaker.

"How do you know? After all this time the water might be just as my grandfather described it," she insisted. "We harm no one by trying to find it."

"Where are we supposed to look? How will we know where to dig?" asked the old man.

"I will read my grandfather's words. You can tell me where to start." Aryeh's enthusiasm was contagious.

"Very well, but first I must finish this shoe. Tell me what your grandfather wrote about the well."

The young woman read, "'My favorite place to stop was a town with a large well that had the cleanest, coldest water for miles around. It was a short walk from the center of the town near a clearing.'" Her voice filled with emotion. "Is this a place to start?"

"No. It is no help at all," said the shoemaker. "The town has grown since your grandfather was a young man. His words cannot guide us to what is no longer here."

Ignoring him, Aryeh continued to read to herself. Then she asked, "Is there a large tree with a curve in its trunk? The well was quite near the tree. Grandfather says he used to lean against the tree and drink the water, feeling as if he were the richest man in the world."

The old shoemaker searched his memory before speaking. "Perhaps if we walk towards the end of the village I might remember something. It all happened so long ago. Does he write anything else that might help us find where it was?"

The young woman blushed as she read, "'It is hot and I sit against this tree watching the prettiest girl in the village milk her goats. I hope that if I look hungry enough she will take pity and offer me fresh goat's milk or perhaps some cheese she has made from it. As she passes, I smile. And hope. Ah, she is looking my way. I will look very weary.'"

"Hmm," grinned the old man, "I don't think that will be of much help. Does he offer any other clues?"

She read the pages as quickly as she could. The faded writing was small and the words were difficult to decipher. "There is something about a view of the mountain. I think he writes that it looks like a bird in flight. Is this possible?"

The old shoemaker nodded. "I think I know the place, but I am not sure. It has been so many years since I even thought about the well."

"Let us go there," she begged.

The shoemaker carefully cleaned his tools, put them in a large basket, and then led her to a grove that was just outside the center of the village where he peered at a mountain range in the distance. They stopped in the midst of a small clearing. On the edge of it were many trees; some so old they looked as if the mere whisper of a wind would bring them to the ground. The young woman ran up to them, inspecting their trunks for the curve, sitting down, looking around, yearning to find the view her grandfather described. Seeing nothing, she asked the old man, "Do you remember anything about the well? Think about the times you used to drink from it. There must be something in your memory that could help us." Her pleading look was more than the old man could bear. "I would so love to drink from the well my grandfather drank from."

"Well, I know it was a long walk from where we lived," answered the shoemaker. "But then I was young and my legs were tired after finishing all my chores."

"Think!" Aryeh pleaded. "How did you get to the well? What was it like? Did you have to step up to it? Was there a dipper?"

The old man shook his head then stopped. "Wait, I do remember one thing. It was hidden in a place no one would ever think to look. The soldiers followed us everywhere, hoping to trick us into revealing the well's hiding place. In the end, they only found it because one day a child forgot to do as he was told and a soldier saw him take water from the well."

He looked around, trying to find something that seemed familiar. "I think it was near a rock. A huge boulder." The two searched but all they found was a rather small rock, flattened by time. The young woman stood on top of the rock and was about to jump off when she thought she heard a sound. Her heart pounded with excitement. Jumping down, she started to dig away layers of leaves and debris buried around the stone but found no trace of dampness, no sign of water. She stopped digging and listened, trying to find the source of the sound.

"What is it?" asked the old man. "Why do you dig there? You will never find the well near that little rock. We are looking for a boulder, remember?"

"This is a little rock now, but a long time ago it might have been bigger. Perhaps the years have covered it with leaves and dirt."

The old shoemaker laughed. "You are stubborn for one so young. It is a great pity you did not know your grandfather when he was your age. You are very like each other." She stopped for a moment, wanting to dig yet wanting even more to hear about the grandfather who had set her on this storyteller's journey.

"While I clear away this dirt, tell me about my grandfather. Please?"

"There is nothing more to tell."

"There must be something. Perhaps you remember a story?" The old man shook his head. "What about the way he told them? Please try. It means so much to me."

"I will help you move the dirt." They worked intently and the pile of earth grew higher but they found no sign of a well.

"This has to be the place my grandfather described. Why can we not find the water?" she asked, hoping the old man would remember something more.

"The well must be filled up. The soldiers threw garbage deep into the opening. Why do you care so much?" asked the shoemaker. "It is only a well. We have other wells."

"I never knew my grandfather yet now I follow in his footsteps. Finding the well he describes would be like finding a trace of him. I want to drink the water he wrote about. It makes him more real to me." She dug until her fingers bled yet even then she would not stop until her fingers refused to move. Disappointed and exhausted, she slumped to the ground.

"We're both tired. Let us rest. Perhaps we will think of something else we might do," said the old man, sinking down into the soft earth.

Aryeh fell asleep dreaming of water spouting from pebbles, of water erupting from the earth, of water spewing forth from the trunk of a tree. She woke suddenly, as if someone had called to her, asking her to lift her head. There was the tree, gnarled and crooked, with a curve in its trunk. No longer tired, she went over to it, staring at the mountains in the distance, slowly sitting down. She called to the old man, "Look! There is the mountain that looks like a bird in flight. The well must be here." The old man sat next to her, closing his eyes, trying to remember what he had known so long ago. As they sat, Aryeh noticed some of the earth was darker than the rest. She dug again but found nothing. There must be a reason for this she thought to herself.

She went back to the tree and opened her grandfather's book, straining to find even one word she might have missed. Suddenly the old man arose and walked to the rock. Standing on top of it, he carefully jumped off as he remembered doing so many years ago. Then, feeling sections of earth, he repeated the jump in slightly different directions. On the fourth jump he landed in the earth that was darker than the rest of the ground around it. Kneeling down, he started pushing aside layers of leaves. She came over to him and asked, "What are you looking for?"

"A large flat stone," answered the old shoemaker, his excitement rising. "I remember now. We used to jump off the big rock and land on the flat stone that served as the cover for the well, but the earth has grown over it. I cannot find it." He rested against the tree, exhausted from so much digging. Seeing the look of disappointment on her face, he said, "I am sorry, I was so sure I remembered where to find it."

Two boys passed them on nearby path. Curious about what the young woman and the old shoemaker were doing, they stopped to watch.

"You rest, I will dig." Aryeh searched for a strong stick and began poking it into the earth. At first, she could barely force the tip into the ground but as she prodded and dug, the earth moved more easily. Soon, she felt the stick scrape across a hard surface. Her excitement gave the old man new energy and he began to dig with her. The boys came closer. A woman carrying a bundle of sticks joined them.

When the top of the rock was free of leaves and debris, they tugged and heaved but neither of them could lift it. They kept digging until they had freed the

sides of the rock. Then, counting and straining, they finally moved the rock a bit, just enough to see what lay beneath. There, bubbling away was the spring that fed the well. They sat and stared at it, too exhausted to move. "It looks clear to me," Aryeh said. The old man eased himself up with painful dignity, cupped his hands, and then gently lowered them into the well. He rinsed away the dirt then brought up his palms filled with clear, sparkling, cold water. After hesitating for a second, he moved his hands to his mouth and drank, slowly. Then he wiped away the tears that filled his eyes.

"How does it taste?" she asked. The old man cupped his hands once more and lowered them into the water. He brought them up and drank once again, to be sure he was not dreaming.

"The water tastes just as I remember," he said, astonished.

Aryeh reached into the well, cupped her hands together, and filled them with water. She looked at it, thinking about her grandfather, how he must have done the very same thing so many years before. She drank the water slowly, feeling more peaceful than she had since finding her parents dead and leaving her home.

When the young boys and woman who were watching them saw the shoemaker drink the water, they whispered excitedly and then the woman sent the youngest back down the path to tell others. Soon villagers quietly surrounded them, moving closer to see what the old man and the young woman had found. The discovery of the well astounded those who gathered around it. Everyone had heard about the old well although most of the young people thought it was just a story or a dream. Word traveled quickly. Soon, half the people from the village were gathered at the well with pots and cups, each wanting to taste the clear, refreshing water of the old, forgotten well.

The young woman and the old man had to tell their story over and over, sometimes twice to the same person. Finally, the shoemaker said, "Please, no more questions, we are tired and I have shoes to finish."

One of the village women said, "The two of you are welcome to have supper with my family. It is not every day we recover what we thought was lost forever." She turned to Aryeh, still flushed from the excitement of drinking from the well her grandfather had written about. "Afterward, we will walk to the mayor's house and sit around the fire while you tell us how it was when your grandfather, the storyteller, walked this road."

"I am not a real storyteller," Aryeh said quietly, thinking of all her grandfather's stories she did not know well enough to tell.

"You are your grandfather's grandchild. That is enough for us," said the woman.

"But I never knew my grandfather. He died before I was born," she protested.

"If you are able to find a well that was buried for longer than most people can remember, I am sure you can tell the stories of your grandfather." As if no further words were necessary, the villager gathered her children and walked off. Aryeh watched her leave, wondering what to do, wishing she could run away.

As if the old man read her thoughts he said, "Have no fear. Tell the words your grandfather wrote that we used to find the well. That will surely satisfy everyone."

Aryeh was not so sure but did not protest as she silently followed the shoemaker. When they were once again in the cool shade of his shop, the old man began working a piece of leather to make a boot. He stopped. "We have spent much of this day together and I do not even know your name."

"My name is…" Suddenly she could not speak. Her old name was too bitter a reminder of all she had lost. She thought of her grandfather Nimah, who had the stories, and her grandmother Nanele, who had the voice. Her parents told her that she must be the one to tell the stories. She now had the voice. She could no longer be Aryeh. She would be *Ni-nan*.

"My name is Ninan," she said. "How are you called?"

"My name is Komas," he replied.

"Thank you for helping me find my grandfather's well."

"Welcome to my village, Ninan," said Komas smiling. "I am pleased to meet you."

Ninan's mouth was dry and her stomach began to ache as she worried about what to say to the villagers. "Komas, tell me about my grandfather."

"It was such a long time ago. I told you all that I remember."

"Please, think some more," begged Ninan. "Try!"

"Well," he said after a time, "as I told you, he had a thick head of reddish

yellow hair and a full red beard, an easy laugh and a quick way with words. He was a tall man, taller than most. All the young women liked him. They brought him food and drink, smiling and laughing, and he laughed back. But when he left, he left alone."

"Why was that?"

Komas shrugged. "Perhaps he thought the life he led was no life for a woman."

Yet his life is the life I must now live, thought Ninan.

"As soon as we saw him, all of us, adults and children, would come round and beg for a story. He'd gather up the littlest ones while the older, taller ones crowded around. Sometimes he would ask, 'So, what kind of a story do you want today?' And we'd shout out, 'Ghosts.' 'Adventure.' Sometimes, we asked for stories we remembered from before."

"Did he ever say no?" asked Ninan.

"Not that I remember," said Komas, "but then I was already apprenticed to my father. There were times when he came and went without my seeing him. My father was a stern taskmaster. Not a man given to letting his son leave work to hear stories." Komas laughed. His laughter was not altogether pleasant.

"What is so funny?"

Komas laughed again, lost in memory. Then his face grew sad. "Ah, Ninan," said Komas as he wiped tears from his eyes, "your grandfather would have been proud of you. Tis a pity the two of you never met."

"Why do you say that?"

"There's a look about you that reminds me of him. He was not an easy man. Quick to take offense, but . . . just as quick to laugh when he saw someone meant no harm. And he was stubborn. Just like you, refusing to give up on finding the well." Komas looked at Ninan kindly. "It is not an easy life being a storyteller, especially for a young woman. But, you are the granddaughter of a storyteller and that is no different from me being the son and grandson and great-grandson of shoemakers."

She started to say that her father had not been a storyteller and that she had not been born a storyteller but was too tired to protest. After awhile Komas stopped working on the boots. "Well, I think this is all I can do for today. As soon as I clean my tools and put them away we can be on our way." Ninan watched, wishing she had tools to take out, use, and put away.

Silently, they walked to the villager's house, pondering the journey that had brought them together. "Ah, I smell food cooking. All this work has made me hungry." He noticed her hanging back. "Come, they are waiting for us." She stood, unable to move. "You need not be afraid. You are young. No one expects you to be perfect. Just tell what you know, any way you choose. Your telling will make us happy. We have not had a real storyteller in our midst for more years than I can remember."

The smell of food and the laughter of excited children welcomed them inside as a young girl opened the door.

THREE
THE STORM'S STORY

The last of the townspeople settled down. Silence fell upon the group as they watched the flickering flames and sipped hot wine spiced with cloves and cinnamon, content to be quiet after the excitement of rediscovering the town well. Ninan and Komas sat on the floor at the edge of the gathering, listening to the snapping and crackling of the fire. The room was small, with a low ceiling that made it seem even smaller. Yet the people who gathered there shared the space with ease, enjoying the physical closeness made necessary by the size of the room. The mayor did not bother to hide his pride in owning such a fine house, the largest in the village. His wife, a thin woman with a worried look, rushed around refilling cups with wine and cider, more like a servant than the wife of the mayor. The smells and warmth made Ninan sleepy. She closed her eyes, unaware that she was leaning lightly against Komas. He held her gently, feeling a companionship he had not known since the death of his wife too many years ago.

Ninan's rest did not last long. The villagers were eager to hear stories of the past, stories once told by a man some of them had known. Soon she found herself facing those who gathered around her. As she started to speak, she noticed the mayor's wife standing against the far wall, ready to fill an empty cup, poised as if she might leave if someone laughed too loudly or became unruly. Ninan could not stop staring at her face for it seemed strangely familiar. Although she could not remember her grandmother, the mayor's wife appeared to be much like her mother's description of her. The woman had large deep-set greenish-brown eyes, which at times were piercing, yet just as quickly, melted into pools of liquid warmth. Then, her worried look softened and the woman's beauty showed through. Although frail,

her dark brown hair was so thick and lustrous it seemed not to belong to her. She
kept sharp watch but spoke to no one.

Ninan averted her eyes to avoid staring at the woman, but there was
something so compelling about the mayor's wife she could not keep her eyes turned
away. She felt the woman was speaking to her, without words, urging her to talk for
her. Ninan was bewildered and tense. She looked at Komas but he merely nodded,
waiting with the others for her to begin. The silence with which people anticipated
the story mingled with the urgency of the woman's mute pleading.

Komas said, "It is time to begin." Ninan felt confused. Her mind raced. The
story she had planned to tell dropped from her memory like a stone sinking into
water without a ripple, and it was too dark to read from her grandfather's book. She
felt ill and faint, but when she opened her mouth to say she was sick and would
have to postpone her storytelling, other words poured out.

nce, long ago, there lived a family that was so poor the
parents had no choice but to sell their eldest daughter into
servitude to rich people who lived just outside the village.
With the money they received, they bought seeds, a cow, and
a goat. The daughter accepted her fate and left early the next
morning to begin life as a servant. She received no wages but each month she had
one day off and was given fruits and vegetables or wine or cheese to take home to
her family.

Each morning at dawn the girl went to the large kitchen where she
prepared the family's meals, washed their pots and plates, and mended their torn
clothing. Between cleaning up after the noon meal and preparing for dinner, she
walked in the nearby fields and forests gathering plants and berries. Some she
ate, a few she used to dye the wool that she spun, others she saved to brew when
someone became ill. She kept to herself, refusing to join the other servants when
they gathered together after their duties ended Her days passed in silence except
for those words needed to answer the few questions she was asked.

She grew from maid to young woman, and although she had come with a
name, no one used it. They called her Mara, the dark one. In time Mara forgot
her birth name and became Mara even to herself. Young men who offered their

hand in marriage found her indifferent and came no more. The cook teased her, warning she would become an old maid, but Mara took no notice and kept on with her work.

One day, as she was gathering herbs, a young man approached and asked the way to the blacksmith's shop. "My horse is in need of new shoes and I must have them to continue traveling." Mara, startled by the sound of his voice, quickly moved away. The man, seeing her fright, said, "Have no fear. I will not hurt you. I merely wish to find the blacksmith." Mara attempted to speak but it was as if she had forgotten how to talk. The more she tried, the more garbled were the sounds she made. She quickly wiped away the tears of frustration that poured down her face, not wanting to look as helpless as she felt. Then she hurried toward the forest.

The young man stood, watching her, puzzled. His horse badly needed shoes but there was a mysterious look in the woman's eyes that haunted him. He walked after her, softly, so as not to scare her. When Mara noticed she was being followed, she began to run. The young man pursued until he caught her hand. Although she tried to escape, he held her firmly. "Please, do not be afraid. I will not hurt you."

Mara looked at him; they were almost the same height, both had dark brown hair and eyes. A stranger passing by might easily have thought they were brother and sister. She pulled away from him, watching carefully. He sat, extending his hand to help her sit, and then offered her water. The cool liquid eased the worst of her fears, and when he asked her name, she found her voice. "They call me Mara."

"What do you call yourself?" he asked.

"I have no name," she said. "I was given one at birth, I think, but I have forgotten what it was."

"My name is Youseph," he said. "I am a stranger here, passing through on my way to Benima." Mara said nothing. "I am a teacher. I have been hired to tutor the three sons of the king."

Mara stood up. "I will show you how to find the blacksmith, but then I must go. My chores do not wait for me."

Youseph rose and said. "I would like to see you again."

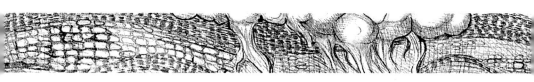

Mara shook her head. "That is impossible. I work until late and begin before sunrise. You will be gone long before that."

"I will wait until you have finished your chores," he insisted.

"Why?" asked Mara. "You are on your way to the palace of the king."

"This is true, yet it is also true I would like to see you again."

She answered slowly, painfully slowly, "I come here after the noon meal to pick flowers and berries. I will be here tomorrow. If you do not come it will not matter." She stood up, turning her back on him, and pointed. "The blacksmith's shop lies in that direction, just beyond the bridge."

"I will be here," he said as he walked to his horse. She left without a word or backward glance.

That night, Mara dreamed she was walking in the fields, gathering herbs, when suddenly the ground she was walking on began to tremble and move. No matter where she ran, the ground shuddered and quivered until it broke apart. She fell into an enormous hole, falling faster and faster. There appeared to be no end to her falling. Frightened, she screamed and woke herself up. Shaking with fear, she sat up in bed, hugging the coverlet to her body, trying to put the sensation of falling from her mind. As soon as she tried to go back to sleep, the falling began again. Convinced it would not end, she left her bed and went outside.

The moon was full, the night was warm, and the chirping of insects calmed her. She walked to her favorite place in the fields, humming as she walked, feeling the terrors of her dream begin to fade. She walked for a long time. Without her noticing, the moon disappeared and the sun's early morning rays began to guide her steps. She gasped when she looked around and did not recognize the surrounding countryside. She realized she was lost and ran, looking for a familiar path, but all the paths were strange and unknown. The terrors of her dream began to haunt her. The faster she ran the more real they were.

She ran until she collapsed on the ground, panting, trying to catch her breath. A horse was almost on top of her before she saw it. "Mara! What are you doing here?" Youseph looked down at her as if she were a ghost.

"I do not know where I am," she stammered, shivering with cold. He dismounted and knelt beside her, taking her cold hands in his, rubbing warmth back into them. She tried to thank him but found speaking too difficult.

Ninan stopped to catch her breath and heard a voice say, "More wine?" She jumped, disoriented by the voice. Looking up, she saw the mayor's wife standing next to her, a pitcher of steaming spicy liquid in her hand.

"No. No th . . . thank you," stammered Ninan. The woman stood, staring at her. The mayor's wife kept staring. People looked at Ninan, waiting for her to continue the story, but she felt confused and uncertain. She had been very deep into the story when the mayor's wife interrupted. Why did the woman persist in her staring? Ninan blushed, remembering how she had stared at the mayor's wife. She looked at Komas but he was lost in thought, drinking his wine. It was as if everyone were under a spell. No one moved or spoke. Everyone appeared to be waiting.

Finally the mayor walked to his wife and whispered to her, "Marya, we have had enough wine. Come sit next to me and let Ninan finish her story."
"I cannot," whispered his wife in words everyone could hear. "I cannot bear to hear her words. They are too real."

"It is only a story," soothed her husband.

"You know better than that," she countered, tears running down the front of her clothing.

"Please, Marya," repeated the mayor, "she is a young woman making up a story."

Ninan felt the woman's agony and spoke softly. "Perhaps I should finish the story tomorrow. The evening grows late."

"You cannot stop now," spoke one of the men, "we want to know how your story ends."

Ninan answered without thinking, "There is no end. There is only a stopping place."

"But what about Mara?" asked a woman sitting on the other side of Komas. "You cannot leave her in the middle of a strange place. We want to know what happens next. Why begin a story you do not mean to finish? That is as bad as never starting one."

Ninan looked helplessly at the mayor's wife. "What would you like me to do?" she asked softly, secretly hoping the woman would tell her to stop.

"You must do as you think best. Are you not the storyteller?"

Ninan protested. "Yes, but it is only a story." Seeking to end the woman's

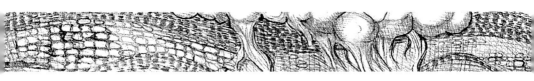

misery, she confessed, "I mean no harm. The words come as I speak."

The woman replied bitterly, "Nothing is *only* a story. A story is always some person's story. I know this too well."

Ninan looked at the mayor who cradled his wife, comforting her as best he could. "But if this is true, I do not know the person whose story I am telling. The words speak themselves. I do not plan them. What shall I do?" she asked.

The mayor hesitated, then spoke gently, to his wife as much as Ninan, "You must finish your story. The others want to know how it ends." He led his wife to the far corner of the room and gave her a cup of steaming wine. They sat slightly apart from the others, shielded by their large dog curling around his mistress, offering his body as protection.

"Finish the story!" boomed a loud voice. Ninan could barely remember what she had been saying when the mayor's wife interrupted. Not only was it not a story from her grandfather's book, she had no idea how it would end. The story was coming from a place so deep inside she knew no way to find it again. The interruption had broken her thoughts; her mind was a jumble of disconnected words and conflicting ideas. If this was what it meant to be a storyteller, she wanted no part of it. She started to stand up but her parents' faces appeared in her mind's eye, reminding her of her mother's curse if she chose not to be a storyteller.

A woman sitting next to her smiled kindly. "Please, tell us the rest of the story."

"Go on. We are listening," urged people. There was nothing to do but close her eyes and wait, hoping the pictures that had formed in her mind would appear once again.

Youseph helped Mara sit up and then, seeing she did not try to run away, put his cloak around her. "I went to the home of the family you serve. They told me you had run away."

Mara tried to tell him about her dream but once again she could not speak the words that filled her mouth. Instead, ugly sounds, harsh and incoherent noises filled the air. The inability to speak filled her with terror. Always before, when she wanted to talk, the words came if she was patient. But now, nothing helped. She had lost her ability to speak.

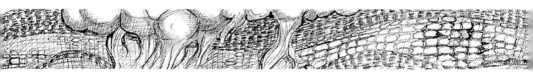

She threw off the cloak and ran blindly, paying no attention to direction. Youseph followed her, catching her arm just as she was about to sink into swampy earth. She struggled to free herself but was too weak to do so for very long. Youseph spoke gently to her. "You are tired and hungry. Perhaps your words will return after you have eaten and slept." Mara did not respond. "I am sure that when you feel better your words will return."

Mara looked at him, wondering what to do. How could she explain her absence even if she did find her way back to the family she served? Youseph led her to his horse. "Come, I will take you back." Mara shook her head. She did not want to return. She did not know how to speak what was in her heart but she knew her days of mute service were finished.

Youseph looked puzzled and uncertain. He understood she did not want to return to the family, to being a servant, but where could she go? How would she live? What would happen to her if she could not talk? He asked her, "Where will you go?" Mara looked down and did not answer. She pushed him toward his horse, as if to say he should not worry about her. He shook his head and said, "I cannot leave you here. We are hours from a village. It is getting colder and I think there will soon be a storm."

Mara said nothing as she once again pushed him toward his horse, walking away from him. "Wait," he said, "my horse is strong. He can carry both of us. I will take you to the village where I am going." Mara shook her head again but Youseph would not listen. "You must come with me, I cannot leave you here." He led her to his horse and firmly helped her up.

At that moment, a bolt of lightning crackled near them. The horse whinnied and lifted his front legs into the air. Large drops of rain and hail pelted them. Youseph shouted above the noise, "There is no time to talk. We must find shelter from the storm."

Huddled together for warmth, Mara and Youseph rode through the heavy rain and lightning. Each time the thunder crashed the horse reared and tried to free himself of his burden. Youseph used all of his skill and determination to keep the horse from throwing them and running off. They rode for many miles before coming to an old cottage that promised to provide shelter from the increasing rage of the storm. Although one side was open and the floor was filled with

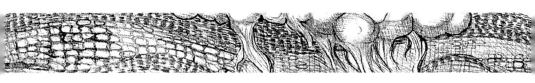

moldy hay, the roof kept most of the rain out. They rested, relieved and grateful to be sitting on a dry patch of ground.

The sound of the rain beating steadily on the roof made them both sleepy, but Mara fought to stay awake. When she saw that Youseph was asleep, she quietly crept outside. The fury of the storm frightened her but she wrapped herself in a piece of old blanket she found near the entrance. Taking a deep breath, Mara plunged into the raging weather.

The wind blew hard and branches flew and fell as if mere sticks being hurled in all directions by an angry giant. The thunder shook her and the lightning was frightening but still she walked, following an unknown road. In spite of her fears, she felt as if the storm outside matched the storm within her, that she could walk forever and feel more peaceful than trying to speak words that would not be spoken. When the road split she stood, not knowing which fork to choose. A tiny rabbit scampered across the road leading to the right, and she followed it.

Suddenly, it seemed as if the storm's fury knew no bounds. Mara felt she was in combat with the chaos of the weather. She yelled at the top of her lungs, "You cannot scare me." Surprised by the roar of her own voice and the ease with which she formed her words, she yelled again, knowing no one could hear.

"Ha! Storm, rage all you like. You will not get me." Despite her lack of sleep, the words filled her with energy and purpose. She felt herself grow strong.

She thought she heard the storm answer her, "I do not want to hurt you. You were born in a storm. You will live in a storm. But, you will die in peace if you have courage." Mara looked around to see who had spoken but saw no one. The words came again. "You were born in a storm. You will live in a storm. But, you will die in peace if you have courage."

"Aieh!" The sudden moan startled Ninan. She looked around to see who had cried out, and saw that the scream had come from the mayor's wife. The others, deep in the story, thought the sound was part of the tale and waited for her to continue. The mayor stroked his wife's hair, as if comforting a troubled child, giving no sign he wanted Ninan to stop. The interruption troubled Ninan. She told herself she must not worry about what to say, that the agony she saw on the face of the

mayor's wife was not caused by her story, yet this seemed impossible. To give herself time, she took a long sip of wine, closed her eyes again, and waited. Then, when the words came, she spoke from a depth that had no name or history.

"Is it courage I need then? Courage for what?" shouted Mara, roaring at the clamor of the wind and the beating of the rain.

Once again the storm answered, 'The courage you need is the courage to remember your real name"

Mara stumbled, thoughts whirling around in her mind as the wind pushed the rains in sheets of wet cold. "My name?" she shouted. "What is a name? One is as good as another. What I am called makes no difference." She pulled the soaking wet blanket closer to her and railed at the storm. "I need no name. What I am called is of no importance."

The storm raged and shrieked. "You must find the courage to remember your name. You cannot live your life without your rightful name. You were born in a storm. You will live in a storm. But, you will find your life if you have the courage to remember what you think has been lost."

Mara looked around, unable to believe the words she was hearing, afraid to know who or what might be speaking. Huddled in the blanket, too tired to continue, too frightened to stop, she kept on walking.

The wind howled louder. Mara shouted. "Who are you? What do you want of me?" She tried to convince herself she had imagined the words yet she could not. The words burned inside her. Cold and tired, she stumbled and fell. The wet leaves received her and she gave herself up to their softness. She had neither the strength nor the will to stand.

From deep within her, the sounds pushed at her, forcing her to sit up. "You were born in a storm. You will live in a storm. But, you must not die in a storm." A bolt of lightning flashed close by. Another came still closer, frightening her to move, beyond fatigue.

She stood up, screaming, "What do you want from me?"

"Remember your name."

"How?" yelled Mara. "How?" Silence mocked her. She staggered forward, with only the roar of the wind and the force of the rain to keep her company. In

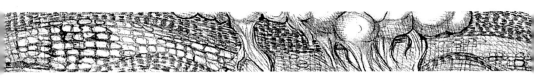

the distance she saw a small hut near the side of the road. With her last ounce
of strength, Mara stumbled toward it. In the back, sheltered from the worst of
the storm's fury, was a small door. She banged on it, hoping those inside would
hear her and be welcoming. At first, there was no response. No sign that anyone
heard her desperate pounding. She banged again, screaming as loud as she could,
"Help! Please help me." Still, no one came. Mara beat on the door with her fists.
"Please, let me in"

The door opened just wide enough to allow an old man to peer out. He
looked at the young woman who stood at his door, shivering, dirty, and wet. He
stood for a few seconds, stunned by the sudden intrusion, then helped her in,
pushing off the filthy, wet blanket. Mara fell, unable to stand any longer. The old
man's wife brought a bowl of hot tea and shooed her husband off to the other side
of the room. Too tired to move, Mara lay quietly as the old woman took off her
wet clothes and covered her with a mended nightshirt and a dry blanket. After
helping Mara to drink the sweet tea, she moved her closer to the fire. For a long
time, Mara knew no more.

The two old people sat and watched her sleep until they too dozed,
comforted by the sight of the young woman who slept so trustingly beside them.

It took all of the night and part of the morning for the storm to find its
peace. The old people moved about quietly, watching the stranger, making sure
she was warm. When she began to stir, curious words came from her, as if against
her will. "I have no name," she moaned. "I have no name."

She dreamed that the old woman gathered her up in her arms and
crooned, "Hush, my darling, hush." When Mara moaned again, the old woman
gently stroked her cheek. "You have a name, my darling. Your name is Marya.
Marya. Your name is Marya." The young woman slowly quieted, and she
dreamed that the old woman's tears dropped on to her face.

When the younger woman awoke and opened her eyes, she saw an old
woman with eyes full of tears that she made no attempt to hide. "Good morning,
child. Are you feeling better?"

Mara, safe and warm in the old woman's arms, remembered the storm and
her journey and the dream. She began to shiver uncontrollably. The old woman
spoke, "Rest, my child. You are safe with us."

The old man brought bread and hot soup. "Have something to eat. You must be hungry. My wife will bring you tea." He put the food down in front of her, watching, waiting.

Mara looked at the food and felt the stirrings of a deep hunger, yet she did not eat. The old man put a piece of bread into her hands. "Eat. You will feel better." His kind eyes reassured her and she put the bread to her mouth. "How did you come to be out in such a storm?" he asked. She began to shiver, trembling with panic. The old man said quickly, "It does not matter. I am a foolish old man to ask questions of a hungry person. You have had a hard time. We can talk later, when you are ready."

The old woman stood up and went to the kettle perched above the fire. She ladled out a cup of tea, spicing it with herbs. "My husband speaks truth. You must rest. There is no hurry." The warmth of the tea and the goodness of the food made Mara sleepy. When her cup was empty, she curled into the soft blanket and drifted into a deep sleep.

She dreamed she was walking in a field of huge rocks and deep holes. No matter how carefully she walked, her feet fell into the holes. The rocks grew larger and higher. Soon she could not see over the tops of the rocks. As she struggled up one, another took its place. When she turned to look back, there were rocks behind her as far as she could see. They began to close in upon her, holding her left foot so she could not move. She screamed but no sound came from her mouth. The silent scream reverberated deep within, filling her with fear. She struggled to free her foot but she could not, the rock was too large and too heavy.

She heard a voice, faint, coming from far away, "Marya. Marya!" There was a long silence then the voice called again. "Marya. Marya." "I am here!" she screamed. "I am here!"

Still dreaming, she felt a reassuring arm on her shoulder and sat up. The worried face of the old man greeted her as he knelt down. "Marya." he whispered, more to himself than to her. She looked at him and felt something stir deep within, struggling to free itself.

The old woman stroked her tangled hair. "Marya" she whispered. Her image began to disappear, yet the name Marya echoed and reverberated. "Marya.

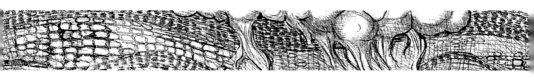

Marya. Marya."

Mara woke up with a jolt. She spoke with a sense of wonder. "My name is Marya. Not Mara. Marya. My name is Marya."

She imagined the name of Mara flying back to those who called her dark and bitter. She had found her name, now would she find her way?

Ninan stopped, too exhausted to continue. Komas filled her cup with hot wine and watched her drink, feelings of tenderness and pride mixing within him. Then he said to those in the room, "This is the story for tonight. It is late. Time to return to our homes." Slowly, still under the spell of the story, people stood to leave.

One woman nodded to Ninan and said, "Good story, miss. Thank you." Others nodded in agreement as they left silently, still feeling the story's magic.

Ninan sipped her wine, accepting their silent appreciation, shaken by the story. She could feel the eyes of the mayor's wife boring into her and knew she would be asked questions to which she had no answers. Komas spoke quietly to her. "Let us leave. I am sure you are tired." He put his arm around Ninan and helped her up.

The mayor's wife spoke, "Komas is right. It is late. I can see you are tired. But I must speak with you. Where did you learn the story you have told?"

"I did not learn it. No one taught it to me. The words just came. I do not know from where. Or how," answered Ninan, filled with shame because she was not a proper storyteller. "The story told itself, from a place deep within me."

The mayor's wife sighed, a strange look on her face, "You have a special gift. You must take care of it. Treasure it. We need to hear your stories. But beware, you may unleash more than you imagine."

Ninan shivered with fear. She did not know how her voice found the words. Where had the story come from? The mayor's wife spoke. "We have many rooms in this house. You are welcome to stay with Youseph and me. We would be grateful for your presence."

Confused, Ninan asked, "Who is Youseph?"

"I am Marya," the mayor's wife, answered quietly. "Youseph is my husband."

Ninan was filled with dread and wonder. Marya? Youseph? How had she come to name her characters the same as the mayor and his wife? Perhaps there was

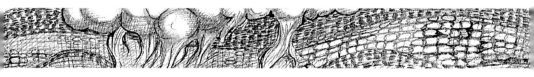

more to storytelling than her parents knew. She shivered, dreading the questions Komas might ask as they walked to his home as well as the questions the mayor and his wife could ask if she stayed.

Komas said, "Stay with them, Ninan. You are tired and the walk to my home is long. I will come for you tomorrow. Rest well. Morning will come soon enough." Ninan sighed and nodded at her new friend's wisdom.

A small sigh of pleasure filled Komas as he walked home, whistling, filling the night air with sounds of happiness.

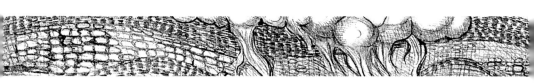

FOUR
A SMALL BIT OF COMFORT

inan sank into the lofty featherbed and sighed with pleasure yet she could not sleep. Although she was warm and dry for the first night since leaving her village, each time she dozed, voices in her dreams woke her up:

"You will never be a wife and mother."

"You must cherish this book. You will wander from village to village, telling the stories of your grandfather and grandmother."

"The shawl will keep you warm when you are cold. It will comfort you when you are lonely and discouraged. Take good care of it and it will care for you."

"You must use your eyes and ears and tongue. This is your burden and your privilege."

She sat up, wanting to stop the voices, and remembered Marya's words: "We will talk in the morning, Ninan. Rest now." What would she say when Marya asked how she came to use the names of Marya and Youseph? How could she explain that she had no idea where the story had come from? Where the names came from. Where the idea came from. Why had her parents not told her she might tell a story that came from nowhere she could explain?

Ninan held her hands over her ears. "Stop," she pleaded. "Surely there is nothing wrong with sleeping in a warm, clean bed." But the voices continued. Sleep was impossible. Ninan caressed the shawl her parents had given to her. She gently wrapped it around her, touching the frayed edges with reverence and awe, feeling herself grow calm. Lighting the candle near her bed, she opened her grandfather's book. The writing was clear, and she nodded when she read his words: I walked until I could walk no more but I found no site where I could stop so I continued walking . . .

Ninan said to herself, "And I thought until I could think no more, but there was no way to stop so I continued thinking." The first pink rays of the sun were chasing the gray. It was time to act. She knew what must be done. With one last glance at the comfortable bed, she got up and quickly dressed. Gathering her few possessions, she crept down the narrow stairs, not wanting to wake those who slept. Her heart pounded as she searched for a way to leave her thanks. She dared not use any paper from her grandfather's book for it was too precious.

As she stood wondering what to say, worrying they would think her ungrateful, Marya entered the room. Ninan jumped, feeling like a thief caught in the act.

"What is it, Ninan? Why are you up so early? I thought you would sleep till noon."

Ninan blushed. "I could not sleep."

"You are carrying your things. Did you intend to leave without a word?"

"No. But I did not want to disturb anyone. Had I the means I would have written a note."

"And what would the note have said?"

Ninan thought for a moment. "It would start: Dear Friends."

"And then?" asked Marya. "Then what would you have written?"

Ninan hesitated, "You have been very kind to me yet I must leave before I am so comfortable I will not want to leave. I hope that one day we will meet again. I will always remember the warmth of your hospitality." Shaking, she looked away from Marya and said, "Then I would have signed my name, put the note on the table near the fireplace, and left as quickly as possible, before I could change my mind." She gazed at a vase holding long stemmed yellow flowers. "You have such a fine home."

"Without even a second thought? Is that what you want to do?" asked Marya.

"No, but I think it is what I must do," said Ninan, looking at Marya for the first time.

"Well, if this is what you wish, do it," said Marya, stepping away from the door. "I will not keep you here against your will."

Ninan felt confused. Why did she not leave? Why did she stand, mute? Why could she not stop longing for the clean, comfortable bed? Ninan looked at Marya, feeling her turmoil yet there was nothing Ninan could say to explain how she knew the story. The two women stood close together yet far apart, neither knowing how to break the awkward silence.

Ninan's words did not reveal her desperation. "I am truly grateful for your kindness. I hope one day to return, to give you something for what you have given me." She draped her grandmother's shawl around her trembling body, nodded her head, and left, afraid to look back, afraid to return.

Marya watched her leave, still upset, still wondering how Ninan had come to know and tell her story. Although she felt betrayed by the storytelling, she knew her husband had not spoken of her early life. Marya shivered, shaking her head to stop unwanted memories yet at the same time, memories of how Youseph had found her and asked her to marry him made her smile.

The cool morning air gave Ninan energy. She walked at a brisk pace. The rays of the sun were warm and comforting. She began to hum, feeling she had narrowly escaped from an unnamed danger, though what this was she did not know. She hoped she would see Komas again. She wanted to hear the whole of Marya's story, to know what had happened to her. Most of all, she yearned to drink from the well, to feel connected to her grandfather. Yet for now, she knew she was too tempted by a clean, dry bed, and good food to trust that she could stay anywhere for a few days and then leave. She dreaded questions to which she had no answers. Had she stayed she might have convinced herself her parents were wrong, that she could not tell her grandfather's stories, that no matter how she tried, she would never be a real storyteller.

She walked for a long time, absorbed in the wonder of all that had happened to her in such a short time. The pangs of hunger came as a surprise. She had not thought to take food with her. Searching the fields for berries, she found some bushes and ate greedily, paying no attention to where she was. As she stepped closer to a bush loaded with fruit she heard a muffled sound. Looking around, she saw no one. She started to walk back to the bush and heard the sound again. This time it was louder and clearer. Someone was crying. It sounded like a child.

Ninan moved toward the source of the sound. Stepping softly, she came upon a small boy with his hands around his head, sobbing. He was lying on his stomach, curled into a little ball. Not sure what to do, she cautiously knelt down next to him and lightly touched his shoulder. "Hello." Startled, the little boy leaned away from her. "Have no fear," said Ninan, "I will not hurt you." The boy, wearing clothes that were patched yet clean, stared at her. His tangled blonde hair caught the sun's rays and shone like gold. He held himself carefully, ready to run. "Have some berries," offered Ninan. She slowly reached out her hand, giving him time to decide what to do, waiting patiently until the boy took three of the berries and put them into his mouth, one at a time. Ninan ate the rest. "Would you like more? I will gather some for you." He remained silent, staring at her, keeping his distance. She wondered if he understood her words.

Sighing, Ninan moved toward the berry bushes. The boy touched the edge of her shawl and said, "Please, do not leave me."

"I am hungry. I have not eaten for a long time, but I will pick berries for the two of us and then I will return. I promise." The boy refused to release his grip on the shawl. Afraid that he would tear it, Ninan sat down. Making sure she would not suddenly leave, he slowly released the shawl, refusing to let go of the last edge.

"My mother said she would return and she did not."

"What happened to your mother?"

The boy looked down at his feet, "She got sick and went to sleep."

Ninan felt her heart go out to him. "When did this happen?"

"I waited and waited and waited but she never came. She promised me she would come back, but she did not keep her promise. She always told me it is bad to make a promise and then break it, but that is what she did."

"Perhaps she thought she would return. Is it not possible she wanted to keep her promise to you and then found she could not?"

"She did not come back to me. She said she would and she left and I never saw her again even though she promised she would never leave me."

"Where do you live?" asked Ninan.

"In the village beyond the next hill."

"Do you have a family?"

The boy hesitated. "I live with my father and his wife. They have a baby. They will not miss me. They are too busy. There is much work to do. The baby cries all the time."

Ninan stroked her shawl, slowly releasing it from his fingers. "What are you doing here?"

"I ran away. I want to find my mother."

"I thought you said your mother was sick and went to sleep."

The boy looked away, "Yes, that is what my father told me. But I think that if I look hard enough, I will find her. She would want me to find her."

"I know how that is," said Ninan sadly.

The boy stared at her. "You do?"

Ninan said simply, "Yes."

"How can you know about this?"

"Both my parents are dead."

"My mother is not dead. She got sick and went to sleep."

"That is what people sometimes tell children when they do not wish to tell the truth. Death is a kind of sleep from which we never wake."

"I want to find my mother. If I keep looking I am sure I will find her," insisted the boy.

"I know what it is like to miss your mother. Yet, if you try, you can still talk with her. My brothers died before I was born yet at times I feel as if they are talking to me."

The boy asked, "What do they tell you?"

"Mostly they give me a small bit of comfort."

"How do they do this?" asked the boy.

"It is difficult to explain. When I sense their presence and their caring, I become calm and still. They help me feel that I am not alone. Soon, I feel…better."

"Would they tell you something to make me feel better?" asked the boy.

"They might," answered Ninan, "but it is hard for them to speak to me when I am so hungry. My growling stomach makes too much noise."

The little boy smiled for the first time, turned, and picked up a small sack. "You can have some of my food. Will this help your brothers' voices tell me how to talk with my mother?"

"I am willing to try though it is hard to say what will happen when I am so hungry. But, this food is yours. I cannot take it. If you are running away you will need all the food you have."

"I would rather have my mother talk to me than all the food in the world."

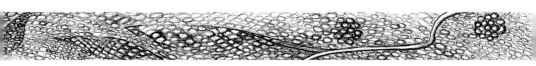

He put his sack in her hands.

Ninan thought it wrong to eat his food yet the boy was so unhappy she took a little and began to eat. He watched anxiously. "Well? Can you hear anything? Have you had enough to feed the voices? What are you hearing?" He waited impatiently for her to begin.

Ninan looked at his thin, unhappy face and said, "Come sit next to me. I cannot concentrate while you are standing up." He sat down, gently running a finger over her shawl. She stroked his forehead and watched his tense body slowly begin to ease. She felt herself move inside to the deepest part of her being. No longer aware of where she was, a story began.

 nce upon a time there was a young girl with hair the color of gold, large brown eyes and a grin that made all those who saw it, smile. She had a soft pleasant voice in which she sang about the things she saw and the people she met.

"And her name was Lara," said the boy.

Lara's parents were farmers and their days were filled with hard work and many worries—weather, animals, getting produce to market in good time. They had four other children, all big strong boys with dark hair and loud voices who worked in the fields with their father. Lara and her mother spent their days cooking and sewing, washing and ironing, spinning and weaving. There was never an end to the work. Each evening after supper, she sang to her parents and brothers as she mended clothes and darned socks. The words did not matter very much. What they wanted to hear was her joyful song, a balm for their hurts and troubles.

So it went, day after day, week after week, month after month, and year after year. One night, after she had finished the last song before they went to bed, her father said to her, "Promise me you will never stop singing."

"I promise," said Lara, who thought her father's words rather strange. To her, singing was as natural as breathing. How could she ever stop singing? Why would she ever stop singing?

One day, the oldest brother said to his father, "It is time for me to marry."

"Are you thinking of someone?" asked his father.

"Our neighbor's daughter," said the son.

"Sofie, that's her name," said the boy. "That is the name of my father's wife. I do not like her. My father should be with my mother."

"Her father's farm lies next to ours. The land that Sofie will bring to our marriage has much value."

"You have chosen well, my son. I will speak to her parents tomorrow after the animals are settled for the night." And so it was arranged. The next month, the son married Sofie, the neighbor's daughter, and they moved into a small cottage on the farm of his parents.

Lara was delighted to have a sister and sang even more joyously as she did her chores. Although the two became friends, Sofie began to be jealous of the attention everyone paid to Lara. She started to hate Lara's lovely voice and easy smile. At first, the twinges of envy were small, but as the family gathered every evening to hear Lara sing, Sofie grew increasingly resentful. She spoke to the girl harshly and told lies about Lara to her husband, hoping he would tell them to his brothers and parents. Her dark thoughts poisoned her tongue.

One night while they were getting water from the well, Sofie said to Lara, "Do you think it right that we should have to listen to you chirp away every evening, with never a bit of silence for the rest of us to talk?"

Lara was surprised. "I did not know my songs displeased you. I thought my singing made you happy. Would you have me stop singing?"

Sofie's anger answered for her. "You need to think about more than singing. It is time you were married. You are only two years younger than I am."

"No one has asked for my hand." She hoisted the pail of water on top of her head, thinking how wrong she had been all these years. Probably her brothers did not like her songs but were too kind to tell her.

Forgetting about her promise to her father Lara thought, Sofie is my friend. I will listen to her. I will stop singing. She is older and knows better what is right for me to do.

The little boy called out, "No, she does not. She is not your friend. She is jealous of you. Do not listen to her. Keep singing." Startled, Ninan felt bewildered by the loud voice of the boy. She felt the familiar confusion, the peculiar unsettled feeling inside herself. Closing her eyes, she waited for the voices and the pictures to resume.

That evening, after the washing up, the family gathered together and waited for Lara to sing but she sat quietly, pretending to pay great attention to her sewing, ignoring how uncomfortable the silence felt. No one talked. No one moved. Sofie knitted with great concentration, only to look up and see the others staring at her. Sofie pretended not to notice. The father spoke to his daughter. "We are waiting for your song, my daughter. Why do you remain silent?" Lara saw that Sofie's mouth was pinched and hard. Sofie refused to meet her eyes. Her knitting needles clacked even faster.

"Father, I am sorry but I cannot sing tonight."

"Are you ill?"

"No," she said, feeling utterly miserable.

"Then what is wrong? Why do you not sing?"

"I cannot say," answered Lara. "I do not have a song to sing tonight."

Her father asked, "Would you deny me my small bit of comfort then?"

Sofie kept knitting. The silence grew thick and heavy. No one moved. Sofie glanced at her husband but he too looked disappointed.

Finally she said, "I am tired. I am going to bed. Come, husband." But he remained seated. Sofie grabbed her knitting and stormed out of the room. The silence was heavy. Everyone was uncomfortable.

Lara's brother was the first one to find his voice. "Please sing, Lara. I miss the sound of your voice. It is not the same, sitting here in silence."

She hesitated. She wanted to sing yet the ease with which she used to sing felt spoiled. She asked, "Are you sure?"

"Yes," said her brother, "I am sure." Lara felt such relief the song danced its way out to those who were waiting. Her sweet joyful voice filled the room and cleared away the heaviness, leaving those who listened happy and peaceful. When the last song became memory, the girl looked up and saw Sofie's angry face peering at her from the doorway.

Lara felt frightened and confused. She had told her father she would never stop singing. She had told Sofie she would not start singing. How could she please everyone?

"Why should she please Sofie? Sofie does not like her. Sofie will never like her. Never. Never. Never. Lara should run away," shouted the boy. "I know what it is like to be told you are bad. I know what it is like to be told to keep quiet. Make Lara run away," urged the boy, desperation in his voice.

Ninan did not know what to do. If she pleased the boy, the story might stop. If she told the story she knew to tell, he might be angry or disappointed. It seemed that telling stories was more complicated than merely speaking words that came to mind. "I have to tell the story as it comes out," she told him.

"No, you are telling my mother's story. Make her run away. Make her run to a place where I can find her. I want my mother. You promised I would hear my mother's voice. What good is a promise if you do not keep it?"

"Perhaps you would like to finish the story?" said Ninan.

"I am not a storyteller," said the boy, near tears. "You said I would hear the voice of my mother. When will I hear it?"

"I do not know," said Ninan.

"You do not keep your promise. My mother did not keep her promise. I will not listen to you." He jumped up and ran off leaving his sack.

"Come back," she shouted. "You left your food." But the boy neither turned nor acknowledged her shouting and was soon out of sight.

Stopping in the middle of a story left Ninan feeling unsettled, as if caught between two worlds, with no place to call her own. She wanted to stop telling stories. It was not enough to tell what came out yet she did not know what else to do when someone asked her to tell a story. She had tried to memorize the stories in her grandfather's book but his words would not stay in her head. She wished she could tell her parents, "I have tried but you were mistaken, I am not a storyteller." Not even the sack of food the boy had left cheered her.

She sat and waited; wanting to sense the presence of her brothers, hoping this would help her feel better, yet nothing happened. Were they angry she had changed her name? Taken the place that should have been theirs? Would she never feel their calming energy again?

Ninan lay down in the grass, wishing she could go to sleep and never wake yet she knew she could not give up. Her parents were not cruel people. They loved her. They had told her what she must do in sorrow, not in anger. And, in some deep place inside her, she knew that someone had to tell the stories. If only her brothers had lived…

FIVE
ON THE MOUNTAIN

The sun was fading and the air grew cool. Ninan shivered as breezes played with the fringes of her shawl, which she had wrapped around her, waiting for the familiar sense of warmth. Even with it tightly hugging her body, she felt cold. She would have to hurry if she was to find shelter before it grew too dark to see. Although she walked quickly on the road that wound around the side of a large mountain, the steepness of the incline slowed her pace. She thought to herself, I am nothing but a liar. I tell the little boy to listen to his heart but when I listen to mine, I hear nothing. Storytelling is just another word for telling lies.

She shook her head, trying to shrug away the dark thoughts. Looking around, she saw, off to the side, a small trail that seemed as if it might provide her with a protected place to sleep. The narrow path was overgrown and her shawl kept catching on branches so she took it off despite the cold, wrapping it carefully in her bag. The hard work of climbing warmed her and she felt a little less miserable. Then, while moving over a dead branch, a limb from a bramble bush hit her in the face. She felt blood run down her cheek and licked its warmth with her tongue, strangely comforted by the taste.

Far off she heard the night call of a bird being answered by its mate. Once again, Ninan felt lonely and lost, without direction or possibility. All she knew to do was walk until she found a place or reason to stop. By now it was almost dark yet she continued to walk, her feet moving along the path as if they determined when she could stop. She bumped into rocks and tripped over tree limbs, yet something inside her urged her on. She silently cursed her fate though she dared not curse her parents. She remembered the warmth and peacefulness of Komas, the comfort of Marya's house, and wished she had not left so precipitously. When she thought about the strange coincidence, telling a story about Youseph and Marya in the presence of the mayor and his wife, Youseph and Marya, she grew frightened. Could it really be coincidence? How had it happened that the names were the same? Why was the mayor's wife so upset by her story? Remembering how the boy had run away from her only added to her misery. Although she practiced telling the stories of her grandfather as she walked along the road, she had trouble remembering them, despite spending countless hours trying to do so. Her head ached from too many unanswered questions. She thought she might feel better if the tears she felt behind her eyes would wash her troubled thoughts away, but she could not make herself cry.

She stumbled, falling down into a soft pile of sweet-smelling pine needles and decided to stop. As she lay, cradled in the needles, trying to savor the last crumbs of the food in the boy's sack, she smelled food cooking and wondered if she was delirious. Annoyed at herself, she stood up and thought she might as well have a look. I will be no worse off if I prove to myself I am only imagining what I wish were so. She walked toward the smell. If food was being cooked, who was doing the cooking? Perhaps this person would not welcome an unknown visitor. Perhaps it was a person she would rather not meet.

She crept toward the scent, stopping and starting, trying to make as little noise as possible. In a small clearing, she saw a man with a white beard and full head of white hair, dressed in the skins of what looked like a bear. She stood watching him, not sure what to do, and flinched when she heard him ask, "Well, are you going to stand there all night looking at me?"

Ninan had to force herself to speak, still uncertain whether to walk toward him or run away. "No sir."

He put a handful of greens in a pot suspended over softly glowing coals. "Then come over here and warm yourself. The night grows cold."

Uneasily, Ninan moved up to the fire, grateful for its warmth. The man stirred the contents of the pot that seemed to contain some kind of stew, but what it was she could not tell. He tasted the liquid, reacting with pleasure. "Are you hungry?"

Ninan looked down. "Yes, I am."

"There is no need to feel ashamed. I do not know many who can say they

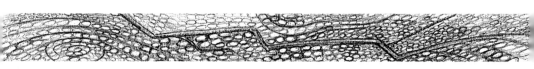

have never been hungry. You are welcome to share my dinner with me." He looked at her expectantly as he moved toward her.

She backed away, ready to run. "What do you want?" she asked.

The man laughed a bitter laugh. His face grew hard. "How is it you come to this forsaken mountain top? It is not likely you were searching for me."

"I was looking for a place to stay the night and smelled your fire. I thought I was imagining it because I am so hungry.

"Why are you not home with your family?"

She suddenly felt afraid, knowing she was alone with a strange man in a desolate place. "I am told I am a storyteller," she said resentfully, surprised to hear herself say it.

"Told? How can you be told you are a storyteller? You either are or you are not."

"Just before my parents died, they gave me the stories of my grandfather and told me I must tell his stories, the stories of our people. I have tried to do this but something bewildering happens. I learn one of his stories to tell but when I open my mouth, another story tells itself. When I say to myself, 'No, this is not the story I wish to tell,' and begin to tell the story I have learned, the story I was telling stops and the story of my grandfather disappears from my memory. How can I be a storyteller if I cannot tell the story I wish to tell?" Why was she telling all this to a stranger? she wondered, wishing she had not spoken.

"I am always wiser after a full stomach. Let us eat first and perhaps we will know more afterward." Ninan sat down near the fire and curled up into herself. She was tired and sad and felt centuries old. He dipped a large wooden spoon into the pot and filled a beautifully carved bowl with food that smelled delicious, giving it to Ninan. "Eat as much as you please. There is more than enough for both of us."

Ninan thought to protest but she was hungry and the man looked at her as if he did not want to be challenged. She ate slowly, wasting nothing, enjoying the sensation of hot food warming and filling her. The white-haired man continued to watch her. When she had emptied the bowl, he poured tea into it, and she drank, relieved to be free from hunger and thirst.

She tried not to watch the man's graceful movement and the surprising delicacy with which he ate, feeling uncomfortable with the way he kept looking at her. When he had finished, he offered her a fur wrap to put around herself. She started to refuse. He was a strange man and she felt uneasy in his presence, but darkness and fatigue decided for her. "I thank you for your kindness."

"You are most welcome. You can be sure of that."

Ninan shivered, trying to hide her fatigue from him, wanting to stay awake until he slept. "Go to sleep," he said. "You will come to no harm here."

Ninan was not so sure. She did not like the way his eyes followed her so she looked for a place to sleep, where she could run if necessary. He wrapped himself in a blanket and settled down near the fire. Ninan waited until he began to snore, then lay down near the edge of the fire and snuggled inside the fur wrap, lulled to sleep by a full stomach and the peaceful sounds of the crackling fire and a friendly night.

The snapping of branches woke her up. She heard his breathing. She felt him touch the fur wrap. Holding her breath, she waited, terrified. She felt him stroke the fur wrap. Then, his breathing grew heavy. Ninan froze. His caresses moved up and down the length of the wrap.

Without opening her eyes, she spoke in a harsh voice, "Go away!" The heavy breathing subsided. The caresses stopped. Then she heard a deep sigh and footsteps walking away. There were no more sounds. Ninan lay awake the rest of the night.

In the morning, the smell of porridge cooking was too much to resist. Ninan arose and washed herself, wondering if he had come to her when she was sleeping. Who else if not him? Had it been a bad dream? He filled her bowl and she ate, amazed to be hungry so soon after such a fine supper, grateful to have food without struggling to find it. To wake up warm and dry, with hot food waiting to be eaten felt like a miracle. "Do you live here alone?" she asked.

"Do you see anyone else?"

The curtness of his reply stung. "Do you miss the company of other people?"

"I have learned to keep myself company."

"But have you no need for someone to talk to?" To love, she thought to herself.

"I have taught myself to live as I do. It is sufficient."

Ninan wondered if this was truly his choice. "How is it you learned not to need people?"

"That is a long story," he replied, stoking the fire, rinsing his bowl and spoon. Ninan sat quietly and waited. Although she could not name what she felt, something about the way he kept looking at her made her apprehensive.

"I would like to hear your story," she said.

"You would, would you? I thought you were the storyteller," he said sharply. "I fed you. If you are a storyteller, is it not time to tell me a story?"

"It is true I have begun to tell stories but I do not know if I am a storyteller. For now, I am merely carrying out the wishes of my dying parents."

"If you don't want to tell stories, and your parents are dead, why do you continue? Why not stop and live your life as you choose?"

Ninan felt like saying, "It is not your concern," but she needed to talk about the turmoil inside her. Besides, she thought, I will never see him again. "It does not seem as if I have a choice. When I do not tell a story I feel shame, that I am betraying a promise, yet after I tell a story I feel lonely. I do not know how to be at peace inside myself. What you have learned is what I need to know. This is why I wish to hear your story."

"If I were you I would not be so sure. Besides, I gave you food and a place to sleep. If I now give you a story what will you give me?"

Torn between curiosity and a sense of danger, she said, "I have nothing to give you that is mine to give."

"You have something that I want." He walked toward her.

"You offered sustenance and I accepted. Nothing was said about repayment. If you tell me a story I will tell you one in return."

"How do I know your story will interest me?"

Ninan picked up her things and started to walk away.

"Wait. What is it you wish to know?"

"What brought you to this place? What is it like to live alone?"

"I do not wish to talk about it." Ninan looked disappointed. "What is one more story among a world of stories? Everyone has a story to tell but does this mean they should all be told?"

"Perhaps only the storyteller knows."

"You tell stories that come from your imagination rather than those in the book of your grandfather. Does this mean you know your stories are worth telling?"

Ninan flushed and looked away. He asked the very questions she asked herself. And to which she had no answers. "What I know is that I would like to hear your story."

"Very well," he said in a flat voice. "I suppose it began when I was a carpenter, traveling from village to village, fixing and mending as I wandered. I had work, food, and companionship in the evenings. I liked meeting new people, traveling to strange places. One day, when I was working in a village I had never been before, I saw a young woman who sang as she worked. Her eyes were full of mischief and she had a teasing way which made everyone smile. I fell in love with her before I knew her name." He paused, a look on his face that Ninan could not read.

"I did the work I came to do but she so filled my heart and mind and soul that I could not leave, so I found shelter. In the morning, I followed her to market. Although I knew nothing about her or she about me, I asked her to marry me, expecting her to make fun of my proposal, to say, 'What, me marry you? A poor traveling carpenter?' But, she took my arm and looked me in the face. I held my breath, hoping she would not find me wanting. 'It is too soon to answer such a question. Stay in our village. There is much to be repaired. When the moon is new, you will know my answer.' I worked hard, and just as she promised, the night of the new moon she came to me. 'I will be your wife.' I hardly knew what to do with my joy. I could not believe my great good fortune. I ignored the jealous looks of the young men in her village. She was mine and I meant to keep her."

His words made Ninan shiver. She watched him take a long drink of water, wondering what he might do to 'keep her.' The man continued without noticing Ninan's gaze. "We traveled and worked together. I did carpentry and she sold baskets that she wove at night. When we knew we would soon have a child, we found a small piece of land that a farmer was willing to let us use in exchange for service. I built a small cottage and worked only as far as I could go in a day. She made a vegetable garden and exchanged produce and baskets for hens. We sold the eggs and soon bought a cow so we could sell the cheese we made from the milk. When our daughter was born, we joyfully welcomed her with love."

Shuddering, he stood up, looking at the mountains in the distance. Ninan hesitated before asking, "Then what happened?"

"One morning, I left to build a storage shed for a blacksmith." He stopped to wipe his forehead. "I was just finishing a large shelf, when I felt a great pain in the middle of my body. For a time I could not move. I collapsed to the ground amazed I could feel such agony and still live. When it stopped for a few seconds, I took a breath, thinking it had ended. The pain returned, deeper and more terrible than before. I lay on the ground writhing, absolutely sure that I was dying. I worried that my wife would never know what happened to me. Then, just as suddenly, the pain stopped. I waited, but nothing happened. The pain was completely gone. Not even a trace remained. My relief changed to fear and I knew I had to go home. People thought I was crazy and I agreed; yet I could not run fast enough. I was afraid to go home but even more afraid to stay."

He paused, the silence too thick to interrupt. "I found the garden torn apart, vegetables strewn everywhere. Scattered feathers were all that remained of the chickens. I yelled to my wife like a crazy man. When there was no answer I forced myself to go into our cottage."

"What did you see?" asked Ninan, afraid to hear the answer.

"My wife and child were covered with blood. In my wife's hand was a piece of material, the kind soldiers wear. Her fingers grasped the material so tightly I could barely take it out of her hand but I wanted that material, the one clue I had to the killer of my family." He stared at the distant mountains. "I dug their graves in the garden."

He glared at Ninan with such a fierce look she found herself wondering if the story was true. Ashamed of thinking this, she asked, "What did you do then?"

"After days of sitting sleepless by their grave, I fell asleep but the nightmares were… I decided to look for a soldier missing a piece of his uniform. The thought of spilling his blood kept me alive."

"Did you ever find him?"

"No."

"Is that when you came up to the mountain?"

"Yes."

"What was it like? Living all alone? So far from people?"

"I could not bear the sight of people. I came up here where I could take out my rage by chopping down trees and carving small things to sell for the food and supplies I needed."

Ninan stood up. "Did you never think to find another wife?"

"I told you a story. Now it is your turn to tell me one, even though you say you do not want to be a storyteller." His words were mocking and the look in his eye was unsettling.

"Your story does not feel finished."

"That is for me to decide, not you."

She walked as far away from him as she thought she could yet still tell a story. "Very well." Too anxious to sit and close her eyes, yet needing time to see the images in her head, she paced in front of the fire, back and forth, waiting for the words to begin.

It was a time of drought. Even the oldest people could not remember such a long dry spell. And the heat made it worse. Children whimpered listlessly as crops withered and animals died. As one villager said, "Even the river has stopped singing." No one knew what to do. Who could think of a solution when the sun beat down on baked earth day after day? Some said the drought was punishment but could not say for what. Others said unusually powerful winds had pushed the rain to other places. But no matter what people said, no rain fell.

Then, one day, a stranger appeared at the edge of the village, dressed in skins of animals, looking almost like an animal himself. And that evening, when he came to ask for food in exchange for work, he was told there was no work, and not much food, for the drought had taken its toll on all living things.

"Well then,' said the stranger, 'if you will feed me, I will make it rain." People laughed bitterly, knowing too well that rain comes and rain goes, but never by the will of man. "I will make it rain, I promise."

"And if you do not, we will have less food, with nothing to show for your promise," said a young woman holding a fretting baby. "If you can make it rain, do so. There is time enough for supper."

"I cannot remember when I last ate," he said.

"That is trouble indeed and I am sorry for your hunger," she said, "but I have troubles of my own. I can barely feed my child and my well is all but dry. Move on if you merely mean to talk. We have no need of false hopes here."

The man said, "I will make it rain if you will spare me a piece of bread." The woman stared at him for a time. Fighting hope. Yet she was desperate. They were all desperate. In the end, she gave him her last crust of bread. He ate it

slowly. Savoring each morsel. She watched the last crumb disappear. Waited for his first excuse. Thinking he would run away.

"I need your help." She wondered what he would ask of her, wishing she had family close at hand. "We must go to the river and sit beside it. Will you come?" Reluctantly she nodded, strapped the baby to her back, and followed the stranger to the river. They sat beside the thin trickle--what was left of the once flowing water. "You must believe if I am to succeed."

"My mind tells me you are fooling me but my heart . . . my heart is foolish."

"Perhaps your heart is wiser than your mind," he said as he began to dig a small hole at the side of the water. The woman watched, puzzled. Then, she crossed to the other side and, without knowing why, began to dig as he did. She watched the water fill her hole and dug another. Water filled this hole as well. All night they dug holes, widening the stream at the place of their digging. Towards morning, the man stood up and sang a wordless song. The woman stood on her side and joined in, harmonizing as the dark slowly lightened into pink.

When the first drops of rain touched her face she thought she was crying. Disbelieving, she touched the wetness with her fingers. Laughed as she licked the moisture with her tongue. Her mind told her she was dreaming but her heart knew better. She looked at the rain, gently falling. Amazed. She thought to thank the stranger but he had disappeared. She had no name by which to call him. There was nothing to do but walk back to her cottage.

"Then what happened?" asked the man.

Ninan shrugged. "I do not know."

"A fine storyteller you are. Maybe you better work harder to learn the stories already told." He put more wood on the fire. Ninan prepared to leave. "Where are you going?" he asked.

"I have taken too much of your time."

The man took Ninan's hand but she jerked it away. "I noticed you admiring the plate and bowl I carved. Stay with me for a few days and I will teach you how to do it. Carving is a useful skill. Of course you need a knife…"

"I have a knife."

"If you are worried about your stories…"

"Even storytellers need to eat."

"Well then, let us begin. First we must make sure your knife is sharp enough. Then I will show you how to choose the wood that is best for what you want to make." Ninan felt a surge of excitement as she sharpened her knife, that at least she knew how to do.

The afternoon passed quickly, too quickly. Ninan concentrated on following the man's advice, surprised when it began to grow dark. Still, she had the makings of a little bowl and was content. After dinner, sitting near the fire, the man asked Ninan to tell him another story.

"I have no story to tell."

"You mean you will not," mocked the man.

"Do not put words into my mouth," she said, standing up.

"Stay! You said yourself it was good to have company. Let us be companions for a time." He smiled at her. "I have a gift I would like to give you, something I thought I would keep forever." He put his hands on the back of his neck and took off a fine gold chain with a small red stone. With shaking hands, he put it on Ninan.

Ninan touched the beautiful necklace, wanting more than anything to keep it. "I cannot accept such a gift. It is too valuable."

"It looks like it was made for you, for your lovely neck. You must wear it," said the man, his fingers caressing her throat. Ninan shivered. "You are a fine looking woman."

"I am still a girl," she said, knowing this was not true.

"I know the difference between a girl and a woman. So should you. Especially when you walk alone. You court danger." Ninan stepped away from his closeness.

"I can take care of myself," she said, thinking about the nighttime visitor.

"Even when you sleep?" he asked.

"I sleep with my knife. It is sharper now than it was yesterday. I am not afraid to use it."

"Perhaps we should have a test. Words are easily spoken."

Ninan took out her knife. "I need no test," she said, trying to sound more confident than she felt. She pointed the blade toward him.

He forced a laugh and said, "Perhaps not," then spoke more kindly. "I do not want you to leave in anger. Can we not be friends?" His look spoke clearly what he meant as he moved toward her, reaching out to touch her.

Ninan was so astonished she almost dropped her knife. "Friends? I think not."

"I am sorry if I frightened you."

"It is too late for sorry." She backed away, struggling to take off his necklace without letting go of her knife. Then she flung it at him. "I want no presents from you."

"Did I not feed you when you were hungry? Give you a warm safe place to sleep? Do these things not matter?" He looked at the necklace lying on the ground. "Put away your knife, you have no need of it with me. I am an old man, I cannot hurt you." He picked up the necklace and walked toward her.

She wondered, how old is too old to hurt? He looked strong. "I believe it is time for me to leave." Keeping her knife in one hand, she gathered her possessions and hurried into the forest. Although she wanted to look back, to make sure he was not following her, she fought the urge. Only when she needed to stop to catch her breath did she dare to turn. There he was, following close behind her.

Ninan ran. She could hear his footsteps coming closer. Although she was tired and out of breath, fear kept her moving. She decided to leave the path, hoping he would not follow her but the thick underbrush made it difficult to cover much ground. Still, it was growing dark and there was no moon, she would find a place to hide. Struggling to regain her balance after falling on a root, she felt his hand on her shoulder. With her free hand she pushed him away and stood up, knife in hand. "You claim to be an old man yet you run far and fast. Your white hair fooled me."

"I took care of you. Now it is your turn to take care of me."

"I thanked you for your kindness. There was no talk of payment so be on your way, old man." She stood, knife in hand, blade pointed at him, forcing herself to meet his gaze without flinching.

When he lunged at her she stabbed him in the chest. "Whore!" he screamed. "You are all whores." Holding his chest, he collapsed to the ground, blood seeping through his shirt.

Ninan gasped, unable to believe what she had done. Without waiting to see how badly he was hurt, she ran back to the path, ignoring his groans and cries for help. This time she did not look back. Spurred by terror, she ran long and fast into the dark night.

SIX
BY THE WARMTH OF THE FIRE

inan covered as much ground as she could for many days before she felt safe enough to put away her knife. She hugged her shawl for comfort, unable to stop reliving the moment when she thrust the knife into his body. She had trouble sleeping though she kept the knife in her hand. Each unexpected sound made her heart race. One night, sleeping near a stream she heard a snort and readied her knife only to see a small wild pig walking toward the water. She lay awake until the first rays of the sun reminded her another day had dawned. She got up more tired than when she first lay down, continuing her journey with only the habit of walking to keep her going.

She tried to think of other things. After the death of her parents she had pretended not to remember her life with them but now she welcomed thoughts about her early life. She recalled times around the table, after supper, when her parents would ask her to tell them about her day, encouraging her to put even small experiences into stories. Although at the time she thought nothing of it, now she realized this was how they decided she could do what they could not, tell the stories of their people.

When the road on which she was walking forked, she stopped, trying to decide which branch to take. It is true, she thought, I do have choices: Left? Right? Straight ahead? Into the forest? Not ready to walk into another forest, she decided it was time to find a village. After making the decision she felt better, especially when a blue jay flew on a branch and began scolding her. She mimicked the scolding sounds and was surprised when he responded, scolding louder than before. Their exchange felt calming, as if she was no longer alone, so she began to listen more closely to birdcalls, imitating them as best she could.

As she walked, she remembered there was a story about birds in her grandfather's book. Lost in thought while trying to think of the story, she tripped on a stone and crashed to the earth with a suddenness that left her stunned and in pain. Adding to her confusion were sounds of laughter. Someone was amused by her misfortune. She looked up to see a young man watching her. "Take your laugh and leave," said Ninan crossly. "I see nothing funny about falling down and hurting yourself." She wiped the blood from her knee with a piece of her skirt but the blood continued to gush.

"Let me help," he said. Taking a rag from his pocket, he pressed it against the cut. Ninan watched as her earlier annoyance gave way to curiosity. He was a handsome man, with thick curly black hair, bright blue eyes, and his grin…. When he had stopped the bleeding, he wrapped the injured knee with care and skill. "Do you think you can stand?" he asked, offering her his hand for support. Ninan was about to take it when, once again, he laughed.

"What is so funny?" she snapped, pulling back her hand.

He laughed again but seeing the anger in her eyes, said, "Look at the road. There is not another stone on it for as far as the eye can see. You tripped on this one as if you were looking for it. Perhaps you were longing to meet me and fell to create your opportunity."

"I was not looking for it or you. Take your laugh for a walk on your nice, smooth road and leave me alone. I am sure you can find many others who will encourage your laughter."

"If this is what you wish then I will do it, though I think you might at least thank me for fixing your cut. If I do say so myself, I have stopped your bleeding, bandaged your wound, saved your skirt from being stained by blood, and . . ."

"Thank you," snapped Ninan. "Would you like me to return your bandage?"

"No," he grinned, "I should like you to keep it as a remembrance of me."

"Hah!" snorted Ninan. "What makes you think I want to remember you?"

"Why not? Surely you are not rescued by the likes of me every day?" Once more he laughed a hearty laugh that rolled up from his center and out through his eyes.

Ninan blushed, unable to think of a suitable retort. Refusing his help to stand up, she hobbled toward the center of the village. Her knee hurt less than her

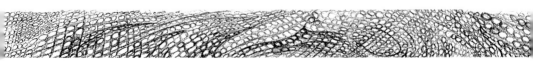

pride and she wished he would disappear, just as much as she wished he would stay.

He watched her limp for a few minutes and then strode over to her. "What is your name?"

"That is none of your concern."

"That is a strange name, Miss That is None of Your Concern," he said, laughing again.

"Why is it you find everything so funny?"

"Aren't you going to ask me my name?"

"No," said Ninan. "I ask a question which you do not answer. Then you ask me to ask you something I have no interest in knowing. I do not want to know your name, nor anything else," she said, knowing this was not true. "Good day. Go away." She wanted to run off but her leg was too stiff and painful.

He kept looking at her and her eyes met his in spite of her determination not to return his gaze. "Go home and laugh at your wife!"

"I do not have a wife," he answered with mock gravity. "But I am looking for one. Will you marry me? I am willing, in spite of your bad temper and lack of proper gratitude."

"No. Definitely not! Now please, go away! I have work to do."

"What is your work?" he asked, genuinely curious.

"If I tell you, will you leave me alone?"

"What? Leave an interesting young woman who can barely walk? "No," he answered. "Certainly not."

"And why not, pray tell?" asked Ninan, exasperated.

"Because I like you."

His grin irritated Ninan. "How can you like someone you don't know? Besides, if this is true, why do you keep laughing at me when you see I am in pain?"

"I laugh because you make me laugh. You make me feel good."

"How? By falling down and hurting myself?" Without waiting for an answer, she limped away from him as quickly as she could. He watched her go and started to follow, but was stopped by the blacksmith.

"Hey, Mikos, my black mare has a large cut on her flank. Can you come and fix her?"

"Now?" asked Mikos.

"If not now, when?" Mikos watched Ninan stop to talk with village women who were washing their clothes on the bank of the river and hoped she would stay for a while. He was intrigued by her sass and quick tongue. "Come now, Mikos," urged the blacksmith, "my mare is suffering." Reluctantly, Mikos turned and followed him.

Out of the corner of her eye, Ninan saw him leave and felt an uncomfortable mixture of regret and relief.

After asking permission to join the women, she took out her dirty clothes and soaked them in the stream, enjoying the feel of the cool water, trying to find a position that did not aggravate the pain in her knee. A woman, younger than the others, wearing a bright blue apron tied around her middle, pounded dirt out of a large pile of clothes, staring at her. "I have not seen you before. Who are you?" Ninan sighed, wondering what to say. Before she could answer, another woman asked, "What is your name? What brings you to our village?"

"Ninan." She answered reluctantly, feeling awkward and uncertain, not wanting to think about the last time she'd told a story. "I…am a storyteller." She liked the look of the young woman who seemed welcoming. "What is your name?" she asked her, rubbing a blouse against a stone, hoping to wash away the stains from when she fell, running away from the white-haired man.

"Natasha," answered the young woman. "A storyteller, how wonderful." The other women murmured their agreement. "Would you tell us a story?" asked several of them.

"Now?" asked Ninan. "While we are washing our clothes?"

"Please," begged Natasha. "If you tell us a story, I will help you wash your clothes"

"I cannot ask you to do that. You have enough of your own to wash."

"Your few clothes will make no difference"

"I would be pleased to tell you a story though you do not have to wash my clothes in return." She took out her grandfather's book.

"I do not mean to be rude," said the woman, "but can you not tell us a story? One you make up just for us?"

"Yes," chorused the others. "Make a story for us that is our very own."

"This is not so easy," said Ninan.

"We will give you food and water. As you eat and drink, you can think about what to tell us. While you are thinking, we will be washing. What could be better?"

"Just like that?" Ninan smiled, delighted by the friendliness of the women.

"Yes, of course," they answered, bringing her a small basket with bread, cheese, and an apple, lined with a beautifully embroidered napkin.

Moved by their offering she said, "I will try, but I make no promises that you will like my story."

"We do not ask for promises, all we ask for is a story." The women nodded and then went back to their washing. As Ninan nibbled and drank, she watched them work. When she began to tell the story, they listened intently, never stopping their pounding and rubbing and squeezing and rinsing, laying out the clean clothes on rocks to dry in the sun.

nce upon a time there lived a small yellow bird. No one knew where it lived in winter. No one knew where it lived in summer. The only time anyone saw it was at noon, rain or shine. Then, the bird would perch on a small fir tree and sing from the top branch. When its song was finished, the bird would fly away, out of sight until noon the next day when it would begin singing the same song it had sung the day before. No one could remember a day the bird had not come.

One day, while the bird was singing its song, a wealthy man came by with his hunters. Hearing the bird sing, they stopped to listen. Entranced by its beauty and song, the man decided to capture it to bring back to his mansion. But, before he could trap it, the bird flew away. "Who knows where this bird lives?" asked the man. The people were silent. "Well? I ask you again. Where does this bird live?"

"We do not know," answered several villagers. "It comes only at noon to sing for a few minutes and then it flies away."

The man turned to his men and commanded, "Tomorrow we will return with nets and rope. I want that bird."

The villagers were upset and stood silently, afraid to say anything. Slowly, they moved away. A little girl said to her mother, "Are you going to let that man take our bird?"

"It is not our bird any more than it is his. The bird comes and goes as it pleases. This is the way of wild things."

"But he says he will capture it," cried the child. "The bird will die."

"It is easier to speak than to act," answered her mother.

"He has many big strong men to help him and the bird is very little. How will it know it is in danger? I am afraid they will catch the bird and then we will never see it again."

"Hush, child, the bird will not be harmed," said her mother.

"How do you know?" persisted the child.

Her mother took her daughter into her arms, hugged her lovingly, and brushed her hair away from her eyes. "Because I know," answered her mother. And with this, the little girl tried to be content, yet she could not stop worrying about the tiny bird and sent a silent message up to the sky, warning the bird of the danger that lay ahead.

"The next day, a few minutes before noon, the man marched to the tree with twenty of his largest, bravest, and strongest hunters. They surrounded the tree where the bird usually sang. People watched from a distance, afraid to come closer. No one spoke. Just as the village bell struck twelve, the little bird flew to a branch, high up in the fir tree and began to sing. "Now!" shouted the man. His hunters threw a large net up to where the bird was, but the bird flew to a higher branch and continued to sing. "Now!" shouted the man again. His hunters threw an even larger net into the higher branches but the bird flew to the top of the tree and finished its song before flying off toward the mountains.

The little girl clapped her hands in delight and laughed. "You were right, Mother. You were right. The bird knows more than all those hunters."

The man overheard the child and walked over to her, menace in his voice. "What did you say, little girl?"

The child was frightened but somehow she found her tongue. "My mother said you cannot catch the bird."

"Hush, child," urged her mother but the man paid no attention to the woman. He moved between the little girl and her mother and bent down.

"And how does your mother know this?" he questioned.

"Because she knows," replied the child. "And she is right."

"We will see if this is truly so," said the man. "When I want something, I get it, and I want this bird." He stomped away, beckoning his hunters to follow him. The men disappeared, creating a wall of dust as they drove their horses out of the forest at high speed.

The child looked at the tree where the bird sang its song and wondered if it was large enough to keep the bird safe from the hunters, but her mother's words, "Because I know," rang in her ears, soothing the worst of her fears. Just to make sure the bird was warned, however, she spoke to it. "Little bird, the hunters want to catch you. Take good care of yourself. Please! We love to hear your song." With that, she hurried to her mother, still wishing there was something she could do to keep the bird safe from the net of the hunters.

The next day and the next, the hunters came and attempted to catch the bird but the tiny yellow bird simply flew to a higher branch. The man grew increasingly angry. "I will have this bird. I will have what I want." He called his men together and told them of his new plan. The hunters agreed to meet the next day with extra nets and special dress.

Just as the bell struck half past the hour of eleven, ten of the hunter's men covered themselves with green cloth and climbed to the highest part of the tree that was strong enough to bear their weight. They settled in amongst the branches and waited for the bird to come. Once again the villagers gathered to hear the bird. When they saw the hunters, already in the tree, they feared for the bird's safety. They knew the bird was in terrible danger. The man, standing beneath the tree saw their worry and growled, "If any of you so much as makes one little sound of warning, I will have you thrown into prison for life. I want this bird and I get what I want." People silently moved away from the tree.

At the stroke of twelve, the bird flew around the tree, looking for a branch on which to perch but just as it appeared to rest, it flew away to settle on another branch. As it came close, one of the hunters reached out to net it.

"No!" shouted the little girl. "No! Leave the bird alone." As if the bird understood, it flew to another tree, even taller than the fir, and chirped merrily.

The man was furious and strode toward the little girl. Her mother grabbed her and tried to run, but the child held her ground even as he screamed. "You warned the bird. You spoiled my chance to capture it. I will have you punished. I will have your mother thrown in prison. I will have you spanked until you cannot walk. I will . . . ." The villagers silently watched from a distance.

The child's mother spoke defiantly. "We have as much right to hear the bird sing as you do. In truth, the bird belongs to no one. If my daughter's cry did indeed save the bird, she acted out of love. You will not harm her or me. Now, let us pass."

When the man ordered his men to grab the child and woman, the villagers surrounded them, protecting them from capture. "She is right. The bird sings for all of us. It is not yours to take."

The man, separated from his band of hunters, could do nothing. The band of hunters refused to attack the villagers. He angrily watched the little girl and her mother walk away, smiling.

The next day, and for several weeks thereafter, the man and his hunters tried every way they knew to catch the little bird, but no matter what they planned, the bird escaped. The villagers watched, hoping the bird would continue to sing. Their silent witness enraged the man and made him try even harder to catch the bird, but the bird always found a way to fly to freedom.

One day, the man did not return. Nor did he come back the next day, or the next week. For a while the villagers continued to worry about the bird's safety yet each day they gathered at noon, and each noon the little yellow bird sang its song. The man never returned to try to capture the bird.

As far as I know, it is still singing.

Ninan paused, opened her eyes, and waited. The women continued to rinse their clothes. "A good story," said Natasha. "Yes, I like this story."

"Why do men always think they have a right to everything they want?" asked a young girl. Some of the others laughed.

An older woman protested, "Not all men."

"No," teased a young woman," almost all. I would like to hear that bird." A chorus of voices agreed with her. One woman chirped like a bird. The other women laughed.

Natasha finished the last of her wash and said to Ninan, "Come, have supper with me and my family. You will be most welcome. Probably they will ask you to tell them a story. We love to hear stories."

"Thank you. You are most kind but I must not linger."

"What is your hurry?" Natasha folded the laundry and put it in a basket.

"Please, do not trouble yourself. I cannot stay."

"Why not? We have food enough to share and we can give you a fresh bandage for your knee." She put the basket on top of her head, balancing it with ease.

Ninan thought about the times she had spent with kind people only to feel pain when it came time to leave. "I must be free to come and go," she said to Natasha. "It is not possible for me to stay with you tonight."

Natasha eyed her shrewdly. "Are you afraid we will keep you from leaving? Please eat with us. Stay the night. Morning will be time enough to be on your way."

Ninan felt torn. She hated saying goodbye. The best way to be a storyteller, she thought, would be to tell a story and leave quickly, without getting to know or like anyone. Natasha took her silence for agreement. "Good! The others will be pleased."

"Others?" asked Ninan.

"Yes," answered Natasha. "We are five; my husband, my brother, the mother of my husband, and our two children. You can see how easy it will be for us to provide food and shelter for one more. Follow me. I will walk slowly so you do not strain your injured knee." She started walking toward her home, humming. Ninan followed, limping. Her knee ached.

The two small children would not let her rest. With weary good humor, Ninan played with them, provided unasked for help in the kitchen, and then at dusk, lit the fire. The small flickering flames grew stronger. Ninan sat by the fire trying to stay awake.

As the family gathered around the table, one of the children asked, "Where is Ninan? I want her to sit next to me." Natasha saw her curled into herself like a cat, fast asleep.

"Mikos, go and wake our guest. She will be hungry if she does not eat." He shrugged, and walked over to the fireplace to wake the sleeping figure. When he saw Ninan, he remembered his encounter with her earlier in the day and smiled as he gently touched her shoulder, wondering what she would say when she saw him.

"Wake up, beauty, the food is on the table. It is time to eat." He took her hand and lightly stroked it, as if she were a small child. Ninan opened her eyes and sat up with a start when she saw who had woken her up. Uncurling herself, she slowly stood up, aware of his eyes on her, unwilling to accept any help from him.

Natasha called to them from the table. "The fire may burn all evening but food will not stay hot forever." Ninan followed Mikos to the table. With one last glance at the fire, she joined the family gathering, talking and eating and passing food.

The mother of Mikos filled a plate and gave it to Ninan who took it, wondering if she would be able to eat. Natasha voiced her concern. "You are not eating, do you not like our food?"

"I think I am too tired to eat. I am sorry."

"Rest by the fire," said Natasha. "When you feel hungry there is food in the kitchen."

"You are very kind but I think it is time for me to find a place to sleep for the night."

"You are sleeping here!" said Mikos, astonished.

"No," said Ninan firmly. "I am not."

"You have an injured knee," said Mikos. "Stay until it is healed. Think of the trouble you had walking here this afternoon. It is swollen and tomorrow it will hurt even more. What are you thinking of? To leave now makes no sense."

Ninan wanted to stay. She wanted to eat with the family and to warm herself near the fire, but she felt if she stayed she would never want to leave. "I cannot explain. It is enough for me to tell you I must leave." Limping slowly, she moved toward the door. Mikos followed her, and then moved between Ninan and the door. "Let me pass." Mikos remained. "Please, let me be."

"What are you afraid of?" he asked. "We are pleased to have you stay. If you are upset about my behavior this afternoon, I apologize."

Trying to hide the tears that filled her eyes, Ninan said, "You do not understand."

"No, I do not."

"It is very complicated," she said.

"Come, sit with me by the fire. I will listen."

He helped her move to a chair near the fireplace. "I had a mother and a father," she began.

"We have all had a mother and a father," responded Mikos.

"True, but not all mothers and fathers are like mine. Just before they died, they made me promise that I would carry on the work of my grandfather, a storyteller, so the stories of our people would not die. They told me I must live alone for only then would I be free to move as a storyteller must, wandering from village to village."

"But why do you have to live by yourself?" asked Mikos.

"Because men do not follow women. Women follow men." Mikos was silent. Ninan looked at him sadly, "Now you know why I must go." Ninan looked and felt wretched.

Mikos hesitated before he spoke. "If you leave because you are afraid to stay the night, what kind of life will you have? If you never know anyone, how will you learn new stories? If you are a storyteller, you must have people to tell your stories to. People who want to hear your stories." He put another log on the fire. "And if you live in terror, what kind of stories will you tell? All your stories will be filled with fear. What about happiness? What about love? How will you find new stories?"

"What you say is true, yet it is not the whole truth. There are many ways for a storyteller to become part of a village, to stop telling stories. My parents warned me there would come a time, many times, perhaps, when I would be so lonely I would be tempted to stop being a storyteller. They begged me to honor their wishes and the tradition of my grandfather."

"Surely staying one night with friendly people is not enough to keep you from telling stories. Your leg is injured. If you keep walking on it your knee will not heal properly. Sit by the fire and rest until morning. No one wishes to keep you from your journey." Seeing the uncertainty in her eyes, Mikos brought a blanket and helped her find a comfortable resting place. Ninan reassured herself she would feel more able to travel in the morning, that it was only sensible to stay. Mikos brought her a cup of tea and a plate of food. She ate and drank slowly, aware of the way he looked at her and how she felt.

"Thank you for the tea and food. It seems I was hungry after all."

"It is nothing," he replied, putting another log on the fire.

"You are wrong. It is not nothing. I appreciate kindness." She gave him the cup and plate, thinking what she might do in return but her eyes closed and she soon slept. Mikos watched her for a while then went to sleep with a heavy heart.

In the morning Natasha went to start the fire and greet Ninan. Not finding her, she called to her brother, "Mikos, have you seen Ninan?"

"No, I thought she was with you. I will ask the others if they have seen her." He returned looking unhappy. "No one saw her leave. No one knows where she is."

SEVEN
THE CROSSING POINT

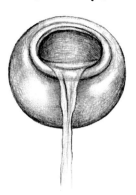

inan walked blindly, oblivious to the pain in her knee, not caring where she went, what she ate, or if she slept. Her grandfather's book felt as if it weighed one hundred pounds. Most days she walked until she was too tired to do anything but sleep by the side of a road. Even the threat of being attacked failed to stir her. She awoke tired, as if she had not slept, as if she were living in a bad dream. Moving from village to village and place to place, she listened and looked, but heard and saw nothing, unable to speak. She kept remembering Mikos' words: "If you live in terror, what kind of stories will you tell? All your stories will be filled with fear. What about happiness? What about love? How will you find new stories?"

One morning, just after waking, she heard crying. At first she thought she was dreaming but no matter how she shook herself, the crying continued. She looked around carefully, going behind rocks and over trunks of trees that had fallen but saw no one. Puzzled, Ninan gathered her things and walked toward the sounds but could not find the source. When she called out softly, "Hello," the crying eased. Someone sighed and took a deep breath. Once more she called out, "Hello," and the crying gradually subsided. Ninan waited until she lost patience and left. Once, she thought she heard someone just behind her, but when she turned she saw no one. The crying sound stayed with her. Though she tried to put it out of her mind, she kept hearing it. Irritated and frustrated, she walked toward what appeared to be a village in the far distance, hoping that whoever or whatever was making the sound would tire of following her.

Although it was early in the morning, the day was already hot, without even a small cooling breeze. Towards noon, she came to the village and looked for water. She stopped some small children and asked, "Please, tell me where I may find water."

"There is none," replied a boy.

"Do you not have wells?"

A girl answered, "The last well went dry yesterday."

One of the children began to cry, "Even the streams have dried up."

"What has happened?" asked Ninan.

"A man bought land upriver from the village and blocked the river to make a lake for his swans to swim. Now there is not enough water to fill our wells."

"But how can he do that?" gasped Ninan.

"He is rich," said a girl. "My father says rich people can do whatever they want. We are poor and the man refuses to talk to our elders. No one knows how to stop him."

Ninan was outraged. "But he must allow water to flow . . . The village cannot survive without water. Surely he will talk to someone. Perhaps he does not know . . ."

A child interrupted. "Many people have tried to talk to him. Not only from our village but from other villages as well. No one has enough water now. We have to walk a long way to find water for cooking and drinking. The animals are dying of thirst. It is very difficult."

"Everyone wants to do something but no one knows what to do," cried a small girl. She stared at Ninan. "Perhaps you know what we can do to return water to our wells."

Ninan shook her head. "No, I do not." The children looked helpless. "I am sure someone will think of something." Her words brought no reassurance. She wished she knew how to help.

She felt the uneasy quiet in the village. Only a few old people walked about, carrying small bundles and bowls. A boy noticed Ninan looking and said, "The old people carry what water they can find but it takes many trips to fill a pot. We cannot stand here and talk. We must help them." They ran off leaving Ninan feeling bewildered.

She could not imagine a village without water. The idea that one man could create such devastation seemed incredible. That his pleasure should be more

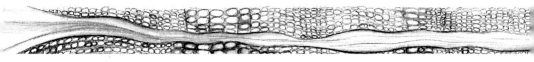

important than the survival of so many people was outrageous, reminding her of the bird story she told to Natasha and her friends. She thought she remembered a story in her grandfather's book about a king who had forbidden people in a village to use the water, claiming it was only his to use.

Left alone, Ninan went to find a shady place where she could rest and read. Although she was thirsty, she was afraid to follow the children and old people. It seemed wrong to use any of their water. As she walked to a large, old tree, she realized her knee no longer ached. Bending it carefully, she noticed it was no longer stiff, and that was one less worry.

Carefully taking the book out of the sack, she looked for the story. She stopped, thinking she heard the crying once again, but then decided she was imagining it even though the sounds were as vivid as if they had been real. "This is strange," she said to herself, unable to imagine what the crying could mean, if anything. She forced herself to put the crying out of her mind and once more, began to read the stories of her grandfather. She was so absorbed in reading she did not hear the approaching footsteps of a large, heavyset man.

His deep voice startled Ninan. "Who are you? What do you want? Why are you here?" The questions came quickly, one on top of the other, giving Ninan no time to answer. "What book are you reading at midday?" He attempted to grab the book but Ninan held it tightly to her chest, ready to run if he grabbed at it again.

"Who are you?" she challenged, as she stood up, moving away from the man, more angry than frightened. "Why do you try to steal my book?"

He stepped toward her. "You are a stranger here. What do you want? Why have you come? We have trouble enough in this village. We do not need any more."

"I am a storyteller," she said quickly. "I tell stories in exchange for food and shelter. I only stopped because I was thirsty and thought to find water."

The man grimaced. "If it is water you want, you will find none here. Our needs are not as important as the pleasures of a man who cares more for swans than people."

Ninan answered softly. "I have heard. Some children told me of your troubles."

The man tightened his fists and spat out words. "Troubles! I could end these troubles in one minute if the others would agree. They are too timid to act."

"What do you want to do?" asked Ninan.

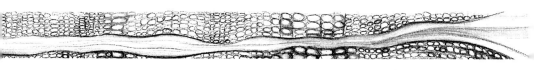

"I will not be telling that to a stranger. What is in that book? There are so many pages."

Ninan echoed the man, "I will not be telling that to a stranger, especially one who threatens to take it from me though it does him no harm." She wanted to walk away, but her belongings lay behind the man, near the tree, and she would not move around him to retrieve them. The two stood staring at each other, as if ready to fight.

He was more than a head taller, with hair and beard as dark as her hair was light. His body told of someone used to hard labor, who did not often take no for an answer. She was sturdy yet graceful. Her presence was strong. She did not look like a person who would easily give up her rights or bend her will to the dictates of another.

Then, once again the crying sounds intruded, filling Ninan with confusion. She brushed her clothing as if to get rid of the unwanted sounds. She muttered to herself, "Go away, I have troubles enough without hearing cries I cannot find."

"What is the matter?" asked the man. "You grow pale."

Ninan blushed. "It is nothing."

"I do not think you speak the truth." His tone of voice softened. "Ach, I am a foolish man to treat a young woman as I have. You are not the enemy. I am sorry for my harsh words."

Ninan nodded. "It is hard to have no water."

"What is hard is to see our water taken from us, to be powerless. We are used to making do in times of drought. I am torn to pieces when I watch my wife walk half the morning just to wash our clothes. I see my old mother using all her strength just to fill a cup with water. This is not right. A man cannot stand by and watch his family and neighbors suffer. Not for any man's whim should we go thirsty. Not for any man's pleasure should we have to bury animals." He looked away.

She followed his gaze, "Is that where the lake is?"

"Yes. That is where he hoards for himself what is not his to keep."

"Is the lake only for his pleasure?" questioned Ninan. "Does he not also use it for drinking and washing? For watering his fields?"

"No, that is why we are so angry. He has many wells, water enough to supply all his needs. He makes a lake to watch a pair of swans." Once more he clenched his fists and smashed some bushes. "This cannot last. We must have water. I will find a

way to make them listen to me or die trying. This is no way to live."

"What can you do? Why will no one listen to your plan? Can they . . ."

He interrupted her, "You say you are a storyteller. What kind of stories do you tell?"

"I tell the stories of my grandfather, from his book. But sometimes I tell other stories, from inside. And sometimes…"

"What does that mean?" he challenged. "From inside?"

Ninan shrugged, "Some stories seem to tell themselves. I open my mouth and the story begins. I tell it to myself as much as to those who listen. But there are other stories…"

"What about them?"

Ninan hesitated. The man had his own worries. Besides, she had no clear way of explaining what happened, even to herself. He was looking at her, his anger replaced by interest. She took a chance. "There are times when I seem to be telling the story of people listening yet I do not know them and I do not know how I know their story. It frightens me."

"But where does the story come from? A story cannot come from nowhere."

"I agree but this is all I can tell you. The stories come if I tell what I see, but I do not know where what I see comes from."

"I would like to hear such a story." He laughed without mirth. "Perhaps we need a story like that. Perhaps there is a way to end our misery we cannot yet see. Come, have food with my family and me this evening. Perhaps a story will take our minds off our troubles, at least for a little while."

"Thank you," responded Ninan. "I would be pleased to come."

Still thinking about what she had said, and unable to make sense of it, the man asked, "But how do you know a story will come out after dinner?"

Ninan was unable to explain what she did not understand. "The stories come if I do not stop them, if I do not try to change what I see in my mind." Once again she heard the crying, louder, more intense. She shivered, wishing the man had also heard the sound.

"How could you stop them?"

"By not being quiet, by not listening . . . By not telling what I see. By trying to make the story do what it does not want to do."

Bewildered, he shook his head. "I do not understand."

Ninan shrugged. "I do not understand it either. I just know I want to tell my grandfather's stories yet the stories in my mind's eye tell themselves."

"What were you reading when I came upon you?"

"I was looking for a story in my grandfather's book that I thought I remembered reading. About a king who claimed the village wells belonged only to him. He threatened to kill anyone who tried to drink from the wells he said were his and his alone."

"What happened?" asked the man eagerly.

"I do not remember. That is why I was looking for the story."

"Ach, I am being foolish. What can a story in an old book have to do with what is happening now, to us?" The man started to leave but Ninan stopped him.

"Perhaps the story will help us to find a way to regain the water."

"Us?" mocked the man. "You are free to leave any time you choose. Us!"

Ninan recoiled as if she had been hit, holding her book close to her. As she started to leave, she heard the crying. This time it was so piercing and insistent she yelled, "Stop!"

"Stop what?" he asked. Ninan was shocked to see the man facing her. She stood speechless. "Have you lost your tongue, storyteller?" jeered the man.

Ninan sighed. "It is a mystery. If I tell, will you promise not to make fun of me?" Curious to hear what she had to say, he nodded. "When I woke up this morning I thought I heard someone crying so I walked toward the sound but could find no one. Since then, the crying has been following me yet when I look, I see no one. I am sure I hear someone crying." Ninan paused. "There, do you hear that?"

"No," he admitted, "yet what you say does not surprise me. There is enough misery around here to make the bravest man weep. What does the crying sound like?"

"Like a woman . . . like someone who cannot bear the troubles she has. The crying is so real. I cannot believe I am imagining it yet you are standing next to me and do not hear it."

"Perhaps it is real," he said. "My mother is experienced in such matters. You must talk with her. She will know what to tell you. I can show you how to find her but I cannot take you there. As it is, I have stayed too long. Those who wait for me will be wondering where I am."

Just then two men came up to them. The older of the two mocked, "So, Elam, this is how you make your preparations? Are we supposed to wait all day

while you talk with a pretty young stranger?" The man's lips clenched tight with fury.

Elam retorted angrily. "I do not tell you how to live. Show me the same courtesy. We have been speaking of important matters."

The younger man sneered. "Important matters? With a stranger? Wasting our time is more like it. We have urgent matters that need our attention. If you need to talk to a woman, talk to your wife. Or have you forgotten you have one?"

"You push me too far, Jochem. I am not a lad who must account for his time. If I tell you we have talked of important matters then we have. Insult me again and you will answer for your arrogance." He curled his fists, ready to fight.

The older man moved between Elam and Jochem. "Enough! Why fight amongst ourselves? It is the lack of water that makes us short-tempered. Remember the face of our real enemy. Remember what it is we have to do."

Elam unclenched his fists and nodded, "You are right, I apologize."

Jochem shook his head, "No, it is I who must apologize. I spoke harshly and too quickly." Jochem turned to Ninan. "Who are you? Why do you come to our village? This is not a place for strangers, particularly young women traveling alone."

"I am a storyteller and I have a book of stories. One of them is about villagers who fought a king who stole their water. Elam thought there might be something in the story that could help you in your struggle."

Jochem asked, "What did they do to save their wells?"

"I know the story is in the book but I forget how it ends so I was looking for it when Elam found me."

Once again Ninan heard the crying. She looked helplessly at Elam who smiled reassuringly. "Go to my mother, she will help you." He showed her the path while the others waited, impatient to be off.

"I will learn the story before evening; perhaps there will be something in it that will help you in your struggles to regain the use of your water."

The three men strode off. Ninan shivered as she watched them go, hearing them argue amongst themselves, afraid their terrible anger would cause them harm. Twice she almost called to warn them to be careful, yet each time she held her tongue. Elam called her stranger. It was not her fight. She was torn between looking for the story and finding the mother of Elam. She missed Natasha and her family, and their warm welcome. She thought to herself, I could have stayed

there for a few days. I could have rested until my knee healed. She shook off her thoughts. How can I miss people I barely know?

The crying sounds came once again and this time Ninan listened carefully to the increased urgency. Something was changing. Ninan hoped the old woman knew as much as Elam said she did. The cries were unsettling. They seemed to be a kind of warning.

Carefully stepping around the deep layers of dust on the road, she walked in the direction of a small group of cottages. No one was about. Had she not known better, Ninan would have thought the village deserted. She noticed footprints in the earth and followed them for a time, seeing and hearing no one. When she was about to give up, she heard voices coming from a small grove of trees. People were arguing, some shouting louder than others, but all were upset. Ninan waited near the trees until someone passed by. Keenly aware of what it meant to be a stranger in a time of trouble, she had no desire to interrupt.

Scarcely had she decided this when the group dispersed and six people emerged from the grove. One hobbled with the aid of a thick stick that he waved in the air as often as he leaned on it. "I tell you it is we who must do it, not our children. They have families. They have too much to lose. We are old. We have lived our lives. We can afford to die."

"Hush," said a woman near him. "It is a worthy thought but without substance. You know we lack strength though we have will. Do not upset yourself for no reason."

"No reason? Life and death is nothing? It is you who should hush. My son has a young son. His wife is carrying their child. He must take care of them. I am old and useless. No one will miss me. How can I sit by and let him face such danger? How could I live with myself if he should die while I looked away?"

Suddenly he saw Ninan and pointed his stick at her face. "What do you want? Who are you? Why have you come to our village?"

Ninan sighed. Always the same questions, yet the man's anger was real. She stepped back. "I am a storyteller. I came upon this village and thought I might quench my thirst with water from your well. I have heard of your troubles. I would help if I could."

The old man retorted, "You? How can you help? Why would you even want to? Leave now. You will find water if you walk far enough along the road."

He was pushed aside by a woman standing next to him. "You have heard of our plight and wish to help. What would you do to save our wells and regain our water?"

Ninan admitted, "I do not know but . . . "

"Then go away," she said tiredly. "Leave us to do what we must."

"I will go away as soon as I speak with the mother of Elam. He told me to seek her out. I have a matter to discuss with her."

The old man jeered. "A matter? What need have you of someone you do not know?"

A woman near him came toward Ninan and said, "I am the mother of Elam. Why do you look for me? What is it that you want?"

Ninan hesitated to speak in front of so many people but no one moved. She quietly told them of the crying and how it followed her. "Elam told me you have knowledge of such matters."

People moved slightly, giving Elam's mother and Ninan room to speak. "This is a serious matter," she said. "I must hear more." She turned to the group, "Return to the village. This young woman is strong. If she does nothing else, she can help us carry water. I will talk with her."

The old man said, "I too will stay."

The old woman said quietly, "No, it is better that you go with the others."

They stared at each other until finally the old man faced the group and said, "She is right. We must leave the matter to those with the strength to do what must be done." Ninan and the old woman watched until the figures were specks in the distance.

"Come, my child, we will walk to a place where we can talk." Ninan wondered why they could not talk where they were. She saw no one. As if reading her mind, the old woman said, "Special talk needs to be spoken in a special place." Seeing Ninan hesitate, the woman said gently, "I never mock what is not understood. There is much mystery in this world."

Ninan followed the old woman through a dense wood until they were surrounded by foliage. She motioned for Ninan to sit though she remained standing. Ninan did not know what to say. The sobbing was so loud she could not believe the old woman did not hear it.

"Speak what you know about the crying. Do not confuse what you think

with what you feel. Close your eyes and let the crying speak through your heart."

Ninan did as she was told. The words, unexpected, came slowly, with great difficulty for the pictures in her head were murky, as if hidden by fog. Her story came from the crying.

hen I was young we lived in the middle of a dense forest, far from any neighbors. My father was a healer and he went as he was called. My mother was jealous of his powers and sought to make them her own. She observed him closely when he mixed potions and ointments, but no matter how carefully she watched, the potions and ointments she mixed did not have the power of his. As time went on, she grew more jealous, hiding her feelings behind acts of caring yet she could not hide them from me. I saw her spite and envy grow.

My mother watched my father teach me all he knew. She tried to force me to tell her what I had learned but I was afraid of her evil side and refused. Her anger knew no bounds, hitting me with sticks until I cried for help, but no one heard my sobs. I was weak and the pain was great. Not strong enough to resist, I showed her how to make a few of the least powerful potions but she wanted to know more. I pretended I did not know any more but she saw through my lies. I ran away but she followed my trail. When she found me she tied me with a rope so I could not escape from her again.

In my father's presence she appeared to be kind and loving. He allowed himself to be fooled by her. I do not know why. His powers were great. Had he chosen to see her true self he would have seen the evil that lay just beneath her pleasant surface. During the times my father traveled, she tortured me. She found my father's books but could not read them. When I refused to read them to her she held fire to my hands until I could not bear the pain. I read the words but made up measures so she would not know the truth. I was a poor liar and she guessed what I was doing. She tied me to a pole and turned me upside down, lowering my face into a well, keeping me there until I struggled no more.

I resisted when I could, but she was clever and without heart. I grew pale and thin. My father mixed potions to heal me and strengthen my body but he did nothing for my spirit. Although I drank them, I did not wish my health to

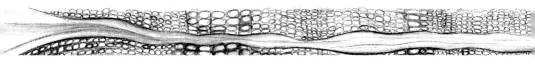

be restored. I did not want to live. My mother grew ugly and less able to hide the evil that she felt. I wondered why my father did not see his wife turning into witch and monster, but she had knowledge of her own and was always able to fool him with her soft talk and good housekeeping.

Ninan stopped. Her whole body ached. She felt she could not continue. The old woman spoke to her, sharply although not unkindly. "You must speak my child, this is the only way you will be free of the crying." And even as the old woman spoke, Ninan heard the crying, as piteously as it had ever sounded. "Take a deep breath and continue your story," urged the woman. Ninan shuddered, her body arched and tensed as if it had a life of its own. She was frightened and did not want to talk any more.

"This is not my story. I do not know what I am saying," complained Ninan.

The old woman ignored Ninan's protest. "Continue the story." And Ninan spoke.

I hated my mother. As she grew crueler, and my father did not stop her evil ways, I felt the love I had for my father slip away. I knew I had to leave but I was trapped so I begged my father to take me with him as his helper. He was growing old and could no longer travel as he had. But the sweet words of my mother convinced him that her need for me was greater than the help I could provide for him. I thought to myself, if you are such a great healer why do you not heal the evil spirit of your wife? Why do you not even see it?

The crying grew louder. Ninan waited in vain for it to stop. Only when she spoke did the crying cease. She felt she had no choice but to continue the story.

I wanted to kill my mother but I knew if I did, she would live inside me. I was afraid I would become like her, unhappy, dissatisfied, unable to be a true healer. I endured her torture knowing I had to find a way out which would not ensnare me in her spirit yet allow me to be free of her and her power. I confess that all manner of terrible actions filled my head and it was with great difficulty that I turned my back on them. I waited, trying not to feel as hopeless and helpless as I felt. One day, an opportunity for freedom appeared.

It was rumored that the landlord's son was ill. The news proved true. My father was called upon to heal the child but he was not at home. The messenger asked my mother to come in his place. Even the healer's wife might be better than no one. My mother knew she could do nothing by herself but consented to come if she could bring me with her, as her assistant. The messenger approved this plan and stayed to help us gather what we needed. His spare horse was to carry us to the sick boy. Before we began, my mother warned me to keep silent, to do as she commanded.

I knew my mother was afraid of horses and offered to mix her a potion that would ease her fear. She hesitated, knowing she could not trust me, yet her terror of the waiting animal was too great to endure without help. Reluctantly she agreed. I mixed up a powerful sleeping medicine that she drank, all the while, glaring at me. I gathered up the herbs and tinctures and got up on the horse. The messenger helped her up, putting her behind me on the horse. I arranged her carefully, almost lovingly. Indeed, it was strange, but I felt a curious tenderness for her now that I knew she was helpless.

"The ride was long and hard. When I felt my mother's body slump against mine I called to the messenger to stop, to tell him that my mother was not well. He helped me lift her down, puzzled, not knowing what to do. I arranged my mother in a soft bower of pines, with food and water. I assured the messenger that we could leave her there in safety until we returned.

"We hurried off to the great house but it was too late, the boy was dead. A great wailing greeted us that matched the weeping inside me. There was no need for me to stay; we left immediately to find my mother. Though we searched carefully, we saw no sign of her. I began to cry. I have been crying ever since. I cannot cease my sobbing until I find my mother. I must end what she began."

The crying grew louder and though Ninan held her hands to her ears, she could not stop the sound. She felt she would go mad if the noise continued. The old woman saw Ninan's anguish and said, "You must help her."

Ninan protested. "How? It is only a story. And why should the girl care about a mother who was so mean to her. Why should anyone want to help someone who was cruel and then lied about it? " She looked at the woman, "Why am I the only one who hears this noise?"

Ignoring Ninan's self-pity the old woman said urgently, "There must be very little time left. I will have to think as we walk. I have a feeling we need to act more quickly than I would wish."

"What does this mean?" asked Ninan.

"We must hurry to the spring. It is far and you need someone to show you." The old woman walked like someone possessed. Ninan wondered how she could keep up such a pace. When they came to the spring, Ninan saw nothing. It was hidden in a copse of trees that had been banked with clay to keep the water from running off. Now, it barely bubbled. Ninan drank and drank and drank. She would have stayed far longer had the old woman not urged her to fill her water skin. "We have to be off."

"Where are we going?"

"Where your feet take us. Stand up! Let your body go as it wishes. Do not worry about me, I will follow you." Feeling awkward and grumpy, Ninan did as she was told. When her body moved, she resisted the impulse to remain in place. As if she were being pushed, Ninan traveled more and more quickly. Bushes and trees appeared to step out of her way. She wondered how the frail old woman behind her was able to keep up, but her heavy breathing told her she was still following, and Ninan did not stop to look.

The way led through the forest to the land belonging to the man who had dammed the lake. Ninan grew frightened but could not stop. She walked to the edge of the lake. Two guards shouted at her but she ignored their words, pretending not to hear them. With increasing urgency she walked up to the front door of the mansion and pounded on the door. "Open the door. Open the door." A man dressed in fine cloth opened the richly carved wooden door and asked what she wanted. Ninan paid no attention and walked up the stairs as if she had lived in the house all her life. Moving from room to room, listening, feeling the doors, searching, she was unable to find what she was looking for even though she did not know what this was.

Behind a huge wooden bookcase she discovered another staircase and began to walk up the steps. When the owner of the house discovered her presence, he shouted at her to leave at once, but Ninan moved even faster. The old woman was frightened, wondering where Ninan was going and what she would find when she stopped, yet she continued to follow her.

The crying grew so loud Ninan thought her ears would explode, and she ran
as fast as she could, hesitating slightly as she touched each door. Feeling the great
heat of an old door, in a secluded room on the third floor, she knew this was the
room she had to enter. Turning the huge brass knob, stiff from disuse, she pushed
against the door with all her weight and strength. When the door opened, she saw
a frail, elderly woman lying on an unkempt bed. As Ninan came closer she saw that
the woman was not old, she was ill.

Without hesitating, Ninan cradled the woman and tried to give her water
from her water skin but the woman was unable to drink. Ninan put three drops
of water in the woman's mouth and massaged her throat until she swallowed. The
owner of the house and the old woman found themselves unable to speak or move.
They watched. Ninan put three more drops in the woman's mouth and once again,
massaged her throat until she swallowed. She repeated this until the woman licked
her lips and drank. As if the two were alone, Ninan gently stroked the hair of the
woman until she fell asleep. She kissed her forehead as she would a child.

After a few minutes, the woman stirred, opening her eyes. Ninan gave her
the last drops of water from her water skin. "Drink slowly. Swallow one drop at
a time. This is all the water I have to give you." The woman did as she was told.
Color began to fill her cheeks and lips.

The old woman found her voice and said to the man, "She must have broth.
Take water from the lake and mix it with the herbs that grow near the bush with
tiny blue flowers. Boil the leaves and berries. Strain the broth but leave the berries
in it. Bring this to me in a small bowl of unfired clay. Hurry! There is little time."

The owner of the house discovered he had no words to protest being ordered
about as if he were a servant and left to do her bidding. In time, he returned,
bringing with him a cup of steaming broth with berries floating on the top in the
shape of a flower. Ninan stepped aside so the old woman could sit next to the bed.
She took the broth and dipped the ill woman's ring finger into it, then put the
woman's finger with the drops of broth into her mouth. The old woman continued
to do this until the ill woman had consumed all of the broth. The old woman held
her until she slept.

Ninan and the man waited, watching. Ninan felt the man's anger and was
frightened by it. When the woman woke and opened her eyes, she looked at the
man standing beside her bed. "Oh my husband, I thought I would never hold you

again." He caressed her, tenderly holding her as if to keep her from disappearing. Disbelief etched his face. Ninan and the old woman stood near the door. Ninan was ready to leave but the old woman gripped her arm and kept her in place.

The man finally spoke to them. "I was told by all our doctors there was no way to save my wife. I left her here for I could no longer watch her die. You saved her life. You have done the impossible. How can I reward you?"

The old woman stepped toward the man, speaking clearly, without fear or hesitation. "We want nothing for ourselves. What we must have is water for our people. Release the dam that stops the waters of your lake. Restore the flow of water to our lands. End the drought your action has created. Give our water back to us before we die of thirst."

The man said, "I will order my men to do so at once."

The old woman put up her hands. "Your men will find angry villagers who have been denied water. They are gathering at the lake, armed with stones and bows and arrows. The guards of the lake must step back, supply the villagers with the proper tools, and tell them, 'Work in peace.' If this does not happen, there will be terrible bloodshed. Your wife will die."

"How can I ensure the peace? I am only one man."

"Only one man, but powerful enough to stop the water," said the old woman bitterly.

"My wife is not yet well. Is your word not enough?"

Ninan glared at him. "No. You must tell your men. They will listen to no one else and they will not act in time. It will take all of us to restore the lake."

"Come now. We have no time to lose," demanded the old woman.

"Go quickly, my husband. They are right. There must be no blood shed," said his wife.

The old woman stared at the man until he nodded and walked to the door. "Hurry," said Ninan, "it may already be too late." With the two behind him urging him to go faster, the man hurried down the stairs and ran toward the lake. Even if he had shouted, no one would have heard. His men and the villagers were battling each other. The noise was deafening. Men lay groaning on the earth, bleeding, crying, and begging for help.

The man stopped. "It is too late. I can do nothing."

"Nonsense," said the old woman. "Find the captain of your men. Tell him

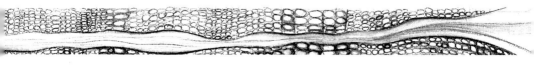

to have his men retreat." She spoke firmly, hoping he would do what now seemed impossible.

Ignoring them, Ninan ran toward the screaming men yelling, "Stop. Stop. The water will flow." No one heard her. She was so intent on stopping the fighting she did not feel the arrow in her shoulder. She kept running, blood streaming down her back. "Stop fighting. Stop. The water…" She fell, unconscious, between the two groups of battling men.

For a moment the fighting men froze, unable to comprehend the sight of a screaming young woman running into the midst of battle followed by an old woman. The captain strode forward. "Who is she?" He glared at the old woman, "What are you doing here?"

The old woman did not bother to answer as she busied herself tending to Ninan's wounds. Only when the worst of the bleeding had stopped did she speak. There was no mistaking what she said. "There is no need to fight. The man has agreed to release the waters."

The captain spat. His men jeered. The villagers muttered among themselves. Elam strode to his mother, shocked to see her and Ninan. "Is this true?" She nodded. "How do you know?"

"Yes, old woman," sneered the captain. "How is it you know so much more than we do?"

"He will tell you," she said, pointing to the ashen-faced owner limping toward the lake.

"She speaks the truth. I came to tell you but I was too late, the battle had begun. Captain, tend to the injured. Everyone else come with me. We will destroy the dam."

By evening, the first of the waters began to flow freely.

By evening, no one was sure Ninan would live.

EIGHT

GIFTS

iven powerful herbs, Ninan slept deeply for several days despite her injuries, cared for by anxious people tending to her wounds. Just before waking, she dreamed she saw the young girl looking for her mother with no success. As she was about to leave the forest, a small dove cooed into the discouraged girl's ear. Led by the dove, she brushed aside thickets and bushes and entered a small grove of trees. There, protected from the weather, lay her mother. There was something different about her face. It seemed softer, less tense. With trepidation the girl made her way to where her mother lay, too weak to move or speak. She whispered, "You have released me from an evil spell. I know no words can express my sorrow for the misery I caused you. You are a good girl and have done no wrong. Forgive me for the pain I caused you."

The old woman's granddaughter asked, "What is the matter with Ninan?"
"She is ill, Amina," answered her grandmother.
"Is she dying?"
"I do not think so, but she will need our help to recover."
"Is her wound not healing?"
"We will have to wait and see what happens. In the meantime, let us bathe her face and neck with cool wet cloths. When she wakes, we will give her broth. Think healing thoughts and be patient." The small girl tried to do as she was told but waiting was a difficult task for her. To pass the time, her grandmother gave her chores, praising her when they were completed, yet all the time both watched Ninan with anxious eyes.

Ninan's shoulder burned and throbbed. She could not move without searing pain. She cried out, "Mother, the pain continues. Why are you still hurting me?"

"Ninan, wake up," commanded the old woman. "It is time."

"Stop hurting me, mother. I beg you," moaned Ninan.

"You are having a bad dream, Ninan, wake up." The old woman washed her face and helped her sit up. Ninan gasped in agony.

"Where am I? What happened? Why is my shoulder hurting?"

"You forgot that real life battles involve real people who use real weapons. A poisoned arrow found its killing voice in your shoulder. For days we worried you would not survive, but now your wound is healing. We are much relieved."

"I have overstayed my welcome. I must leave." She tried to move her right arm.

"This is now your village. We are your people. You are one of us. This is the way it is." Ninan's eyes filled with tears. The old woman cradled Ninan's head against her. "You need to rest. Do not worry about the length of your stay. No one here will keep you against your will. When you have healed, we will help you on your way, but for now, eat and drink the water that once more flows into our wells. Without your help, many would have died. Our wells would still be dry." She sighed. "Who knows what would have happened then."

For days, the old woman tended to Ninan's wounds, refusing to sleep or eat except when villagers came by and insisted she rest and take nourishment. Yet the constant vigil was taking its toll. "You look tired," said Amina to her grandmother. "Go and rest. I will stay with Ninan. When she wakes, I will call you."

As her grandmother rose, reluctant to leave, she said, "Ninan may talk in her sleep, shouting words you do not understand. Answer her as best you can in a calm voice. Do you think you can do this without fear?"

"Yes, Mima, I can." Her grandmother smoothed the child's hair away from her eyes, kissed her forehead, and left. For a time, Ninan slept so quietly Amina had to put her cheek against her chest to make sure she was still breathing. Then, Ninan began to thrash violently. Amina worried she might hurt herself. Afraid to leave and get her grandmother, and afraid do the wrong thing, she watched helplessly.

Suddenly Ninan cried out. "I will. I will. I have not forgotten. I promise."

"What have you promised?" asked Amina. "What is it you have not forgotten? You can tell me." The child climbed on the bed and awkwardly patted Ninan's cheek.

Her voice grew louder and more urgent. "I will never forget. I will do as I promised."

Amina was afraid Ninan would fall out of the bed and tried to think what her grandmother would do. In her best grandmotherly tone she crooned, "Hush, child. All is well, rest." She kept repeating the soothing words, wondering if Ninan could hear her. Pretending to be her grandmother gave her courage. "Hush, my child. All is well. Rest for now." Ninan kicked the coverlet so wildly she frightened Amina. Forgetting to be calm, the small girl yelled, "Hush, child. All is well." The loud voice startled Ninan and quieted her nightmare. Time passed slowly.

When the old woman returned, Amina and Ninan were fast asleep, the small girl curled like a little kitten, encircled by Ninan. The two were breathing in unison. A deep sigh of contentment escaped from the old woman as she watched them sleep.

Word of Ninan's condition spread quickly. The villagers, grateful for her assistance, expressed their wish to help her. To all of them, Mima said the same thing, "There is nothing you can do for the moment. She needs to rest." The old woman stroked Ninan's hair and sang old ballads in her deep, clear voice until she felt Ninan grow calm. Then Mima spoke softly. "It is time to wake, my child. It is time to face the forces of the dark." She repeated her words, quietly waiting. Ninan moved away from the old woman but Mima held her firmly. When Ninan opened her eyes, she could not remember the old woman or where she was. "It is time to wake, my child. It is time to face the dark spirits."

"I am tired. Let me rest."

"You will have no rest until you enter the dark time. This is why you are ill. I know you are afraid but you are not alone. We will help you."

"What are you talking about? What do you mean, dark time?" complained Ninan.

"I am old and spent much of my life running from what I did not want to see. I have learned we cannot run from ourselves no matter how we try. Some people think me wise, and if this is true, it is wisdom born of pain. I have learned to take back what is mine."

"What does this have to do with me? Let me sleep."

"You told a story which came from deep inside you."

"I am a storyteller. Storytellers tell stories."

"Not every storyteller carries a book of her grandfather's stories. Not every storyteller fights who she is or fears what she knows."

"Did I not act when action was needed? How can you call me coward?"

The old woman put Ninan's shawl around her shoulders. "I will bring you a cup of broth."

"No. I want to sleep."

The old woman sighed. "Very well, sleep. Do what you must do. Should you want my help, you know where I am." She walked slowly away without looking back.

Ninan knew the old woman was right, but her fear was too great to put into words. Unable to sleep, she watched the travels of the moon. Despite the pain, she sat up, waiting until the dizzy feelings passed. Then, even more slowly, she stood, holding on to the wall, willing her weak and shaking legs to support her body. Her throat constricted and she wished she could cry, but no tears came. Instead, she felt darkness caught inside her, like a huge lump that would neither stay down nor come up. Breathing was difficult. Sitting back down on the bed, she rested for a few minutes and then forced herself to stand up, by herself, without leaning against the wall. Sweat beaded her face but she refused to give in to the dizzy feeling. It was hard work.

Voices bombarded her. "You alone of all our children have survived. You must tell our stories before the people forget what happened, before there is no one left who remembers." Ninan put her hands over her ears trying to stop the sounds.

"I am telling stories, just as you have asked. I am keeping my promise. Do I not go from village to village as you bade me? Do I not turn my back on friendly people? I am injured. Do I not deserve to rest? Why do you haunt me? What do you want?" Her words grew louder as she tried to stop the inner voices.

Hearing the shouting, Mima came to Ninan's bedside, listening to the words that poured out of her. "Why do you plague me? Have I not kept my promise? Why will you not leave me alone? Go away . . .I am so tired . . .Please . . ."

Mima brought her a cup of water. "Drink this." Ninan took the cup but her hands shook uncontrollably and she spilled most of the liquid. She looked apologetically at Mima who tried to comfort her. "Do not worry. There is more, thanks to you. I will refill the cup." She propped Ninan up with pillows and left.

The voices continued.

Ninan was troubled by Mima's kindness, by the caring of her family and the people in the village. Traveling was so much easier when she did not take time to talk with people like Komas and Natasha and the little boy who wept for his dead mother. Would the voices scream forever? Would the voices continue to fill her dreams to keep her from staying in a village? The more friendly people were, the louder and more insistent the voices became. Even now, fully awake, their messages pounded her. "Time to move on. Time to leave. Do not love."

When Mima returned with more water, she saw Ninan's anguish, her body tense, poised to protect herself against attack, and felt her heart lurch. Ninan looked young and defenseless. Mima steadied the cup so Ninan could drink. "Drink as much as you like. Quench your thirst. We have enough water." Drinking the water felt as if she were making an unknown promise. The feeling she was betraying her parents was almost overwhelming. She tried to push it away.

"I cannot stay for long. I think I will not feel well until I leave."

"I think you will not be well until you talk to the voices that fill your dreams and make your heart heavy," said Mima.

"The voices scream I must not forget my promise."

"What voices? What promise?" asked Mima gently. "Look Ninan, the dawn is coming." The two watched in silence as black shadows turned to gray, then slowly filled with hues of pink and gold. Birds chirped, singing their welcome to the new day. "Stay a few more days. Surely the voices will grant you this." She saw the bewilderment on Ninan's face. "Tell me, what is troubling you my child? I know how to listen."

Ninan hesitated, unable to speak what filled her mind. Instead she said, "How shall I address you? You answer to many names."

"Some people call me Old Woman. Others call me Grandmother. I would like you to call me Mima as my grandchildren do."

"Is this your real name?" asked Ninan.

The old woman sighed, "What is real?"

Ninan remembered Mara's struggle to remember her name. "Each of us has a real name. Is yours Mima?" asked Ninan, wondering why the old woman looked so troubled.

"No, but it is what the people I hold dearest call me." She ladled soup into

a wooden bowl and gave it to Ninan. "Taste it. Tell me how you like my soup."
Ninan wished she had the courage to ask Mima more about her name and how she
came to be called Mima. The soup smelled delicious. Pangs of hunger reminded her
she had not eaten for a long time.

Ninan smiled shyly. "You make good soup, Mima."

As Ninan grew stronger, she and Mima worked together, drawing water from
the well, cleaning, washing, cooking, baking, and picking herbs. Few words were
spoken between them but the silence was healing. Ninan noticed Mima watching
her but she was not yet ready to speak about her troubled dreams and worrisome
thoughts.

One night, Mima invited Ninan to sit in front of the fire and drink tea
while she sat nearby, rocking in an old rocking chair. The sound of the rocking
was soothing, and for a time they said nothing. When Mima did speak, Ninan was
startled for her thoughts had taken her far away. "My husband made this rocking
chair for me when I was expecting my first… Elam. He said that rocking cured
almost everything. When I feel in need of comfort, I curl myself into this chair and
rock and hum. After a while something inside me feels lighter."

"Are you telling me that if I rocked in your chair I would feel better?"

Mima smiled and poured them both more tea. "I believe you need to
discover this for yourself."

"What I need, is to leave tomorrow. I have never stayed in a village for more
than one night. I have been here many nights."

"What will happen if you stay a few more days?" asked Mima. "You know
you are welcome here."

"I am grateful for the kindness shown to me."

"And we are grateful for your help."

"You did what was most important. You knew about the herbs and how to
use them."

"And you enabled us to regain the flow of our water. This is a great gift. Who
knows what would have happened, how many more people would have died, had
Elam and the other men carried out their plans to use force to restore our water.
There was so much anger and frustration. It is hard to remain reasonable when
there is no water." Mima stood up. "Try. See how you feel after you have had a

good rock." She stood up, beckoning Ninan to sit in the rocking chair.

Ninan hesitated, almost afraid, but once she began rocking, she found the rocking motion calming. Mima asked again, "Why must you leave a village after one night, Ninan?"

The rocking motion eased Ninan's fear of speaking. She told how she had come to be a storyteller. "When I stay in a village for more than a day I meet people. They tell me stories of their lives. It is hard to leave yet I know I must continue on to other villages, new places, if I am to be a storyteller. What is most difficult is when I see young men and women looking at each other in ways I envy. I have to pretend I am not interested. I have to force myself not to see what I see. No man will follow me as my grandmother followed my grandfather. This is not the way of men."

"You keep moving because you do not want to care about the people you meet? Is this how you believe your parents meant you to live? You think this is the right way to live?"

"I do not know if it is right, it is all I know to do."

"Your parents entrusted you with a powerful legacy. They saw that you had a gift they did not themselves possess. You have chosen to use your gift, but you have not chosen how to use it. This is why you are afraid. But, you are a storyteller and you will find your way of telling stories. Of this I am sure," said Mima kindly.

"How?" asked Ninan urgently, "how do I do this?"

The old woman walked over to Ninan and ran her fingers over the smooth wood of the rocking chair, stroking it tenderly, as if the touching would reveal her answer. "No one can tell you this but I believe it is necessary for you to stop running. If you are not part of the lives of people, the source of your stories will dry up. Like small streams feeding a river, the stories of others become yours. Even now, you say you tell your own stories more often than you tell the stories of your grandfather. I do not believe you could stop telling stories even if you wanted to. You are not a storyteller because your parents told you that you were. They merely recognized you possessed a gift for telling stories, but they knew you as their child, not as a storyteller, and they were not able to help you learn to use your gift. Now, like all of us, you must choose your own way. Only after we do this have we really lived our own lives."

"All choices are not mine. If I choose to have a child, it would not be

possible for me to travel from village to village. If I am to be a storyteller, I cannot
tell stories only to my child."

"Women travel with children. Women travel without husbands."

Ninan wondered if Mima, for all her wisdom, understood what she was
talking about. "You have lived in this one village all your life. You have not had to
make the choices I must make if I am to keep the promise I made to my parents."

"You know nothing about my life."

Ninan blushed. "Forgive me. I spoke out of turn," but even as she
apologized, she saw powerful and violent images of a child being beaten, of a
girl being stoned. She shook her head and opened her eyes to make the images
disappear, but they continued. A man was screaming. A woman was crying. People
were running away. The story pushed the words out of her mouth, slowly at first,
gradually taking on a life of their own.

here was a village. It was near a lake. A blacksmith lived there
with three sons by his first wife who died giving birth to his
third son. He had a daughter and two sons by his second wife.
The trouble began when the daughter grew into a lovely young
woman. Two of her brothers stared at her with looks that were
not brotherly. Her father could not keep his eyes off her body, could not stop
touching her golden hair or looking into her hazel eyes. He found reasons to wipe
smudges from her face and brush flecks of dirt off her clothes. Her brothers teased
her, finding reason to come too close. Their attention made her uncomfortable but
she did not know what to do about it.

One day, while she and her mother were at the lake washing clothes, she
wanted to say, "Mother, I do not feel comfortable around father and my oldest
brothers." Instead she asked, "Mother, is it not time for me to find a husband?"

"You are still young," said her mother. "What is your hurry?"

"I am sixteen. Surely this is old enough."

"Very well, I will speak to your father. He will make the arrangements."

"No, do not ask him. I was being foolish." They finished washing the
clothes and no more was said.

The next morning, while his daughter was weeding a vegetable patch, her
father strode over to her and grabbed hold of her, dragging her out of the garden.

"Father," she screamed. "Let me go."

He slapped her so hard blood poured from her nose and mouth. She tried not to cry but tears poured down her face. "What have I done? Why are you so angry? Why are you hurting me?"

He hit her again and this time she crumpled to the ground, shielding herself from further blows. He fell on top of her, rubbing his hands over her body, muttering incomprehensible words. She felt his hands under her skirt, his tongue, forcing itself into her mouth. Struggling to escape, she thrashed and kicked until she heard him cry out, moaning as he rolled off her. She ran to her mother.

"What happened?" she asked, washing the blood from her daughter's face and clothing.

"I was weeding. Father came to the garden. He was angry at me but I do not know why." She started crying, still feeling her father's hands and mouth on her body.

Before she could tell her mother what happened, her mother said coldly, "I will not listen to your lies. Your brothers told me what you did. You should be ashamed of yourself. No man will want a woman who covets her brothers."

The girl was stunned. "My brothers? My brothers?"

"You pretend to be so innocent. Why should I believe you? They have given me more than enough proof. I cannot bear to look at you. Finish your work while I think what to do."

The daughter tried once more to tell her mother what really happened but she would not listen. Too stunned to think, she left her mother, knowing she could no longer live in the same house as her father and brothers. When her mother was not looking, the daughter took food from the pantry and left. Thinking she had escaped unnoticed she took no care to hide her tracks. She did not know her brothers watched her every move.

As she walked toward the edge of the village she looked up and saw a group of young men staring at her, their faces contorted in anger. Out in front were her oldest brothers. She stopped, frozen with fear. Each man seemed to be holding something in his clenched fists.

The first stones hit her body as she ran, looking for a place to hide. The men followed after her, aiming now at her face. She ignored the small stones that found their mark until a sharp pain on the side of her face tumbled her into

blackness. When she woke her clothes were torn. Every movement created new agony. Blood covered her legs. In her left hand was a piece of cloth she knew well. It had come from the shirt of her oldest brother.

She lay on the ground, moving in and out of darkness, wishing she were dead. How long she lay there, she did not know but in time she dragged herself to the lake and fell in. The icy cold water quenched her thirst and washed her body. She lay in the sun, covering herself as best she could. When enough strength returned, she stood up and walked away from the place of her birth.

Mima broke the silence, asking sharply, "Where did you hear this story?"

Ninan looked at her. "I do not know. Have I offended you? Is something wrong?"

"I beg of you, tell me where you heard it."

"I did not hear it. I am sure of that."

"Then where did the story come from? Stories do not come from nowhere."

Ninan got up from the rocking chair. "It came to me as I rocked. Please, Mima, do not be angry with me. I did not mean to upset you."

"Your story stopped. Is there more?"

Ninan nodded, hoping Mima would sit and rock. She drank a glass of water feeling Mima's eyes boring into her. "I do not have to tell it. I do not want to displease you."

"What you want is not important. How does the story end?"

"I do not decide what happens. The story tells itself."

"I want to hear the rest of the story." Mima's voice was so cold Ninan shivered.

"Sit in the chair. I will stand," Ninan pleaded, wanting the Mima she knew to replace the angry cold woman who stood in front of her.

"Do not concern yourself with where I sit. Finish the story!" demanded Mima.

"Very well," said Ninan feeling helpless and afraid.

The girl avoided people. All she wanted was for her life to end. She slept unprotected, waiting for wild animals to make a meal of her. They did not come. She waded into wild streams hoping the current would take her to a resting place

where she could breathe her last breath. The current refused to take her. Wanting to starve herself to death, she was unable to stop gobbling berries whose thorns tore her tattered dress and bloodied her legs and arms.

Each morning she threw up the little she ate. At first she thought she was ill but it soon became apparent, she was with child. She remembered too well her fear and the pain of her mother as she helped deliver her two brothers. Who would help her? Did she want help? No, better she should die in childbirth like her father's first wife.

The months passed slowly. The young woman felt no love for the baby within, pushing its way into a world that would not welcome a child born of rape. When her pains let the woman know the baby was coming, she rested in a grove of grasses at the edge of a river, bearing the labor pains in silence, afraid to cry out for fear someone might hear her. The child took its time, as if it did not want to be born. The woman writhed and bit her tongue. Still the child did not come. Desperate to be rid of her agony, the woman pushed with all her remaining strength until she felt the baby slowly make its way out of her body. Instinct took over. As soon as she could move, she crawled to the edge of the water and threw herself and the child into the river. When she woke she knew Death had refused to do her bidding.

Hearing voices, she tried to hide but a group of women, coming to wash their clothes in the river, saw her. Too weak to protest, too numb to care, she allowed them to tend her. They asked no questions for which she was grateful. In time, her body healed. She became part of the village. A man offered his hand in marriage and she took it gratefully for it gave her place and purpose.

When she was once again with child, she hid her nightmares and the ever-present memory of hurling herself and her child into the water, hoping this new birth would ease the shame she felt. At least these sons and daughters would enter the world welcomed by loving hands. Although she was a loving wife and mother, a few saw the pain in her eyes, the distance in her no one could breach.

As for the woman, she never forgot the sight of her first child flying through the air, received by the swiftly flowing current, as she cursed the waters that would not have her, that would not end her misery.

"And do you judge this woman?" asked Mima, an edge to her voice.

Still in the story, Ninan sighed. "I do not judge, I merely tell."

"But if you met this woman and knew it was her story, what would you tell her?"

"I would say that throwing herself and the baby into the water was like throwing the past out of her life. It was an act of desperation for which she paid dearly."

"How do you know?" demanded Mima.

"She is a kind woman with a loving heart. Had the baby been conceived in love I am sure she would have nurtured it. But this was not what happened. She was condemned, though innocent, violated through no fault of her own, and left to die. It is a wonder she survived."

"What is the woman's name? You did not tell it," asked Mima.

Ninan shivered, hoping Mima would stop asking questions. "I tell what I know."

"And when you tell it again, will you name the woman?"

"I do not know if I will tell it ever again."

"Why is that?" asked Mima, her voice less tense.

"The stories I tell have a life of their own. They come through me. I have no idea why or how the words find their way to my voice. I do not plan what I intend to say. This story happened because you and I are together, in this room, just the two of us." But even as she spoke, Ninan knew there was more. Just as she had told the story of Marya and Youseph, she knew she had told Mima's story, and was frightened. How did she know it? Why did she tell it? How could she keep this from happening? Why could she not memorize the stories in her grandfather's book? She yearned to ask Mima for her thoughts but dared not.

Mima took Ninan's face in her hand and looked into her eyes. "Are you sure?"

"Yes, Mima, I am very sure."

Ninan's shoulder was healing. Mindful of her aching heart, Ninan asked Mima, "Are there words of wisdom you can give me? Something to help me in my travels?"

"When you understand that loving does not stop your stories, you will choose your own way to be a storyteller. But this will take time, and it will not be easy for your fear is great." She smiled with kindly. "It seems you know how to run,

perhaps too well for your own good."

Mima's words emboldened Ninan to ask the question that most worried her. "Mima, the story I told, it scares me. Sometimes, I tell a story and it is as if I know something that needs to be told so I speak what comes to me, but it brings no joy. Not to the hearer. Not to me. After, I feel wrenched from myself. How is this possible?"

"I believe there is something in you that connects with the untold story, a story that needs to be told. In some way I do not understand, you find the words to tell the story."

"But why me?"

Mima shook her head. "Perhaps your parents knew you better than you know yourself."

"These stories leave me spent. I have no wish to tell them." Ninan shook herself, as if trying to be rid of the mystery. "How do I learn new ways?"

"You sound just like Elam when he was your age. Growing from a boy to a man was difficult for him."

"What did you say to him?"

"I told him growing up to be the person you want to be takes time and courage and the ability to love. " Ninan's thoughts flew furiously inside her as she rocked in the chair as if her life depended on it. Mima sipped her tea, enjoying the fire as flames flickered gracefully, feeling a strange and welcomed peacefulness

Abruptly, Ninan stopped rocking, "I do not think I can continue as I have. I know you are a wise woman. I have to trust you." Trembling, she forced herself to say, "I ask for your help." Mima took Ninan into her arms and gently hugged her. She felt Ninan's fear-stricken body and stroked her back until Ninan rested more easily.

"I believe you need to leave your grandfather's book and your grandmother's shawl with me. I will keep them safe. Think of my cottage as your home. Return to our village when you wish to rest or when you want to be part of our family. Do not be afraid to make a mistake; you will do what has to be done when you are ready. Of this I am sure."

Ninan shuddered. "Go without my book? Without my shawl? I cannot do this. I need them. How will I live without them?"

"You only think you need them. The book and the shawl belong to the way of your parents and grandparents. Until you are free of them you cannot use them.

They use you."

"Can I never take them with me?"

"Of course, but only when you are ready to do so with love, not fear," said Mima gently.

"You said it would be difficult. You did not say it would be impossible." Ninan stroked the smooth wood of the rocking chair. "I can hear you thinking nothing is impossible."

"I am not so foolish as to say nothing is impossible, but what I say to you is possible. I have faith in you and your stories. Otherwise I could not be so sure of what I tell you. You know more than you think."

"I cannot imagine walking without my book and my shawl. So many times they have kept me going. What will I do for comfort?" She avoided looking at Mima. "I have many dark thoughts. Sometimes I feel I will fall into them and die. How will I keep myself safe?"

"That is a question only you can answer, but I believe you have more strength and courage than you know. You will find comfort in other ways."

Ninan looked up. "How can you be so sure?"

"I feel it in my bones." She looked into Ninan's eyes. "Perhaps the same way you know stories without knowing where they come from."

"Is there anything else your bones tell you?"

"Yes. I have been sitting too long. I must get up and move around while I still can." She stood up with difficulty and Ninan thought to help but as she moved toward the old woman Mima waved her off. "No, I must do this by myself. You will not be here forever." She walked to the fireplace and stirred the pot.

"I will do as you suggest. I do not know what else to do. Tomorrow morning I will leave without my grandfather's book and my grandmother's shawl."

"Ach, Ninan, you are too hard on yourself. You do not need to leave tomorrow. Stay and enjoy the Sabbath with us, the next day will be soon enough. Besides, Amina will be terribly disappointed if you leave without seeing her and saying goodbye. She loves you."

"But she just met me."

"Children know what is in their hearts."

The next morning Ninan was awakened by a squiggly, squirming bundle of excitement bouncing on her bed. "Wake up, sleepyhead," laughed Amina as she

tried to find Ninan's ticklish spots. "Time for you to wake up. We have already had breakfast and done our morning chores." Ninan tried to protest but the child's delight was too much for her to do anything but enjoy the fun. She pummeled Amina with pretend ferocity until the little girl, giggling with joy, fell out of bed with a loud thump. Startled by the sound, Mima came to see what was happening and smiled, leaving quietly, knowing the smells of brewing coffee and baking bread would soon bring Ninan to the table.

Amina waited impatiently for Ninan to finish eating and then said, "The table needs flowers." Ninan nodded, amazed at the small child's attention. She had never known such affection and wondered if the child's delight would survive her long absence.

Armed with a jar to keep the wildflowers moist, Amina showed Ninan her favorite spot. "What did you like to do when you were my age?" It seemed so long ago Ninan had trouble remembering, but Amina kept peppering her with questions. "Where did you live? What did you play with? Did you have brothers and sisters?" Ninan laughed, picking Amina up and dumping her in a patch of daisies, but the child was quick and pulled Ninan down beside her. "What was it like when you were a little girl?"

All of a sudden Ninan remembered a time when it seemed to have been raining forever. She was tired of staying indoors but she had been promised a surprise if she kept at her sewing with no further complaints. Her excitement changed to wonder when she saw her mother return, soaking wet, with a bunch of tall grasses in her hand. She watched her mother twist the wet grasses into a small doll, even before she dried herself. Ninan was still more impressed when her mother braided tiny blue flowers into a wreath for the doll's head and then into a necklace that she wove around the doll's neck. Ninan played with the doll for the rest of the day. When the rain finally stopped, her mother casually suggested that Ninan might make her doll a doll friend. Ninan remembered telling her mother she did not know how to do this and her mother had smiled and said, 'I think you can do it. Try.' And Ninan had tried, many times, and in the end her mother had been right, she did make a doll, slightly lopsided and not quite put together in proper doll shape, but Ninan loved her dearly, especially when she sewed a small dress and hat for it. Other memories rushed in, as if a gate had been lifted, a barrier opened, and a wall broken down. She felt as if her brothers were smiling, sending her loving thoughts.

She looked around, searching for tall grasses like those her mother had used. "Would you like a doll to play with, Amina?" The child looked puzzled. Ninan laughed as she began cutting lengths of grass, handing each stalk to the young girl. "I think we have enough. What do you think?" Amina nodded. "Here, take a strand and do what I do," said Ninan, excited by the prospect of making a doll for the little girl.

It had been a long time since she had made grass dolls and at first, her fingers stumbled and pieces she tore were too short. Amina did the same, still not knowing what Ninan was doing. Ninan let her mind drift back to when her mother first showed her how to make a grass doll, and as her memories became clearer, her fingers deftly wove the strands of grass, as if her mother were beside her, giving instructions. Soon, the figure of a doll emerged and Amina whooped with delight, even more excited when she saw her own doll take shape.

Ninan picked tiny yellow flowers and showed Amina how to twist and braid them into hats and necklaces. The little girl found a broad leaf and turned it into a skirt, held in place by a flower chain and said, "I will name my doll Miryam. What is your doll's name?"

"I think I will call her Miryama. The dolls look so much alike perhaps they are sisters?"

"Yes," said Amina, "they are sisters. But I think they need a mother and father and a brother or two." She twisted more strands until she had made two larger dolls while Ninan made two that were quite small. Amina arranged the dolls in a circle, naming each doll.

"Tell me about the family," requested Ninan.

Amina spoke as if she had known them all her life. "The father is a blacksmith and he makes shoes for horses. Sometimes he makes goods like candlesticks and weather vanes to sell at the market. The mother makes candles to put in the candlesticks, but there is one set she will not sell, ever, because her husband made it for her as a wedding present. Miryam is the oldest and she has to milk the goats and make the cheese. She hates the smell of goats and cheese. When the sheep are sheared she spins the wool and makes cloth for their clothes. The two boys are still very little so they mostly stay near their mother, but when they are bigger, they will help their father and when they grow up they will be blacksmiths."

Ninan was unnerved. Amina's story was so close to the one she had told

Mima and yet, the child had told it with love in her voice. She wished she knew more about where stories come from and how a story comes to be told.

Mindful of her decision to leave the next day, Ninan found herself reluctant to enter into Amina's story, trying to keep herself from fully enjoying the child's loving. Amina took no notice of Ninan's occasional and abrupt withdrawals; she simply hugged her way back into Ninan's good humor, taking for granted that Ninan loved her as much as she loved Ninan.

While Ninan and Amina enjoyed their day together, a young man came to the edge of the village. He had passed through often enough in the past for his appearance to cause no questions. People smiled at him, chatting briefly before continuing on their way. He listened to their talk, saying little. Although his eyes searched continuously, he gave no outward sign that he was looking. Moving with grace, he wandered about for a few hours, then left, as quietly as he had come. He would return.

NINE
GATHERING STRENGTH

Elam and his family gathered around Mima's table, eating the evening meal with great humor and joy. After everyone had finished eating, Amina clapped her hands.

"Now it is time for Ninan to tell us a story, a bedtime story for me. Please."

Luna cautioned her daughter, "You are not the only person sitting here. Perhaps the others do not want to hear a bedtime story. It is not our bedtime." Amina looked stricken.

Ninan's heart melted and lifted the child into her lap. "Will a bedtime story for Amina please you all?" Heads nodded, only Mima looked concerned. "What kind of story would you like to hear Amina?"

"A Once Upon a Time story," she answered, giving her a hug. Ninan felt Mima's eyes on her, as if reminding her of their talk. There was nothing to do but begin the story.

nce upon a time there lived a small child, very much like you, Amina. She lived with her mother at the edge of a small village. Her father had been away for many years fighting in the king's army. There were no other children. It had been so many years since the child had seen her father she no longer remembered what he looked like. Her mother, whose tears had long since dried up, never talked about him. Each day the child helped separate the strands of flax as her mother spun them into threads. Then, with great skill, she wove fine cloth that was much in demand. They had enough to eat, their hut was dry, and the months and years passed with little to alter their days except for the changes each

season brought.

One day, the child saw men coming toward the cottage. She ran inside to tell her mother. The woman put the kettle on and took off her apron. The child hung back, behind her mother. Visitors to their cottage were few, especially strange men who wore colorful uniforms and carried weapons.

"Good day to you, madam." The men strode in, stooping to avoid hitting their heads on the low ceiling. They did not try to hide their curiosity as they looked around. The mother and her daughter waited for them to speak. The child stared at their fine clothes and shiny boots.

"Do you not wonder why we are here?" asked the captain.

"I am a poor woman and have few visitors. What brings you to my cottage? What is it that you want?"

"The man answered curtly, "What we have to say will not take long. It is well known that you have great skill in spinning and weaving. The king's daughter is to be married soon and the king has need of those who spin and weave to make clothes for the wedding. We are here to help you pack your things. You will be provided with spinning wheels and looms." The child moved closer to her mother, suddenly afraid.

"It will not take me long to prepare. My child and I have few belongings."

A heavily built man spoke harshly. "We said nothing about your child. You will be too busy to take care of her. She must remain behind."

The woman struggled to contain her horror. "I cannot leave my daughter. She is too young to live by herself. If she is not welcome, I will not come." She put her arms around the child and stood resolute, staring fiercely at the men.

"You have no choice. When the king commands, his subjects obey. He is your lord to whom you are sworn allegiance, to follow without question."

The woman said, "Many years ago I had a husband who went to serve in the royal army. I have not seen him since that time. Surely we have fulfilled our obligations to the king. I will not leave my child. I will not come with you. Please send the king my regrets. Where there is no welcome for my daughter, there is no place for me."

A third man sneered, knocking over a chair as he strode toward the woman. "You speak foolishly. The king has given orders for you to attend to his needs and this will be done. You should be grateful that he notices you."

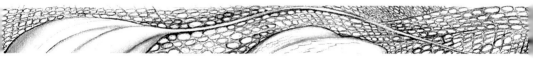

"Then I am without gratitude," said the woman. "I will not leave my child for anyone, no matter how high in rank he stands."

"We could force you to come with us," said one who had not yet spoken. "We are four strong men. You are only a woman." They moved menacingly toward her as the little girl cowered in fear, clinging to her mother.

"A woman has strength that men do not recognize. Tell the king I cannot come. I will not leave my young daughter."

The captain laughed hollowly and said, "Come, come, we are wasting time. Pack your belongings. We have no time to lose. The king awaits your presence. Your daughter is of no concern to us."

The woman forced herself to pour a cup of tea. "Either you are deaf or foolish. I have said I will not come unless my child comes with me. Now, please leave, my work is waiting for me. Threads do not weave by themselves. Good day." She took a sip from her cup and sat down at her loom. "Daughter, bring the yarn which has been drying outside. I will soon need it." The child hesitated, afraid to leave her mother. "What? Is deafness catching? Go and fetch the yarn. Do as I tell you. I will soon need it."

The child stared at the four men standing in front of the door, waiting for them to leave. She walked toward them slowly, hoping they would move out of her way. They remained where they stood.

She spoke softly. "I must fetch yarn for my mother. Please let me pass." Despite her fear, she fixed her clear, frightened eyes on them.

The captain had a daughter close to the age of the child and he said to the others, "Let the child go. Our quarrel is not with her." As she moved to open the door, they made way for her. When the child was out of sight, he said, "Madam, we will give you one day to find a home for your child. We return tomorrow and you will come with us. I warn you, if you try to flee you will be caught and punished. Be ready. We have talked long enough."

The woman watched them leave and did not return their farewells. Sipping her tea, she wondered what to do. By the time her daughter returned, the mother had made her plan.

"Have they gone?" asked the child.

"For now, but they will return tomorrow morning. We must be ready. Do as I tell you and ask no questions." The woman took a small box from where

she had hidden it under a pile of flax. Opening it, she took out a gold chain so
delicate the child could hardly see it. The woman held it in her palm and stared
at it for a long time. She brushed away her tears and gathered her daughter into
her arms. "This was given to your father when he was a young man. His father
had been given it by a grateful king whom he had bravely served. Wear it now
around your neck. Never take it off. Never, ever!"

"If anyone should ask you how it is you wear such a chain, you must say,
'It was given to my father by his father who received it from his king for services
rendered. I too would give such service were I allowed.'" The mother took her
daughter's small face in her hands and warned, "Do not forget these words. Your
life depends on them." Trembling, the child repeated the words as her mother
put the chain around her neck.

The woman worked all day and far into the night, preparing for the
return of the soldiers. Every detail had to be considered and thought through.
She rehearsed her daughter, trying to anticipate problems that might arise. Most
of all, she made sure the child knew what to say when the time came for her to
speak.

Slowly, she packed, tidied the house, and readied the child. Too tired to
move, the two fell asleep in front of the fire.

"Open the door. Open the door in the name of the king." Taking a last,
quick look around, the woman took a deep breath and walked toward the door.
The knocking grew louder and more insistent. "Open the door in the name of
the king." The woman calmly opened the door and stood quietly in the doorway.
"We have come to take you to the king," shouted the soldiers as they stormed
into the small cottage knocking over everything in their way.

"You do not have to shout. I know why you are here and I am ready." The
men pushed past her and picked up her belongings, two huge piles of flax and
a sack filled with her few possessions. The child was nowhere to be seen. The
woman did not look at the men, afraid to reveal her anxiety.

"You need not take your flax with you," said the captain. "The king has
the finest flax in the kingdom. We will leave it here."

The woman spoke calmly. "You would not let me bring my child. Surely
you will not refuse to let me bring the flax for which my spinning is so famous."

Afraid to make a mistake, he reluctantly agreed. "Very well. Men, load the

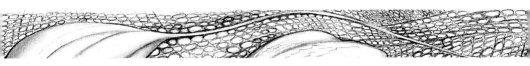

horses." The soldiers grabbed the bundles.

"Stop!" she yelled. "The flax is fragile. It will be ruined if you do not take care. If it does not arrive in good condition I will not be able to spin my yarn properly. The king will not be pleased. Surely you do not want to feel his wrath."

She stood beside the men as they tied her bundles to the horses, making sure they placed the flax on the horse as she directed.

A soldier complained. "This is the heaviest flax I have ever carried."

The woman smiled sweetly. "That is because it is so special. It is why I must bring it with me. Without it my threads and cloth would be ordinary. The king would surely find them wanting." When the last horse was loaded, the woman mounted and they left for the palace.

They moved slowly, the woman insisting the flax be checked often. When they stopped for water, the woman wet the flax. "I must keep it from drying out," she explained. When they stopped to eat, the woman once again inspected the flax.

One of the soldiers sneered, "Do you plan to feed the flax as well?" The woman made no reply. Her quiet dignity silenced their crude jokes. Dusk had long since fallen by the time they reached the palace.

The woman did not wait to be told what to do. "Please put the flax in the room where I am to sleep."

A soldier asked, "Do you rest your flax before you use it?"

Ignoring him she announced, "I will carry this bundle of flax." Happy to have less to carry, the soldiers readily agreed without argument. The way to her sleeping quarters was long, up many steps and through narrow corridors. Although her arms ached, desperation gave her strength. When the other bundles had been thrown down on the floor, she placed her own bundle on top of them.

The captain said, "There is food and water here. The king's advisors will call for you in the morning." The woman nodded and was silent as she watched them leave. When she could no longer hear their fading footsteps, she still stood, as if the slightest motion or sound on her part would bring them running to her room. When she was completely satisfied she was alone, she unwrapped the flax, carried out the second stage of her plan, and fell asleep.

"But what about her daughter?" cried Amina. "Why did she leave her child behind? Ninan, what about the little girl?"

"Let Ninan finish the story," said her mother, taking her daughter into her arms, wondering the same thing.

Mima nodded. "You must have faith, Amina." She spoke to the child but she looked at Ninan. "Please, continue."

Awakened by the rays of sun, which shone through a tiny opening near the top of the wall, she made her final preparations and waited. To calm herself, she hummed a song she had learned from her father.

The door was opened with no announcement or knocking. In strode six guards and a well-dressed woman who entered and stood just inside the room. The woman stared at the flax. "The king has prepared a room for you to spin and weave. You must have all the flax spun within three days. The cloth is to be finished in seven days. Leave your flax here. You will not need it. The room is well equipped. The guards will take you to the place where you will weave."

The mother spoke calmly, "I must spin my own flax."

The king's serving woman disagreed. "Nonsense, you will do as you are told. Leave your flax here."

The mother stood next to her flax. "I will not work unless my flax comes with me. If I am to spin the yarn for which I am famous, I must work the flax I know best." The two women stared at each other, neither giving in. No matter how the serving woman glared, no matter what she said, the child's mother would not be intimidated. The mother asked, "When the king goes to hunt, does he not take his favorite weapon? Why should I not take my favorite flax? Why should I not have what I know best to use? Surely the king wishes me to make the finest cloth possible. Let me speak to the king, perhaps he will grant my wish."

"You? You talk to the king? He is much too busy to waste his precious time speaking to a poor weaving woman. You will do as you are told."

"Please, take me to the king. Let me plead my case before him."

When the serving woman saw the woman was not afraid and would not do as she was told, she snarled, "If you go to the king, you will surely anger him. He has sent people to the dungeon for lesser offenses than this. Take care what you ask. You may well regret your impertinence."

"I mean no offense. I merely wish to use what I know best. Surely the king

will want his daughter to have the finest cloth possible."

"I have done my best to warn you." She turned to the guards. "Take the woman to the king. I will tell him of her disobedience." She strode out of the room, leaving the guards to do as she commanded.

One of the guards pleaded with the child's mother to reconsider, to do what she had been told, but she remained firm. "I have done no wrong and mean no offense. I am ready to see the king." She showed the guards how to carry the flax except for one heavy bundle, which she carried herself. The guards, taking pity on her, offered to help but she refused saying, "I am the only one who knows how to carry this bundle. Though it is heavy, I will manage." They took her to the king, knowing she could come to no good end.

When the woman was finally admitted to the royal chambers, she was exhausted, yet remained clear in her mind. The plan was working well. When the flax was stored, she gently rested her bundle on the floor in front of the king and approached according to custom, waiting for him to speak to her. He was astonished that such a poor weaving woman would be so obstinate and spoke sternly, "What is it that makes your flax so special you would disobey your king?"

The woman went over to the bundle of flax she had carried, picked it up, and placed it closer to the king. Carefully and quickly, with shaking hands, she uncovered her small daughter. Taking her by the hand, she brought her to the king. Paying no attention to the gasps of the king's advisors, she put her arms around her daughter. Her presence gave the mother power and calmed the child.

The king roared his displeasure. "What is this? You were told to come by yourself. You have work to do. You have no time to care for a child. Guards take her away! I will not countenance such disobedience."

The mother gently moved her daughter toward the king. The child took a few steps, curtsied, and said sweetly, "The answer to my presence, your majesty, lies around my neck." She came close enough so he could see the chain. Then she repeated the words her mother had made her memorize. "This chain was given to my father by his father who received it from his king in return for services rendered. That king was your father. I too would give such service were I allowed." The child curtsied and returned to her mother who hid her smile.

"Come here, child. Let me look more closely at your chain." The child walked to the king who took the chain in his hands and stared at it. The mother and daughter watched and waited.

The king looked at the mother who spoke without fear. "I would not leave my daughter to do your service. No loving mother could. But just as my husband served you in your army, we will do the same. We are prepared to weave our best cloth for you and your daughter if you will let us be together. My child is as precious to me as your child is to you. A king does not love his children better than a weaving woman just because he is king."

The king's voice was husky as he spoke. "You are a brave and wise woman. Your child may stay with you. I will give orders that this be so. Guards, take these two to the spinning room."

And so the mother and her child spun the fibers into thread and made beautiful cloth for the daughter of the king. When the work was finished, the King rewarded them with fine presents. They returned to their small cottage with great honor and much happiness.

"Did they live happily ever after?" asked Amina.

"Certainly," smiled Ninan. "And now it is your bedtime."

"Will you put me to bed, Ninan?" The child snuggled close to Ninan's heart.

"Yes, if you wish." As they left the table Ninan said to Amina, "I will not be here when you wake up tomorrow."

"Where will you be?" asked Amina.

"I will be telling stories in villages, just as I have told stories in this village"

"Will you come back to us?" asked Amina.

"Yes, I will, but I cannot tell you when. Still, I promise I will return. And, when you worry, wondering if you will ever see me again, think of the mother, refusing to leave her child and know that I am coming back to you." When Amina began to cry, Ninan wiped away her tears and caressed her hair. "I will stay with you until you fall asleep. The child snuggled against Ninan who watched over her with a love she hadn't known she could feel.

Mima and Ninan walked back to Mima's house arm in arm, neither talking about what was on their mind. While Mima stoked the fire, Ninan caressed her grandfather's book. Just the thought of leaving it behind left her feeling bereft. What would it be like not to have it. And the shawl, could she really leave it with Mima?

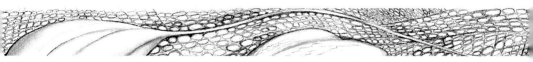

"If I am to leave my shawl and my grandfather's book, where shall I put them? I need a place where they will be safe for as long as I am gone. Who knows how long that will be? She tried not to think about what it would be like to leave without her only source of consolation.

"Put them here, in this wooden trunk. My husband made it for me as a wedding present. I keep the things I value most inside it." Ninan opened the trunk. Inside were finely woven blankets and two pillows stuffed with goose down. As Ninan picked up the pillows, thinking to put her book and shawl underneath them, she saw what looked like remnants of tattered clothing. Stained. Ninan stared, a sense of horror made moving impossible.

"What are you looking at?" asked Mima.

"The blankets. Did you weave them?" she said, trying to steady her voice.

"Yes," said Mima curtly. She walked to the trunk, closed the lid, and sat on it. "Before you leave, tell me, how did you know what happened? I told no one."

Ninan felt helpless. "You must believe me. What I spoke came to me from the pictures in my mind. If I had my way I would never tell such stories again but…"

Mima sighed, stoked the fire, and sat in the rocking chair, rocking steadily, staring into space. "Your parents saw you better than you see yourself. You have a gift, a terrible and wonderful gift, a blessing and a curse. Be careful, Ninan. Learn to use it wisely or it will use you."

The next morning, Amina arrived at her grandmother's house early, hoping to see Ninan before she left, but she was too late. The old woman saw her small grandchild staring so unhappily at the empty road she gathered her into her arms. Their tears mingled.

TEN
JOURNEY TO A PATH

inan woke before dawn, upset about having to say goodbye, wondering if it was really safe to leave her shawl and book in Mima's old wooden trunk. Even though she trusted Mima, she was not at all certain that leaving them behind was what she needed to do to feel better. As she got out of bed her foot touched a basket that had not been there the night before. Ninan thought to leave without it but Mima's words came back to her, "Do not ignore your feelings. Welcome new people into your life. You are a storyteller. How else will you hear their stories? How else will you have new stories to tell?" Ninan knew the basket and its contents was an act of Mima's caring and to leave it behind would be unkind, but even as she picked it up she felt as if she was entering a new country where she knew neither the language nor the customs. She talked to herself. "My life is different from everyone I meet. Would that one of my brothers had lived." She remembered the many evenings when her mother had lit the candles, singing a blessing before her father sang the prayers. She wondered if she would ever feel such peace again.

Outside, the cold air was bracing; her arms and neck felt unnervingly light without her book and shawl. Many times she felt a stab of fear, worried she had left her belongings someplace, ready to search, only to remember she had chosen to let Mima keep them for her. She wondered what would comfort her in days to come, but as she walked, she admitted to herself, it might be more difficult but it was not worse, at least not yet. Refusing to think about what the future might hold, she walked with energy and anticipation.

By mid-morning she grew hungry and stopped by a small stream. Sitting under a huge tree, she opened the basket and found not only food and water, but a delicately woven shawl of wool dyed in many shades of blue. Ninan could not believe her eyes. It was the most beautiful shawl she had ever seen. Light, yet warm, and unlike her own shawl, resilient rather than fragile. She put the shawl around her shoulders, reveling in its softness and beauty. She held it out to the sunlight, watching sunbeams play on it, the colors like water glimmering with sunlight. Tears came to Ninan's eyes as she walked back to the tree and her basket, unaware that someone was watching her every move.

With her shawl covering her, Ninan lay down for a nap. She dreamed she was walking in a rich, verdant countryside, a place that was familiar yet unknown. Although the hills were high, she walked up and down as if walking on level ground, covering vast amounts of territory with no effort. At first she enjoyed the power to move with such ease, but gradually, when she wanted to slow down, she recognized her body was moving on its own, with energy she could not control. Although she was not tired, when she realized she had no power and no idea where she was going, she tried to stop herself by grasping a tree, but the tree came with her. She jumped into a lake, but the water moved with her. Terrified, she called out but no sound left her mouth. Gathering speed, she moved too quickly to walk. At first she was running, but then her feet left the ground and she was flying over mountains, through clouds, into storms. There was nothing to stop her and no one to help her. Gradually, her fear transformed into pleasure. Flying was fun, especially when she learned to direct her course a little, leaning to the left side of this peak, heading over the top of that one. Although she still had no idea where she was going, she delighted in the air caressing her face and the feeling of her body soaring into space. Perhaps I might find a landing place, she thought. Scanning the countryside she saw what looked like a small patch of green meadow. "That looks nice," she said to no one in particular, "I will try to land over there." As she flew lower, she saw the small meadow was a huge field but still, it looked safe and inviting. Gracefully, she spread her arms and legs, gradually floating safely down to earth.

Contentedly Ninan opened her eyes, knowing her travels had been a dream, yet not ready to begin walking. Several times, she thought she saw someone observing her, but when she looked, the face was gone. "Ah well, it must be my imagination," she said. "I suppose it is time to be on my way." She walked with

an unusual sense of lightness and well being. Once again she sensed she was being followed, yet no matter how carefully she searched, she saw no one. Was her mind playing tricks? How safe was she walking alone in dark places, knowing no one? Shivering, she vowed to be more careful, although exactly what that meant, she was not sure. She took out her knife, just in case.

Toward evening she reached the outskirts of a small village and her earlier lightness of spirit disappeared. I am not ready to meet new people, she thought. I have no stories within me and no book to help me. I will wait until I have a story to tell before I enter a village. When it grew late, and the villagers were asleep, she crept into the village, refilled her water bag, and walked until she saw no more cottages or signs of habitation. This became her pattern for the next few weeks. At first, she consciously avoided people, but after a while, it became habitual. Although loud noises and unexpected movement frightened her, she walked at night and slept during the day.

One evening as she was getting ready to leave, she heard loud drunken voices. She hid in the bushes, hoping whoever it was would not find her. When a hand clapped over her mouth to keep her from crying out and another hand pressed her tightly against his body, Ninan tried to remain calm, hoping she could find a way to free herself. The man threw her to the ground with great force, her head barely missing a sharp rock, landing on the side of a log. Blood dripped down her face. She quickly rolled onto her back and kicked the man in his groin as he bent down. In the seconds it took for him to react, Ninan rose, holding the rock in her hand. "One step closer and I bash in your head," she warned, hoping she sounded convincing. The man, taller by more than a head, well built, but very drunk, tried to stand up. Ninan threw the rock, aiming at his head. Without waiting to see if she hit him, she ran. Hearing him follow her, she headed for a patch of dense underbrush but when she stumbled, he lunged, catching the end of her skirt. Ninan grabbed it out of his hands, picked up another rock, and threw it. His groan told her this one had found its mark though she still heard his footsteps following her. She ran for as long as she had breath, and then, unable to control her loud gasps, sank down into a mossy patch between bushes, and waited. At first, she heard him looking for her, his calls for help from his friends reverberating in the darkness. Then she saw him as he searched for her, tripping over rocks and roots, cursing, threatening. When his back was turned she ran again, this time toward the

road. Running until she had no more breath, her sides splitting with pain, she hid behind another clump of bushes, her breathing heavy and loud. Not trusting the silence, she waited, ready to run once again.

At first light, still hearing nothing, she tried to retrace her steps, hoping to find her belongings. It was the snores than attracted her attention. The man was sleeping, his head on her basket. She stared, trying to think, her mind jumbled with fear. Afraid to move his head and unwilling to leave without her basket, she looked for a stone that was the same size. Terrified that she would wake him, she found one, picked it up, and carefully moved toward him. He moaned, expelling stale putrid air. Ninan tried not to breathe. When the snoring started again, she waited until she hoped he was sleeping deeply. Then she placed the stone under his head, pushing the basket aside. She fled, holding the basket in front of her. Running hard. Running from the stink of his breath. Wishing she could run from the feel of his hands on her body.

Needing to put as much distance between her and the man, she walked until it was late afternoon. Then, too tired to take another step, she found a protected place to sleep and dropped in her tracks. It was already dark when she finally woke up and started walking, knife in hand, listening to every sound and movement, afraid to sleep. It took many nights without incident before her fears lessened.

Ninan did not know when the change happened or why. Somehow, she no longer felt the need to be alone. Something inside her seemed less troubled, calmer. She began waving to those she passed on the road but was not yet ready to stop to speak. Although she missed her book and shawl, she became aware of a new sense of space inside her, ready for new stories to form. She paid attention to the landscape, noticing sunsets and sunrises, as if seeing them for the first time. Teaching herself to whistle, she spent hours imitating the sounds of birds. No longer alone or lonely, all of nature kept her company. Despite rain and cold, her spirit flew out to all she encountered. Often she was tempted to return to the village of Mima and Amina, but she kept walking, knowing in her heart it was still too soon to return. When she was ready, she would not have to decide; her feet would know the way and begin walking.

One morning she was awakened by sounds of people laughing. She noticed

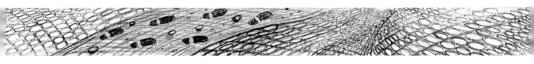

animals and people walking briskly. She could not remember when she had seen so many people at one time. Curious, she joined the throng. No one paid much attention to her, yet people were friendly, sharing their water and food in exchange for small labors like catching straying animals. Ninan had little to trade but when a small child complained he was tired, she offered to carry the boy as both parents were already carrying large loads of goods carefully and delicately balanced. The tired child curled happily in Ninan's arms and was soon lulled to sleep by the sound of Ninan's whistling. Ninan, glad to be able to help, was reminded of the boy who ran away from her when he did not like the story she told him.

The mother of the child did not seem much older than Ninan but already she had three children and a fourth on the way. The two walked beside each other for a while, each too shy to ask questions. The silence was friendly as the two took each other's measure and then began singing songs remembered from childhood. Ninan wondered what it was like to have three small children, be pregnant with a fourth, and at the same time, share the burden of making and selling baskets.

Towards noon, the family stopped to eat and invited Ninan to join them. She sadly refused, "I have no food to share with you, though I do have water." She felt shy around this family—they reminded her of what she was unlikely to experience.

The man said, "We would be pleased to have you share our food. You have been of great help. Our son is too young to walk the long distance to the market yet we had no choice; we had to bring him. This market takes place only once a year and it is a great opportunity for us to sell our baskets and woodenware. The money we earn will last us a long time."

Ninan wondered if she was ready to tell stories. Even thinking about this made her feel queasy. Maybe I should learn a trade. Maybe I could learn to make baskets, she thought. Maybe I could practice carving bowls and plates. Thoughts of the man on the mountain made her shudder. "Where is the market?" she asked.

"Outside of a small town that is two full days' journey from here." He looked at his wife and children, shaking his head with worry. "We have already been on the road for more than one week. Traveling has been difficult, but people have helped. We will have an easier journey home if we sell our goods, but I do not know how well we will do if we cannot arrive for the opening. The best days to sell are the first two and they start the day after tomorrow. Our children are too small to push them any harder." He playfully ruffled his son's hair. "They are good children; they do their best." The man walked to the kettle, boiling over the open fire. "Have a cup of tea. Whenever I am discouraged I find that drinking tea makes me feel better." Ninan took the cup and sipped the steaming liquid. Warm as the day was, it refreshed and soothed her. The man and woman arranged sleeping places for their children and then the woman nursed the youngest, her eyes closing with fatigue. The man cleaned and put their possessions in order, ready to move as soon as the children woke. Ninan was surprised to see a man do these chores. Wisps of wonder danced around her singing, what if . . .? She pushed them away. Such thoughts held out the promise of what could never be. Then, an idea came to her, too incredulous to mention. She dismissed it but the idea kept coming back, like a ball on a string tied around her thumb, which she kept sending off into space, only to have it rebound into her palm. Twice she stopped herself from speaking, but the third time words rushed passed her resolution to remain silent.

"I am in no hurry. If you are willing, I could walk with the children while you and your wife travel more quickly. I think the oldest two would stay with me. I know I am a stranger, and have nothing to give you to assure their safe arrival, but I will take good care of them for you. I give you my promise"

The parents looked at each other, astonished by her unexpected offer. Ninan walked to a nearby tree, giving them time alone to talk between themselves. The wife said to her husband, "I have watched her with the children and she is kind. We have great need of the money yet if we continue at our present pace, we will not arrive in time for the opening of the market."

Her husband responded, "I could go on ahead, by myself, and sell, but I promised I would never leave you." They held hands gently, each wondering what to do. The oldest boy cried out in his sleep and Ninan went to him, stroking his forehead as Mima had stroked hers. She felt strangely peaceful even though something within her was stirring, a new feeling she had no words to describe. She let it rest, peacefully, within her.

When the children woke, the family and Ninan started walking on the road to the market. Ninan watched to see how she could help, quietly doing what was necessary. The two older children, a boy of four and a girl of six, enjoyed Ninan's whistling and soon she was busy teaching them to mimic birdcalls, happy just to be with them. When they hopped and skipped back to their parents, Ninan took

some of the load from the wife so she could carry her youngest son more easily. They walked in companionable silence, not wanting to use energy on speech. The children, assured of being carried when they grew tired, walked more quickly than they had, even singing songs to Ninan in return for her songs to them. By dusk, they had covered a long distance and the parents looked less worried. Although Ninan hung back, not wanting to intrude, she helped set up camp for the night. Mima would be pleased, she thought.

That night, when the children were asleep, Ninan and the couple sat together, enjoying the peaceful warmth of the fire. "I am Taya. What is your name?"

"Ninan."

"What brings you on this road to the market."

Ninan smiled shyly. "I am a storyteller. And you? Where do you come from? What has your life been like?"

Taya answered, looking into her cup of tea, as if her story lay in the leaves. "Kurro and I grew up together. We became friends when we were children. I never looked at any other man; even as a young child, I knew he was the only man I would have to be my husband."

Kurro touched his wife's fingers, "I, too, grew up knowing I wanted to marry Taya but this seemed utterly impossible." He sighed deeply, his face creased with pain. "Perhaps it is just as well we cannot know our future."

Taya touched her finger to her husband's lips, "Those times are finished. You must stop thinking about what happened. We tried to be careful and kind."

"The memories are strong; they will not let me rest."

Ninan spoke softly. "I would like to hear your story."

Kurro hesitated, "We have never talked about our lives to anyone. We agreed this was not safe. Yet sometimes I feel a need to speak."

"Perhaps if you tell what happened, the memories will fade and thoughts about those times will become less painful," suggested Ninan, thinking this was what Mima might say. "For a long time I too was silent. Then, I met a wise woman who told me it was not good to keep everything to myself. I have noticed that when I do not talk, my feelings grow so strong I cannot think clearly. I do not recommend silence, not at all. Her advice has helped me."

Kurro nodded. "I agreed to keep silent because I thought it would keep us safe but now I do not feel good. Misery takes up too much space inside me." He turned toward his wife. "Do you mind if we tell her, Taya? A storyteller is not easily shocked. Perhaps if we speak about what happened we would feel better."

Taya spoke first. "My father owned much land, more than anyone else, and this made him an important man in our village."

Kurro continued, "My father worked this land and as payment, gave half of what he grew to Taya's father, leaving our family with no money to save to buy land of our own."

Taya spoke. "On my sixteenth birthday, my father betrothed me to a man whose land bordered my father's. I knew he coveted the excellent farmland with its many streams because it would provide water needed to irrigate the crops. What I did not know was that he wanted to own it so badly he would do anything to make it his. As the only daughter and oldest child, he knew he could use me to gain possession of it. Since my mother died giving birth to my brother and my stepmother was timid, there was no one to help me."

Kurro put his arm around Taya. "We first began to play with each other when we were small, too young to be noticed. This was easy when we were little, but when I was old enough to work in the fields with my father, meeting became more difficult. We worked from sunrise to sunset and there were always overseers watching."

Taya sighed. "My father and stepmother tried to make me feel that being married to this man was a great honor for I was not beautiful. They talked about the fine dresses I would wear and the many servants I would have to help me keep our estate, but their words did not impress me. I wanted to be with Kurro. Fancy dresses and gold jewelry did not matter to me. I was afraid to tell my father about my love for Kurro because I thought if he knew, he would have him sent away or cause him to have an accident. Anything was possible if it helped my father acquire the land he so badly wanted. Days passed quickly, plans were made. I grew more desperate. I finally told my father I would not marry the man of his choice because I loved another man. He called me foolish and stupid. I was his daughter and he had made a fine match for me. I would do what I was told."

Her voice faltered. Kurro continued. "He said she was his daughter and it was her duty to be obedient and serve her father. She would marry the man of his choice."

Taya had tears in her eyes. "Foolishly, I told my father I would run away

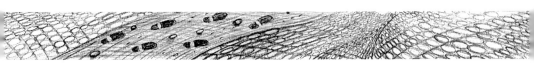

rather than marry an old man. He ordered his men to guard me day and night to make sure I could not escape." There was a painful silence.

Ninan asked, "What happened?"

"At first, while the guards were watching, my father spoke harshly but did not touch me. When he saw his words had no effect, he threatened to have me whipped if I did not do as he demanded. The day was set for my wedding, and with no way of escaping from the ever-present guards and servants, I became frantic. The notes I sent to Kurro were found and torn up without me knowing he never received them. I begged my father to give me a little time. I even pleaded with my future husband, but he was my father's friend and just as determined as my father that the wedding take place as planned. I thought about killing myself but with someone watching all the time this was not possible. I finally decided my only choice was to refuse to eat since life without Kurro was a kind of death. Although not hearing from him made my struggle more difficult, I never doubted his love for me. This gave me the strength and courage to do the little that was in my power to do."

"But it all sounds impossible. How is it you are now married?"

"Taya stopped eating two weeks before the wedding was to take place," said Kurro. "At first, no one noticed, but when she grew too weak to leave her bed her father called a doctor and discovered her refusal to take nourishment. He cajoled and yelled and threatened, but Taya refused to eat, sipping a little water when she thought no one was looking. I still do not know how she managed to keep going."

"At the end of the month, the man who was to be my husband still insisted on having the wedding. Since I had been told the marriage was postponed, I had eaten a little, just enough to keep from dying. When I found out I had been tricked, I was too weak to prevent being dressed in my wedding finery and carried to the ceremony."

Ninan gasped. "Oh no!"

"When I saw my intended husband I vowed to remain silent. I would not say, 'I do.' Without these words there is no marriage, even with a father such as mine. Everyone who gathered for the wedding ceremony came in vain. I refused to marry him. I would not be his wife, ever, no matter what happened to me."

Taya's mouth was grimly set as Kurro continued. "All this time I was sick with worry. I sensed that Taya had not received my messages and I could not find a way to be with her. Even servants who had been my friends refused to help. Her father had sworn them to his service on pain of death. Those servants who did not agree to help him were discharged. When I heard the marriage was taking place I felt hopeless. Although I tried to hide my suffering by day, apparently I cried at night in my sleep. I was ashamed that my father heard and asked the cause of my distress. I felt weak and foolish but he was strangely kind and listened carefully as I answered his many questions. When I had no more to say, he asked how much I loved Taya. 'She is my life,' I told him. Then, he talked about my mother for the first time. He told me how much he had loved her and that when she died, part of him died as well. We sat, quietly, each of us thinking about the woman we loved. Then he stood up, clearly determined, and said, 'You shall have your chance.' It seemed impossible. How could I meet with the woman I loved when there was no way to send a message? But, my father was a clever man and my distress moved him. As we talked through the night he thought of a plan, and when morning came, we set our words in motion."

Taya smiled. "The day after the ceremony was to have been held, I was lying on my bed, too weak to stand up. No one was allowed to talk to me and the house was deathly quiet. When I heard my father talking to a person who sounded like an old man, I waited, curious and afraid. What was he telling him? What was this old man going to do? In a few minutes a figure, heavily shrouded, came walking into my bedroom, followed by my father. The figure said in a cruel voice, 'You are an insolent daughter and this cannot be allowed. Your father has hired me to teach you to be obedient. I will make you honor the will of your father, as any loving daughter would. To that end, you will come with me. In one week I promise you and him, you will freely consent to marry the man your wise father has chosen or you and I will suffer the consequences.' I was too weak to protest and it would have done no good. My father was determined that I would marry the man of his choice. They tied me up and threw me on the back of a horse behind a heavily armed man who spoke in curses. I could not imagine what was going to happen to me, terrified to think how I might be made to consent, supposedly of my own free will, to marry my father's friend. As the old man gave instructions for us to leave, my father said, 'Here is the first third of your compensation. The rest, as we agreed, will be given to you when you have returned my daughter and the marriage has been consummated.' The old man nodded. 'This is indeed the contract to which we have

both agreed.' Then he got on his horse, shouted a command in a language I did not understand and we left my father's lands. I tried not to think about the horrors that awaited me."

Kurro grinned. "They traveled all day, not daring to stop except to untie Taya and let her sit more comfortably behind the armed man who was my brother. The old man was my father. After two days, I met them in the agreed upon meeting point we deemed to be safe. Taya was exhausted but we managed to continue traveling until we reached the village of distant relatives of my father where we married and remained until Taya regained her strength. Then, we traveled until we found a place to make our home, hoping to be safe from her father's wrath."

"And we have done this without his money," said Taya. "Although compared to the life I lived with my father, we are very poor and have little in the way of worldly goods, somehow, we manage. Everything is possible as long as we are together."

"How did you have the courage to fight against your father? To refuse to do as he wished?" asked Ninan. "I would have been too frightened. I think eventually I would have given in when I thought I had no chance of being with Kurro."

Taya shook her head. "I do not believe we can know what we will do if we have never been in such a situation. When you love someone as much as I love Kurro, there is no lack of courage. Our love was all that mattered to me. And," she giggled, "I could not bear the thought of sleeping with that old man."

"Did your father ever find you?"

"We never gave him the opportunity. We live quietly, far from my father's estate, in another part of the country. I am known by my husband's name."

"What about your father, Kurro? What happened to him?"

"He lived with us until he died since he did not dare to return," answered Kurro. "To avoid suspicion, my brothers left before Taya's disappearance became known. This was the only way we could make sure her father had no chance to retaliate. But in truth, there was nothing to keep us from leaving. Her father took the best my family grew. There was always too little left no matter how hard we worked."

Ninan grinned. "So in the end, you got even and took the best crop her father grew."

They laughed companionably, watching the fire, each lost in thought. It was

late when they banked the coals and prepared to go to sleep. Taya knelt down next
to Ninan, "We have thought about your offer. If you are willing to help us as you
have been doing, we think we will reach the market in time for the opening. But we
realize this is a lot to ask of a stranger, though you do not feel like a stranger. And I
must also say that you were right about our need to talk; keeping silent for so long
has not been healthy. You listen without judgment; otherwise we might not have
been able to talk so freely."

Ninan blushed. "I am the one who must thank you. You have given me
much to think about. Since I usually travel by myself, I am learning how little I
know."

Taya smiled. "That is true for all of us. Can you imagine? I was once a rich
man's daughter, brought up to consider myself better than everyone. Maids dressed
and undressed me. Clean, freshly ironed clothes appeared as if by magic. When I
married Kurro I did not know how to make a fire or cook or wash clothes or sew.
Even now, just when I think I know exactly how to make a basket, I find new vines
and have to learn all over again. But, I think this is good. It makes life interesting.
Perhaps this is how life is supposed to be. Ach, it is too late for philosophy. I will see
you in the morning. Good night."

"Good night," said Ninan. "I will be prepared to leave when you are ready."
Taya nodded and left. Ninan was exhausted yet she could not sleep; her mind was
full of the events of their story. She watched the moon's light gradually make way
for the sun and it was almost morning when she fell asleep. The children's noises
woke her and she rose sleepily, unaware that the stranger was once again watching
her.

The next two days were among the happiest and busiest Ninan had ever
known. She fit herself into the rhythms of the family, cooking, carrying, caring for
the children, and helping set up camp for the night. Although they talked little
after the first night, a closeness grew among the three that Ninan had not thought
possible. Even with the children, they walked at a good pace, covering many more
miles each day than they had before Ninan joined them. At lunch Taya joked, "You
should live with us all the time, Ninan. Look how much the three of us can do
together." Ninan felt her heart lurch. A great sorrow overwhelmed her.

She tried to make a joke, to push away the hurting. "I am only a storyteller;
you would soon find me useless." She stood up and walked off to wash her cup.

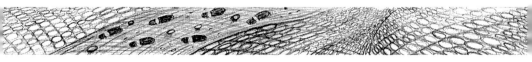

Taya followed. "Why do you say *only* a storyteller?"

Though she tried not to, Ninan burst into tears. Taya put her arms around Ninan, "I am sorry if my words offended you."

Ninan shook her head and briefly told her story. "I am afraid that if I let myself love a man or a village I will want to stay. I will stop telling the old stories and they will be forgotten. I could not bear this. I would like to love a man yet I have never seen a man follow a woman. I keep moving so I can tell the stories that need to be told, but the faster I move the more confused I am. I find feelings painful. It is much easier to live without feeling."

"And are you still moving?"

"Yes, but these few days with you and your family have shown me that, Mima, the grandmother, is right."

"Grandmother?" asked Taya.

"I wandered into a village whose water supplies had dried up and without knowing what I was doing, helped them regain their water. But before I could leave I became ill. Mima and her family took care of me. To assure them, and myself, that I would return, I left the book of my grandfather's stories, and my grandmother's shawl with her. Mima said I could not run forever, that feeling was part of life, but in this she is wrong. If I do not feel, I do not have to worry. I can keep going for as long as I live."

"This does not sound like a happy way to live," said Taya.

"There are worse, believe me. I am trying not to keep running. I believe what Mima says, that this is no way to live, yet it is all I know to do."

Kurro walked over to them and laughed. "We are ready to leave. Are you two going to stand here and talk forever?" Taya teased him with a kiss and picked up her baskets.

"You are coming with us, Ninan?" Ninan looked at the family, an ache in her heart. Then she nodded, and prepared to leave.

That night, they came to the edge of the village where they joined other people who had come to the market to sell wares, arriving early enough to find a choice place to make their camp. The three adults made easy work of the chores, and Ninan could not help noticing how much she enjoyed being with Taya, Kurro, and their children.

The stranger watched Ninan.

That night, as they sat around the fire, Kurro said, "I believe it is time for you to tell us a story. Did you not say something about silence not being good for the soul?"

Ninan grinned. "Yes, that is what I said when I was giving you advice but my life is not as interesting as yours and I have not told stories for some time. Still, I will try."

t was a time of drought. And with drought comes famine. Parched fields yield no crops. Even the river was mostly muddy swirls where tiny pools of trapped water lay helpless, powerless under the unrelenting rays of sun. People began to leave the village, hoping to find water and food.

In time the village was deserted except for one young woman who was too weak to travel. She prepared herself to die as others had done, lying on clean bedding left behind, too heavy to carry. In the evening, alone, she lay on her bed, waiting for death, sipping the little bit of water villagers could leave with her. But death did not come. Nor did it come the next day. She was tired of waiting.

Standing up, she was puzzled to discover she could still walk and made her way unsteadily to the dried up river where she sank her feet into the still moist sludge. The cool mud revived her spirits and she thought about how she might find food and water though she knew other villagers had found none.

She was standing so still when the bee settled on her arm she watched it without fear, amazed that it was still alive in this place of dying. When the bee flew off, she followed its path, standing quietly when she could not see or hear it. The bee returned from where it had gone and rested on her arm. She did not know how long she followed the bee but it felt as if the bee was leading her to a place of life. Each step led her away from the place of dying.

Yet she was weak. In time she fell and could not rise. The bee came and went several times, depositing tiny drops of honey on her lips that she licked gratefully but could only murmur, "Thank you," as she lay on the ground. Time passed slowly.

Then, in the distance, she heard a strange sound that got louder and

louder until it sounded like bolts of thunder. Dark clouds covered the sun's rays, cooling the air. She never saw the bee drip honey on her parched lips nor did she see the hundreds of bees that followed. But when she awoke, she was covered with sweet sticky drops of honey. Licking her fingers and wrists and every part of her body she could reach, her strength began to return. When she tried standing up, rivulets of honey ran down her legs. Catching every morsel of the precious liquid, the woman ate until her strength returned. She did not die.

After a bout of puzzled silence Kurro asked, "And then what happened?"

Ninan shrugged uncomfortably. "There is no more."

"But there is no ending. What happened to her? What about her family? Did anyone return? How did she live if she was all alone?"

"I do not know. I tell the story as it comes to me. This is all that came." She stoked the fire, not knowing what else to say.

"But you are a storyteller," said Taya, "you can say whatever you want."

"That is not the way my stories happen. They tell themselves."

"But they do not have to. Try," urged Taya. "Imagine what might have happened. Give the woman a name. Tell us about her family. We want to know more."

Ninan felt a surge of anger. They had asked for a story. She told them a story. Why ask for more simply because they did not understand the ending. For her it was a perfectly satisfactory ending. The woman was dying, the bees gave her nourishment, and she lived. "I told all I know. There is no more to tell." She put another log on the fire. "It has been a long day and I think we are all tired. Good night."

Kurro and Taya looked at Ninan, puzzled by the sharpness of her words. They were uncomfortable with the tension. Taya got up and followed Ninan. "Is something wrong? Why do our questions upset you? We wish to know more about the woman, is that so terrible?"

"No, it is not terrible but you do not understand. Perhaps you have heard other storytellers and they can do as you have asked. I do not know any storytellers so I cannot say. When people ask me to tell a story I see images in my head and I tell what I see. When the images stop, the story stops. I cannot tell a story if I have no images."

"Have you ever tried?" asked Taya.

"No," admitted Ninan.

"Then why not try?" asked Taya.

"You ask more than you know. But," she said, remembering Taya's kindness, "I will think about it."

"Do not be upset with us, please?"

Ninan wanted to go to bed and forget the story. "I am tired. Goodnight, Taya."

"Goodnight, my friend." Taya left, feeling unaccountably sad.

When Ninan closed her eyes she saw the woman in her story. Alive. Staring at her. "Go away," she muttered, but the image remained.

"You saw more. Why did you not tell what you saw?" said the woman in her mind's eye.

Ninan got up and walked around the sleeping family but the voice followed after her, accusing, demanding. She walked into the forest hoping to leave the voice behind. It would not be stilled. Ninan thought to out-walk the voice but it continued, even as the darkness softened into gray. Why had she stopped the story? Why had she said she told all she knew to tell? Where had the story come from? She had not experienced drought or famine. Her head ached.

ELEVEN
A WAY OF BEING

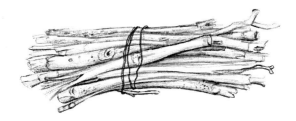

The excited sounds of villagers greeting each other crashed into Ninan's misery. Although Mima's blue shawl was wrapped around her, cradling her with warmth, she felt no comfort. The day was cool and sunny, a good temperature for the activity going on around her. She felt someone poking her. "Are you going to sleep all day?" giggled the children. "Get up or you will miss the best part." Taya was just behind her children, the baby strapped to her back.

"Why are you in such a rush? It is too early to get up," complained Ninan. "I need to sleep." The two children jumped on her back and started tickling her. Ninan evaded their pokes until she could not help laughing. "I give up. If you get off me I promise to get up." The children, giggling with pleasure hesitated, wondering whether to stop. Ninan stood up so quickly the children rolled off her onto the grass, laughing, delighted with themselves. With the blue shawl to ward off the early morning chill, she stretched her arms up toward the sky.

Aware that Taya's eyes were fixed on her, Ninan blushed. "Why are you staring at me?" She hoped Taya would not mention their conversation about the story.

"You are so beautiful. I could watch you for a long time."

"Beautiful?" gasped Ninan. "Your eyes must still be asleep. Beautiful . . . my goodness." Shaking her head in disbelief, she quickly changed the subject. "What shall I do to help you get ready for the market?"

The children shouted gleefully, "Everything has been done. It is time for the promenade. Hurry, Papa said we will lose our place if you do not come at once."

"What is the promenade?"

The children were barely able to keep from running off. "Come, Ninan. Now!"

Feeling out of sorts, Ninan followed the children and Taya as they made their way among crowds of people walking around stalls and blankets filled with fruits, vegetables, woven goods, jewelry, meats, furniture, and tools. Ninan had never seen such a large market before and felt disoriented by the sights and smells and sounds and movement. The aroma of freshly baked bread was too good to ignore. "I will stop here. The smell of the bread is too much to pass by."

The oldest child protested. "You cannot buy anything now, this is the promenade. The people who buy and sell are walking around looking at the goods before the market is officially open. Is there something you would like to buy, Ninan? If you could, that is?"

"I wish for a slice of bread with cheese and butter and jam and a cup of tea. Then I would like to have some of the fruit over there and…"

Taya teased, "Do you live in your stomach?"

Ninan grinned. "I cannot resist such wonderful smells. How long do I have to wait before I can buy something to eat?"

Taya took Ninan's hand and said, "Look at the blankets."

"Oh," gasped Ninan. "How beautiful they are." She touched one gently. It was so soft that when she brushed it with her cheek it felt like a breeze caressing her. "This must have taken months to weave."

She turned, her eyes caught by the baskets skillfully placed by Taya and Kurro to show off their individual and unique designs. "Taya, where did you learn to weave wood? I have never seen such variety. And to think you were a rich man's daughter . . ." She stared at the baskets; each so different and beautiful she forgot her hunger.

Taya's face clouded over. "I remember the first time I saw the great vines growing in a large forest near where I lived. I was so entranced by their shape I cut a few vines and began intertwining the thicker trunks to make the frame and thinner branches to weave the insides. My work was clumsy and fragile, yet I felt a surprising satisfaction. Without thinking, I brought my first efforts home but before I could say anything, my stepmother chastised me. "Taya dearest, do not bring those dirty vines in here. You will mess up the carpets. Have you no sense?" Before I could speak, my stepmother had taken the baskets, thrown them into the fire, and called for a servant to sweep up the twigs that fell onto the rugs. I stood frozen with fury, looking at the fire, suddenly blazing with my baskets. I turned to leave the room as my stepmother asked, 'Did you want to tell me something, dear?' I swallowed my anger."

'No,' I replied, taking care to hide my feelings.

"She asked me, 'Why on earth did you bring those messy vines in here? We have maids to gather our kindling. What were you thinking? Have you forgotten who you are?'

"I said what she wanted to hear: 'You are right, it was a mistake. I will not do this again. Forgive me for making a mess. I apologize for causing the servants extra work.'

"My stepmother gave me a kiss on her forehead and said, "Do not worry, they are paid to do our bidding. You are my sweet, good little girl.'

"From then on I said nothing. Although I kept making baskets until they were good enough to satisfy me, I never again showed them to anyone except Kurro who took them to sell when he went to market. He kept the money I earned in a special place, to be used when we could be together. Instead, Kurro and his father used the money to buy material to make the costumes for his brother and father so they could play the roles that made it possible for me to escape from my father's house. I wove my way to freedom and our life together."

Sensing pride and defiance in her voice, Ninan asked Taya anxiously, "You are so brave, yet your eyes are filled with sadness. Did I hurt you when I called you a rich man's daughter?"

Taya shook her head. "No, you said nothing wrong. Sometimes, a small bit of hurting can last for a long time. Yet, now that I am a mother, I believe my stepmother did not mean to hurt my feelings. She was not an unkind woman. I think she would have helped me when I was in trouble but she too was afraid of my father's temper.

The children, sensing their mother's unhappiness, came and leaned against her. Taya stroked their hair and said to Ninan, "How can I dwell on the past when I have such joy in the present? Right now I think I am the richest and most blessed of women."

Ninan sighed, feeling a yearning deep within her. She wanted to be part of a family, but what part she did not know. She felt separated from herself.

The ringing of a loud bell brought an abrupt change to the pace and activity of the promenade. People moved quickly to their stalls and areas. Hordes of people seemed to appear from nowhere. The crowds were so large Ninan could not focus. The bright colors and shapes dazzled her eyes. Several times the noise and tumult made her hold her hands over her ears and eyes. Still, she was pleased to be there and looked forward to helping Kurro and Taya sell their wares. Towards noon, the smells of food cooking over small fires made Ninan dizzy with hunger and anticipation. Everywhere she walked, a new smell delighted her. "I must find a way to earn money," she thought, walking to the stall of an old couple grilling meat on a bed of white-hot coals. They looked tired and an idea came to her.

"Is there something I might do for you in exchange for a bit of your food" she asked, uncomfortable yet trying to appear friendly and at ease. The old couple continued to wind the spit as they talked the matter over with each other. Several times they looked at Ninan. Had she not been so hungry, their earnest consideration would have made her laugh. There was so much talk just to answer a simple question.

When they apparently came to a decision, the old man turned to her. "We can always use more branches. Bring us a good pile of sticks this big," he said, moving his hands to show her the size he wanted, "and we will feed you this afternoon." Ninan brightened at the thought and smiled hopefully. "Could you spare a small taste before I begin? Your food looks and smells delicious and I am hungry."

The simple request provoked more discussion between the husband and wife, and Ninan was tempted to leave but her growling stomach was embarrassing. Eventually, the old woman nodded and gave Ninan a few juicy chunks of roasted lamb. Eating food that tasted as wonderful as it smelled created a sense of well-being in Ninan as she walked toward the woods, ready to collect wood for the couple's fire.

Gathering small sticks was not as easy as she had assumed. People had been collecting twigs and branches since the previous day and she had to walk longer than she planned before her stack was large enough to bring back. The cool morning air gave way to a bright hot day, and when Ninan saw the river, she could not resist. Taking off her clothes, she waded in, luxuriating in the cool, clear, fast moving water. The warmth of the sun and the rocking of the water lulled her into a

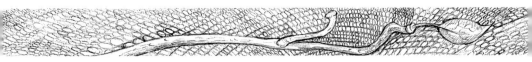

drowsy state. She got out of the water, leaned against a soft pillow of pine boughs, and soon fell deeply asleep.

The man who had been following Ninan for the past weeks was no stranger to many of the market folk. He moved easily among the crowds, smiling at people seen only once a year. He made sure she would not see him yet he was close enough to hear her talk to the old couple. When she left, he followed, staying far enough behind so she would not sense his presence. His long years in the woods hunting animals taught him how to move in silence, without disturbing his prey. He was in no hurry. When he saw her fall asleep near the water, he watched, willing to wait until the right moment to reveal his presence. He sat at a distance, content to feel the sun on his face.

When a large frog plopped itself on a rock near Ninan's face, the splash woke her. The great big green frog seemed to be saying she had used his space long enough, now it was his turn. Ninan laughed and made faces at the frog as he took a long graceful leap into the water. She whistled as she dressed, picked up her load of branches, and began walking back to the market. Gradually, she became uneasy, sure she was not alone; yet when she looked around once again, she saw no one.

Unable to find the source of her anxiety, yet unwilling to dismiss her thoughts as mere imagination, she stopped and started, feeling cross and irritated. Then a branch snapped and she turned around quickly, half expecting to see a small animal scurry away, half anticipating she would, as usual, see nothing.

"Hello, Ninan."

"Mikos!" Words and thoughts and feelings flooded her mind and body. "What are you doing here?" She picked up branches that had fallen off her pile.

"How is your knee?" he asked.

"My knee has healed well. You gave me good care." She wanted to walk back to the market. She wanted to eat the promised lunch. She wanted to touch Mikos. She wanted to jump into the water. Ninan held the branches so tightly they began to crumble. "I better collect more sticks; these few will not earn the meal that awaits me." Feeling shaky, she picked up branches. Mikos worked silently beside her until they soon had two large piles. "Thank you for your help. This wood will last the old people for the rest of the day, perhaps even until tomorrow," stammered Ninan gracelessly.

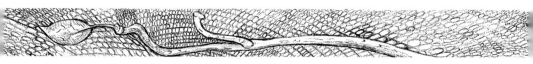

"I am happy to help you gather more wood," he said.

Ninan demurred. She wanted to ask how he came to be in the woods with her and why he was looking at her so intently. "What brings you here, so far from home?"

"I come to this market every year." They walked in silence, each lost in thought. The old people, delighted by the size of the wood piles, gave Ninan and Mikos as much food as they could eat, urging them on when they showed signs of stopping.

"Come, Ninan," said Mikos, when neither of them could eat another morsel, "let me show you a favorite place of mine." He took her hand and led her under an arbor of wild grape that shielded a small green area, almost like a canopy bed. Ninan felt his strong calloused hand and her skin tingled with pleasure. Mikos held a bunch of vines aside and the two of them walked onto a small patch of moss-covered earth. Rays of sunlight dappled through the vines making patterns of sunshine and shadow on the leaves.

"Oh!" cried Ninan. "How wonderful." The sounds of the market were barely audible, drowned out by the songs of the birds. Ninan looked at Mikos, so close she could see the pulse throb in his neck. "It is good to see you again."

Mikos nodded. "In my heart I knew you would be gone the next morning, yet I hoped I had persuaded you to stay. Natasha longs to see you again. We all miss you, each of us in our own way." He touched the back of her hands with his finger.

"What is there to miss? I fell, you laughed . . . that is not a lot to miss."

"You do not tell all that happened."

Ninan blushed and moved away from him, hoping he would tell her what he had missed and what she had not told.

"Did you not miss us? Not even one of us?" he teased.

She brushed a spider off a grape leaf, feeling the warmth of Mikos' breath on the back of her neck. They stood there, she facing the leaves, he looking at her back. "It has been many months since I was in your village. I did not walk on a straight road. Why have you come?"

Mikos gently turned Ninan around until they stood face to face. "When you left, a great sadness filled me. At first I laughed at myself. It was silly to think that spending part of one day with such a prickly person could make a lasting impression. Yet this is what happened. I began to miss you. More than I could have

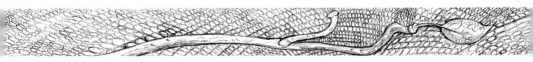

imagined. I grew irritable and unpleasant to be around. One day Natasha told me
if I did not try to find you, she would do so for me and then I would have to take
over her chores and the care of the children. I protested but she said she could not
look at my long face for one more minute. She packed a basket of food and ordered
me to leave."

Mikos spoke with a teasing tone yet his eyes were serious. He took Ninan's
hand. "I have many skills. I can work as a blacksmith or a carpenter. I know about
healing cuts and mending broken bones. On the road, when I offered my services, I
also asked if anyone had seen a young woman storyteller pass by. Often, I lost your
trail but eventually I talked with someone who knew or had heard of such a person.
I passed through one village and met a friend of yours, a little girl named Amina.
She told me how you helped them when their wells went dry and that you almost
died trying to stop the fighting. She said you promised her and her grandmother
that you would return to her village."

Ninan blushed.

"I wished I had been there to help heal your wounds."

"They took good care of me. I…" She did not want to tell him how long she
had stayed there. "Why did you just follow me? Why not let me know you found
me? "

"I was content to keep out of your sight until it felt right to speak. Many
times I opened my mouth yet the time seemed wrong. I do not know how I would
have known the right moment but fortunately for me, the branch took matters into
its own hands." He looked at her intently, as if memorizing her features.

Ninan remembered the attack in the woods. Now Mikos was telling her
he had followed her without her knowing though she had often had the feeling of
being observed. Would she ever feel safe walking by herself again? "Frequently these
past few weeks I felt someone was watching me but I never saw anyone. When you
saw me upset, looking around, why did you not speak then? I was a woman alone,
did you never think about that? Sometimes I was so frightened I kept walking long
past the time I would have stopped. Once, I was attacked. Did you watch that,
too?"

"No. If I had seen your attacker, I would surely have come to your aid." She
did not look convinced. "I did not want you to run away from me again, yet I was
not prepared to tell you what was in my heart. I thought I would watch you and

learn something of your life. I am sorry I caused you worry."

"And now, having seen the way I live, what have you learned?"

Mikos answered forcefully. "I want to be with you for the rest of my life."

"Who is it you want to be with? You do not know me. Perhaps you are still laughing at me, thinking I am a foolish person who does not know the difference between teasing and truth? Do you think I will stop telling stories just to be with a man?" She moved away, her back to him.

"I am speaking my heart's truth. I have tried to live without you and I do not like it. And neither does my family. You are special, Ninan, a strange and wonderful woman. Beautiful . . ."

"Please, do not use such words. What do you want from me?"

"I want to share what you experience. I want to listen to your stories. I want to walk with you on your road."

Ninan sat down to calm her racing heart. She rocked herself to quiet her inner turmoil, speaking quickly, out of fear and yearning and hope and despair. "Men do not follow women who walk their own paths. This much I know. I want no promises you will not keep."

Mikos knelt beside her. "Have I not followed you since you left my family's home? Have I asked you to come back with me to my village? Have I said you must not tell stories? What makes you so sure that your parents' wisdom is every man's truth? You do not know who I am or what I want or what I feel yet you judge me fiercely."

Ninan stopped rocking. "I do not see men following women, do you? I do not notice husbands walking on their wives' roads, do you? I cannot know what I do not see. Men want to lead. Women are taught they must follow. I cannot live my life in this way and be a storyteller. I cannot change my life to suit a man. So, leave. Find a woman who will follow you." Ninan saw that her words angered Mikos but she was caught between hope and disbelief.

"Is there nothing I can say that will make you believe me?" Mikos took a deep breath and spoke again. "Words cannot change your experience, Ninan. I ask only that you let me prove the truth of my words. Permit me to walk with you and share your life. Give me the opportunity to prove that what I say is what I mean and what I want. Surely this is little enough to ask?"

Ninan sat quietly, voices battling deep within her. She wanted to say yes. She wanted to say no. She did not believe him. She was afraid she would learn to love him and then he would leave, tired of following her way in the world. She shivered although the day was still warm. The small mossy space threatened to suffocate her. "It is late. I have to leave. Kurro and Taya will be wondering where I am."

Mikos put his hand on her shoulder. "You have not answered me."

Ninan reluctantly removed his hand. "I do not have an answer. I cannot say yes and I cannot say no." She stood up to leave, determined not to continue the conversation.

Mikos stood in her way. "Why not? Let me travel with you, spend time with you, as you are. If this means walking the countryside next to you, I am prepared to do this. I have not asked you to do anything differently. I have not asked for anything in return. I have only asked . . ."

Ninan interrupted him. "Stop repeating yourself. I hear your words. You make your offer sound simple and natural, but it is not simple or natural for me." She could not look at him.

Mikos persisted, not willing to lose her again. He watched the turmoil play on her face. "What are you thinking, Ninan?" When she did not answer he asked again, "Do you not like me? Do you prefer not to know me? Shall I go away and leave you alone forever?"

"No. I would be lying if I said I do not want to know you or I never want to see you again. I have thought about you ever since I left your village. Meeting you was why I could not stay there, even for a few days. But I do not want to lose my stories. Have you ever heard of even one family who travels from village to village, where the wife and mother is the one who tells stories? You are not the first man who says what he needs to say in order to have a woman do his bidding. How can I trust what I do not see, do not know, and most certainly, do not believe?"

Mikos clenched his jaws to contain his anger. "You have my word. I am only one man and I can only speak for myself. It is up to you to decide whether you can trust me."

They had spoken all that could be said by either of them and yet, Ninan felt the power of his presence, the intensity of his wanting to be with her, the attraction she felt for him. "You have chosen your words with care but I need time to become used to your presence. I have agreed to help my friends Taya and Kurro sell their wares. Will you spend the time with us or must you have your answer at once? Now or not at all?"

Mikos forced himself to speak softly. "I thought you did not believe in friends." Without waiting for Ninan to reply, he took one of her hands in his and gently caressed it. "Since you have promised to help your friends, I am willing to wait. All I ask is that you see me, Mikos, not just a man who will say anything to get what he wants."

"Then it is settled. Come and meet them." She ran out of the enclosure, like a rabbit freed from a trap. Before he could say another word, she rushed toward the market as fast as she could. He raced to catch up with her.

Taya had been looking for Ninan, and when she saw her, she blurted out, "Where have you been? We looked everywhere for you." Her tense face and worried look frightened Ninan.

"Is something wrong? Are the children . . .?"

"They are fine. We thought you had gone."

Ninan was shocked. "But I promised to help you. Besides, I would never leave without saying goodbye."

Taya smiled. "People have heard you are a storyteller. There will be a fire tonight in the big circle, after the market closes. Will you come and tell a story?"

"Why not?" she said, deliberately challenging Mikos. "Am I not a storyteller? A storyteller is always ready to tell stories."

Mikos did not react. Instead, he left to greet people who surrounded him, wanting to know how the past year had gone for him, eager to tell their own news. Shouts of laughter assaulted her as Mikos and his friends hooted and regaled each other with exploits, marriages, and births. Although this was what she wanted, time for herself, Ninan felt jealous and was relieved when Taya and Kurro needed her to sell their goods, asking no questions, though she knew Taya had seen her with Mikos. She wished she had not mindlessly agreed to tell a story in the evening, keenly missing her grandfather's book. Even though she seemed unable to tell his stories, having the book gave her courage.

All through the afternoon she tried to think of a story but none came; not even the beginning of an idea. She sold Taya's baskets and Kurro's woodenware in a daze. Several times people asked if she was ill. She began to panic. What if I have no more stories inside me? Then who will I be? She considered running away but knew this would not help for long. All the while she worked at the market, helped with chores, and tended to the children, her mind was focused on finding an idea for her story. When evening came, she went to the fire, dreading the moment when everyone's eyes would be on her. She had to find a way into the story.

Sitting on a bale of straw, she covered herself with the blue shawl. The night was warm yet she could not stop shivering. When everyone had gathered around her, and the silence made a space for her words, she closed her eyes. No images. No words. Desperate, she opened her eyes and said to the market folk, "Let us be still for a few minutes, to allow the events of the day to begin to fade." She closed her eyes, took a deep breath, and waited. Pictures formed. Words came.

ong ago, in a place far away, there lived a widow whose children had left to make their own ways in the world. She lived simply and quietly, earning what little money she needed by selling eggs and milk. Living alone, she welcomed the occasional visits from neighbors and tinkers coming to sell her pots and tools and other goods. The woman, neither young nor old, had grown used to days filled with work, caring for her animals, tending her garden, baking bread, and keeping her cottage and animal shed in good order. She did not yearn for a different life.

One night, just after she had finished washing up the supper dishes, she heard an unfamiliar noise outside. Someone or something was trying to get into her house. She picked up a lantern and opened the door just wide enough to peer out. There lay a young man, covered with blood, moaning in great pain. She bent down to question him but the man had used all his strength to move toward her light. He said nothing. He saw no one.

Although he was much larger and heavier than she was, she managed to drag him inside, next to the fire. Panting from the effort, she put water on to boil and found clean rags to stop the bleeding. She felt his body but found no broken bones. Pressing various parts of his body brought no loud cries of pain. When she had stopped the bleeding, she cleaned and bound the cuts, wiping away as much of the dirt as she could. The moans gradually stopped and he slept peacefully. The widow went to her bed but was unable to sleep. Annoyed that she could not still her racing thoughts, she got up and sat in her rocking chair and watched him. He slept all night and most of the next day.

She was feeding the chickens when he awoke. He looked around, recognizing nothing. He tried to stand up. The loss of blood made him dizzy and he sat before he fell. He laid back on the blanket by the hearth, remembering nothing of the past few days save for the image of the huge bear lunging at him, claws slashing at his body, his desperate attempt to save himself. He had no idea how he survived the bear's attack. He did not know where he was or how he came to be in this clean, warm cottage. Too tired and weak to move, he lay where he was hoping someone would soon return. When he heard the door open, he tried unsuccessfully to stand again.

"So, you are up, are you? How are you feeling?" The man did not answer. "I will heat a cup of broth." The man watched her, a short woman with a strong, capable body that reflected years of hard work. Her dark brown eyes looked at him with a directness that made him flinch. He managed to sit up.

"Where did you find me?" he finally asked. "I remember nothing after the bear attacked me. How did I come here? Who are you? Who lives…?"

"Sip the broth and then we will talk." She filled a cup with hot, strong soup and put two slices of bread and butter on a plate, watching with satisfaction as he gobbled down the food and emptied the cup. Silently, she refilled the cup and plate three times, busying herself, waiting until he was prepared to talk.

"What is your name?" he asked.

She sat down in her rocking chair. "Zyah. And you?"

"Melum. I thank you for saving my life. Although I have nothing to repay you with, perhaps when I am stronger . . ."

"You owe me nothing. What I did was freely done."

"Still… Saving a man's life is no small matter. I wish to give you something in return. This is only right."

The widow shrugged. "You need to rest and regain your strength. There will be time for talk later. Lie down. I will put clean bandages on your cuts."

For many days the man stayed with the widow, gradually becoming stronger and more able to move without reopening the deep injuries. The worst wounds were on his arms where he had fought to save himself from the bear. He bloodied many bandages until he learned to be patient, to let the cuts heal in their own time. He took to rocking in her chair, watching the woman as she worked, admiring her strength and calm. They talked little.

One day, a burning log rolled out of the fireplace and without thinking, Melum pushed it back in, putting more wood on top of it to hold it in place. He noticed the wounds did not bleed. Cautiously, he opened the door, brought in a small log, and waited. The scabs remained closed. He felt a surge of joy and began carrying in logs to fill the bin. His excitement gave way all too quickly to exhaustion, yet as he sat and rocked, he thought about the woman who had cared for him for so long without complaint.

Zyah came in and noticed the filled woodbin. Her eyes asked what her mouth did not.

"My wounds are healed. I have lifted and carried and there is no more bleeding. You have taken good care of me. How can I thank you?"

"I have told you, your words are thanks enough. Too much gratitude is as bad as none."

Melum sat, confused by what he felt. His body had healed well enough, his strength was returning, yet he had no desire to leave. He liked being with this strong capable woman though she was old enough to be his mother. He wanted to care for her as she had cared for him.

That evening, he sat by the fire long after she had gone to bed. When he knew what he would do, his only wonder was what her response might be.

In her bed, Zyah tossed and turned, exhausted yet unable to sleep. She re-braided her hair, threw a shawl over her sleeping clothes, and walked outside. The night was clear, the stars shone with dazzling clarity. Comforted by their familiar brilliance, she went inside and put the kettle on to boil. Melum was asleep by the fire, his young face, peaceful and innocent. She remembered such a look on the face of her husband and was shocked when she realized she had lived without him longer than they had lived together. Her years as wife and mother belonged to the distant past and she had learned not to dwell on what she no longer had. Still, the sight of Melum made the years of discipline and denial seem a period of drought.

Thoughts she fought to keep from thinking flooded over her until she put a fist to her mouth to keep from screaming. I must not forget he is almost the age of my sons, she reminded herself. I will not allow his presence to disturb my settled feelings. I shall ask him to leave tomorrow. He is well enough. The longer he stays, the more difficult it will be for me to say goodbye. She drank her tea slowly, resolved to restore her inner peace. Without thinking, she carefully knelt down beside him and gently kissed his cheek. As he stood up, he smiled in his sleep. The look was a stab of pain to Zyah. She chided herself. Foolish woman, stop this childish nonsense. You are middle-aged and he is young. His whole life lies before him. She returned to bed, resigning herself to restlessness.

Toward morning, she fell asleep and slept long past her usual waking time. At first Melum went to her bed, thinking her ill, but after satisfying himself that she was peacefully sleeping, he watched her for a few minutes. He liked looking at the lines on her face and the softness of her hair as it caressed her pillow. Shaking himself, he left to feed the chickens, milk the cow, and prepare breakfast.

When she woke, she sat up, bewildered by the unaccustomed brightness of the day. She quickly dressed and rushed to go outside but Melum stood in her way. "Good morning."

She smelled the warmth of his body and spoke sharply, "I have slept too long; I have much work to do. The eggs need to be . . ."

"There is time for you to eat the breakfast I have made. I have done the morning chores." He led her to the table and before she could protest, brought her food and poured tea for both of them.

"There is something I would like to tell you," he said.

Zyah did not want to hear what she thought he was going to say. "I thank you for doing my work this morning, but now that you are healed, I think it best that you be on your way. You are a young man; a small cottage with a widow woman is no place for you. I will pack you food for your journey."

She took her cup, leaving her food untouched, and went to prepare herself for his leave-taking.

He followed after her. "This is what I wish to talk with you . . ."

"There is no need to talk," interrupted Zyah. "You have your whole life before you and you had best get on with it, as I must do with mine. Winter is coming and there is much to do. The seasons wait for no one."

Melum looked at the tightness of her mouth and the slight trembling of her hands and took them in his. She jerked them away as if hot coals had burned her. "Why do you touch me? I have asked you to leave."

She tried to pull her hands from his but he held them fast. "I do not want to leave. I want to stay with you. I am happy here."

"I am almost old enough to be your mother. I have raised two sons who are now grown. Please leave quickly and say no more."

"I want to be with you, to help you just as I have done this morning. You are the woman I have wanted to live with. Please do not ask me to leave." She removed her cold hands from his warmth and forced herself to smile.

"You are a kind man. I understand you feel indebted to me but there is no need for repayment. I freely gave you care. Your restored health is compensation enough. Let us talk no more. While you prepare to leave I will make food for your travels. I have washed and mended your shirt and pants; the bloodstains and torn places are barely visible. I will give you a shirt that belonged to my husband. Neither he nor I have use for it now."

She tried to control her trembling and wanting, knowing it was best for both of them that he leave quickly, before she admitted how much she wanted him to stay. Twice, she almost cut her finger as she sliced cheese. Melum took the knife out of her hand and moved the food.

"I do not ask to stay out of gratitude though I am grateful. I choose to stay because I do not want to leave you. I feel strong and whole when I am near you. I want to share life with you. I need to be with you. I cannot speak more plainly. I like to look at you and work with you and talk with you. Your age makes no difference to my love."

"Hush! What you say may be true for now, but soon you will want to be with a young woman. You will want to have children of your own. This is only right and natural. If I feel pain seeing you leave now, later it will be unbearable. I have learned to live my life alone. I manage well enough. It is best you leave now."

"You have not said you do not like me. This would be reason to leave. Do you want me to go because you do not care for me?"

Zyah blushed and looked away. "I cannot say I do not care for you." She forced herself to face him. "But, I have learned to live by myself. I do not have the courage to learn to do this a second time. It is best that you go now. In a short time you will meet a young woman and you will forget about me."

"Do you think I have never known young women? Do you truly believe I want to be with you because I cannot find a woman my own age? You do me a disservice, but I will leave immediately if you tell me to go. If not, I have courage enough for both of us. What is in my heart gives me strength."

Zyah flared with anger. "This is easy for you to say. Our time together has not been long. How can you talk with such certainty? This only proves you are too young for me. Please, I beg of you . . ." She turned away, slicing the bread with trembling fingers.

"Let me stay. Give me a chance to show you what I feel. Or," he asked, "is it that you fear the talk of neighbors?"

"My neighbors are my friends. They want what is good for me."

He grinned. "Give me one month to show you I am good for you. If, after this time, you are not convinced, I will leave without another word."

"One month is a short time. I have been a widow for more than twelve years. I have lived alone since my sons left. I am not used to living with anyone any more." She struggled to find the words to ask him once again to leave, but they would not come. He had touched her heart and she could not stop the feelings he now stirred.

Melum sat quietly, waiting. The silence lasted a long time. She felt unable to say what she knew she must say.

Perhaps it was the sounds of the birds or the rustling of the wind . . . Perhaps it was another chance to feel the fullness of life . . . Zyah knew she could not honestly tell him to leave.

She gathered her hopes and dreams and desires, and then lightly placed her hand next to his. "Your words are rain on parched earth. I will take the chance. The future will take care of itself. May I be strong enough to bear what it brings."

Their hands touched. The rhythms of life flowed between them.

Ninan sat without moving, her eyes still closed, waiting for the pictures in her mind's eye to fade. Those gathered around her sat in silence. In each person lived the image of the man and the woman, ready to begin an uncommon life. Women wondered what would happen; men speculated as to what they would have done. Although as usual, the story left Ninan drained, the silence of the audience left her apprehensive. Her story had none of the adventure or action people were used to hearing. She wrapped Mima's shawl around her more tightly and breathed deeply, relieved she had had a story to tell.

She felt Mikos staring at her through closed eyes. She heard him ask, "What happened when the month was over? Did they live happily ever after?"

Ninan looked to see if he was teasing her, ready to protect herself, but his eyes were clear and she saw no sign of his familiar, mocking laughter. Standing up, she faced him, taking his measure, and her own. She saw others, waiting to hear her answer. In a strong, sure voice, staring at Mikos, she spoke. "Yes, they did. They made a life for themselves that lasted."

The audience sighed with pleasure. Now it seemed the story had a real ending. They left quietly and peacefully, satisfied in some profound place deep within themselves yet Ninan wondered why she had spoken so quickly. She had no more pictures. She had no idea whether the man and woman would live together happily. She had said it to please Mikos and this did not please her.

Taya and Kurro looked at her as if she were a stranger. Ninan greeted them cautiously, uneasy about the expression on their faces.

"Your story pleased us very much," said Kurro. "Does it please you?" His eyes took in the presence of Mikos standing close to Ninan.

Too shy to say much, Ninan said, "Yes."

Feeling out of place, Mikos moved away from them but Ninan said, "Mikos, do not leave." She held out her hand. "Kurro, Taya, this is my friend, Mikos." Kurro and Taya smiled as she introduced them. Mikos took her hand in his.

There was an awkward pause as the four stood, tired yet unable to leave. Ninan was keenly aware of Mikos yet too shy to include him in their sleeping arrangements. It was Kurro who looked at Ninan but asked Mikos, "Would you like to join us? There is room for one more."

Mikos glanced at Ninan who said nothing until the silence grew too tense to bear. "You are welcome," she said, finally. The tension eased. The four made their way to the sleeping children.

TWELVE
A NEW SUN RISING

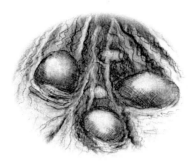

Mikos followed Ninan to the place where he could sleep, close to where she would lie but too close to the children to talk. He knew better than to suggest a different arrangement. The two lay separately, each wide-awake. Ninan wondered why she had said the couple lived happily ever after. She had no idea what happened after she ended a story. She could hear Mikos tossing but made no move to speak to him.

After a time, she walked through the moonlit woods to the river and stood at the edge of the bank, thinking about how her life had changed since the last time she had bathed. Watching water swirl around rocks before whooshing down slight drops, she felt the power of the flow match the confidence of the river's direction. Shivering, she undressed and waded into the current. Surprised by the strong current, she fell and was carried by the stream until she regained her footing. Gasping and laughing with pleasure, she exulted in her joy, which was for the moment, unfettered by old fears, untouched by new worries. When she finally made her way upstream, she felt healed of an undefined and unknown wound. Whistling as she put on her clothes, Ninan was pleased to be alive. She had just put her foot on a large rock, ready to walk back to her friends when she looked up, not pleased to see Mikos. Her look demanded an explanation.

"I followed you," said Mikos.

"Why?" asked Ninan.

"Did you not say you felt fear when you walked at night, all alone?"

"Yes."

"You do not seem pleased I am here."

"I do not believe you followed me just to protect me."

Mikos sat on the rock and gently touched Ninan's foot. "What do you believe?"

"I believe you want something I am not prepared to give."

"And what might that be?"

Ninan pulled her foot from Mikos' hands. "If you do not know, I do not need to tell you." She stood up, moving away from him.

"Why are you so unfriendly? I thought we had an agreement. Was I not to follow you?"

Ninan felt uncomfortable. Her body tingled, still cold from the river. She wished she could lean into his warmth but his banter irritated her. She felt she was losing a battle she did not know she was fighting. "It is almost morning. I am going back. Do as you please."

"What I please is to give you a hug." He held her close, feeling her resistance melt.

Ninan hated feeling so torn. She spoke softly as she moved out of his arms. "Thank you, I am much warmer now." Giving him no chance to speak, she ran back to Taya who was cooking mounds of dough on a stick. The smell of baking bread greeted Ninan. All too soon, the children were up and ready to play. She swung the oldest around and then grabbed the second child, spinning the two of them in the grassy field. Unable to hold their combined weight for long, Ninan fell to the ground laughing with the children. Taya took pity and came over to help. Ninan playfully pushed the children off her and noticed Taya was not quite able to conceal her anxiety. "I worry when I wake and do not find you."

"I went to the river to have a bath. I did not want to wake anyone up."

"When I saw you were gone I was afraid you had left."

"I told you I would not leave without saying goodbye, I will not disappear, I promise."

"You are like the sister I never had. I did not realize how much I missed having a woman friend until I met you. Although I love Kurro, and we talk often, talking with a woman is different. I wish you were my sister. I could teach you to make baskets and you could tell stories at markets . . ."

"I wish we were. I wish we could. But, I am sure we will see each other again. I know we will. Let us promise this to each other." She took Taya's right hand. "I,

Ninan, do hereby vow to remain a lifelong friend to Taya, to be her sister by choice.
Now it is your turn."

Taya took Ninan's right hand, holding it as if in a formal ceremony. "I, Taya,
do hereby vow to remain a lifelong friend to Ninan, to be her sister by choice."
Although the children had no idea of the meaning of the words, they sensed the
exchange of feelings and stood quietly, watching the two women.

Closing the market was hard work, made easier by the unexpected help of
Mikos who spoke little, making no attempt to ease the strain between him and
Ninan. When the time to say goodbye inevitably came, Ninan experienced a sharp
sense of loss. It took all her self-control to keep from screaming at them not to
leave. Although she and Taya had promised to remain friends, the uncertainty of
their lives made seeing each other again seem impossible. What good were promises
if their paths never crossed? Knowing she could not simply walk away, Ninan
searched for something to give to Taya. She wanted to give her the blue shawl but
this belonged to Mima. She wished she had the shawl of her grandmother.

Taya, feeling the same need, found the answer for both of them. She put
her arm around Ninan and walked with her to a place where they could be alone
for a few minutes. Both women were crying, knowing neither could say when
they would next see each other. She put her present into Ninan's hands. "Here is a
basket that is half made, with all the reeds you will need to finish it. I would like
you to complete it for me and use it until we meet. Then, I will use it until we
see each other again. It will be a remembrance of our friendship and a useful help
at the same time." She gave Ninan the basket and showed her how to weave the
remaining vines, taking pleasure in watching Ninan weave a few strands. When
she was satisfied that Ninan knew enough to complete it, Taya said, "Good! Finish
it tomorrow or whenever you like. You know enough to work on your own. Every
time I work on one I will think of you finishing our basket."

"I wish I had something to give you, something of me to have as a
remembrance. I would give you this blue shawl but it is not mine, and I have
nothing else to give."

"You have given me your stories. They will live within my heart forever."

"Those stories were for everyone but you have given me an idea. I will give
you a special story; one that only you will hear. And, one that only you can finish."

"But I do not know how to tell stories. How can I finish it?"

"If I can finish a basket, you can finish a story." They sat in silence until Ninan spoke.

here was darkness in every direction. Before light was brought to the people, they moved around using only touch and sound. No one strayed far from the places that were known. To do so meant death from cold or starvation or loneliness. No one asked if this was all there was. This was the way the world was. Everyone knew this. Until one day.

A creature suddenly fell from the dark sky. Bleeding. Hungry. Almost lifeless. No one had ever experienced anything like it. Some people were frightened and moved away. Others stood, not knowing what to do. Two women moved slowly toward whatever it was, feeling their way, listening to the sound of its cries, smelling its spilled blood, waiting to see if it would rise by itself. It did not.

The two women touched the creature lying quietly, at the edge of life, and knew they must act quickly if it was not to die. Even then they knew it might not live. One woman gently cradled the creature, hoping her warmth would be soothing while she stopped the bleeding. The other brought water and food which she crushed with the water, making it into a paste which she placed on the creature's beak, gently wetting its mouth with the nourishment.

It did not move. The woman tenderly opened its mouth and dripped water into its throat. Then she massaged the creature's throat until it swallowed. While her friend cradled it, she slowly fed it until the paste and the droplets of water were gone. Then there was nothing to do but wait. And hope.

All day the two women cared for the creature, waiting. Sensing its struggle to breathe, hearing its rasping breath, though it did not move. The women fell asleep with the creature cradled between them.

Some time after they had been sleeping deeply, fluttering awakened the women. The creature was moving. The women fed it more water and food, feeling awe as the creature took a few steps. The women held their breath, afraid to startle it. The creature shook itself and flew over the women, returning to the space between them. When the creature first spoke the women did not understand its words, but it continued talking until the women learned. What the creature told them was amazing.

"I come from a land of color, from light and warmth. I will show you where it is. You will never be cold again."

"You are small and we are big," said Yanina.

"What is color? What is light?" asked Alora.

"It is true that I am small and you are big but if you do what I say, all will be well." Yanina smiled. She was ready. "I cannot tell you what color is, you must see it for yourself. And light too. I can only say it is not what you know and nothing I can describe."

"I will follow you," said Alora, "to the color and light."

"We will follow you," added Yanina. "Tell us what to do."

When the two women told the others they were going to leave, that they planned to follow the creature wherever it took them, some people cried and begged them not to go, predicting they would suffer terribly. Others said they were foolish. A few, very few, only two actually, asked if they could come. Although the women agreed, when it came time to leave, only Alora and Yanina held on to the creature's tail as it flew over a landscape they could not have imagined.

This they did, for a long time, longer than they knew. Then, one day, when they awoke, it was not dark. Something made their eyes hurt. They covered their eyes but their curiosity and excitement was so great that when they heard the sound of the creature, they opened their eyes and saw what they had never seen and for which they had no words. This world was beautiful, exactly as the creature promised. The women looked as hard as a thirsty man might drink.

This is how the women first saw a bird, and color, and light, and sun. And the two women, who were as close as any two people could possibly be, decided that color and light were so wonderful they had to share it with all those who lived in darkness. But, if they stayed together, it would take them twice as long to bring color and light to those without. Could they separate? Could they bear to live, each without the other? It was a difficult decision for they loved each other deeply.

Ninan stopped, grinning. "Just as you asked me to finish your basket, I ask you to finish my story. But not now. Think about it. And, when we next see each other, I will give you your basket and you can give me your story. What do you think?"

"Given that I am not a storyteller, it will take me until we meet just to decide what happens to the two women. Yet when I think of your story I will feel close to you. I thank you for your gift. Before we leave I want to describe where we live. When—notice I do not say if—you come, you will easily find us for there are vines and baskets in every stage. Wood and shavings and woodenware are strewn around our cottage."

Ninan listened intently, memorizing every detail, hoping she would forget nothing.

There was nothing more to say. They parted in sorrow-filled silence. Ninan watched the family walk down the road, growing smaller as the distance between them increased. Her chest ached and she blinked hard to avoid the tears that threatened to drown her face.

Mikos put his arm around her as she waved goodbye to Taya and Kurro, blowing kisses to the children. He rubbed Ninan's shoulders as she stared at the slowly disappearing figures. When they were gone from sight, he spoke. "It is hard to say goodbye to people you care about. It is not something I like to do. In my village people seldom leave and I think this is good."

"Perhaps it is, for some, but traveling is my way of life, though I admit, I find it difficult at times." Feeling a pang of disloyalty, she added, "But it is the way of storytellers."

"Could you not stay in one village and tell stories? You would still be a storyteller." Ninan did not answer immediately. The thought was tempting and yet, she felt annoyed. Already he was asking her to change her ways.

"Perhaps there are different ways to be a storyteller, but my grandparents traveled from village to village, telling old stories, learning new ones. I think their way is the way for me."

"You have tried this, could you not try another? Perhaps the one I offered?"

Ninan looked at Mikos, his strong body, his dark welcoming eyes, and his wonderful smile. Living as a storyteller in his village would make life easier, yet she did not think she could do it. Not yet, perhaps not ever. "I must continue as I am, Mikos. It is the right way for me."

"But can you not think of the other?" He saw her staring at him, challenging

him, as if to say, 'I told you so.' "I will not plead. I want you to do what is best for you."

She could feel his yearning mix with her own. "I will think about it."

Walking with Mikos was a new experience for Ninan. She had not realized how she emptied her thoughts of one story so she could be open to the next as she walked by herself. Accustomed to spending days at a time without talking to anyone, she walked in silence with Mikos, wondering what it was like for him. He came from a large family where someone was always talking, usually on top of two or three others, everyone wanting to be heard at the same time. Although she was not surprised when he began to whistle, the sound irritated Ninan and she walked even faster, to get away from it, not stopping to ask if her pace was too fast. Mikos responded by whistling and walking more quickly, seemingly unbothered.

She asked herself if being with Mikos was such a good idea. Life was less tumultuous when she traveled alone. Yet, when they stopped for the evening to make camp, she appreciated the ease with which the two of them gathered wood and made the fire to cook supper. When the night creatures hooted and howled, she was glad to have his company. What was not good quickly became apparent. Mikos prepared the two sleeping places next to each other. Ninan moved hers away yet when she returned, they were once again as they had been, touching. Ninan did not know what to do and was devising a plan when he put his arms around her, hugging her with an intensity that was disturbing and welcoming. She felt the warmth of his body pressing against her. Although her body responded, pressing close to him, she said, "No. I am not ready. I prefer we first learn to be friends. I know so little about you."

"This is true," he teased, "and that is why I am giving you a chance to know me better."

"This is not my way of knowing," she said, moving away from him. "I have been living alone. I need time to get used to being with you." She moved her sleeping place away from his and wrapped her shawl tightly around her, turning her body away from his.

He stood, looking at her, wondering what to do, feeling the ache of emptiness as he yearned to hold her close.

The next few days were strange for both of them. Ninan walked quickly to ease the intensity of her feelings, to lessen her sense of being 'filled up,' and to mourn the loss of Taya and her family. Mikos followed, as he promised, not knowing how to reach Ninan. It was as if she built a wall around her, blocking all feeling. Although Ninan, for the most part, enjoyed being with Mikos, she sensed his discomfort with her silent way of traveling. In the past, when she felt troubled, she avoided people, walking away from villages, living off the land. She knew Mikos was different. He liked people and looked forward to talking with them, even as he worked. Being alone made him feel lonely, yet he had promised her he would follow beside her, travel as she did, and live as she lived. She hoped he would keep his promise.

Ninan felt the difference in their ways of being when he asked if she wanted to fill their water bags in the next village. She was unprepared for the suggestion; the thought of meeting new people so soon after saying goodbye to Taya upset her. "I still have water in my bag but if you need to fill yours, I am sure we will soon come to a stream where you can replenish your supply long before we come to a village."

"It is not only about filling my bag. I would like to meet some of the people who live there. I have heard they make interesting objects from wood."

"Are you unhappy with my way of walking?"

Mikos chose his words carefully. "I am not unhappy, it is just that your ways are not mine. I have to try them for a time before I can say I am not happy." He avoided looking at her

"I knew you would soon tire of my way of living."

"You are quick to come to your conclusion. It seems you know my mind better than I do. I did not know you were a mind reader." He stormed off but Ninan ran after him, calling his name. He stopped but did not turn.

"I am used to living alone. You are used to being in the midst of many people, to being the center of attention. How could you possibly enjoy my way of living? Already you use the excuse of filling water bags to be with people. Why not admit this is so? Why do you pretend to be happy if you are not?"

"Are you choosing to make my decision for me?"

"No. It is just that I do not understand how you can possibly want to live a life so different from what you have known. You like to be with people all the time. I know this and I make no judgment, but I am tired of wondering how you are feeling, if you are lonely. I did not ask you to come and yet I spend most of the day worrying about you."

"There are many ways to live one's life. Even you might find another way if you were willing to give yourself a chance. You think you are no longer afraid but I see fear in your eyes."

"What you see is your imagination. I am not afraid. What I am is tired of being with people right now. I need to be silent and create space inside me, to make room for new experience. Is this wrong because it not your way? How can you insist you know me when we have spent so little time together? What do you mean when you say you know me?"

In spite of his anger, Mikos laughed. "You look as cross as you did when I first met you."

"Laugh as much as you please. I do not need to stay around to be the target of your jokes."

"Oh Ninan, Ninan, Ninan . . .you are such a funny little . . ."

"I am almost as tall as you are. I would not call you little." Mikos laughed again.

"What is so funny?"

"What is so funny?" repeated Mikos. He hesitated. "I think you are funny because you get so cross so quickly, even when I am trying to help. You remind me of a bird I once had. No matter how hungry, it refused to eat as long as I was looking at it. The moment I turned my eyes away it gobbled everything in sight. But, if it saw me looking, the bird would stop eating and make noises, as if it were scolding me. I laughed then and I laugh now."

"Perhaps this was the only way the bird had to protest your tyrannical ways."

Mikos took Ninan's hand and said quietly, "It may be that we are having trouble learning to be with each other, but this does not mean we cannot learn to change. Come, lie with me."

"I have changed enough for awhile. I hardly know myself as it is."

Once again Mikos laughed. "Oh Ninan, I love you."

"We are so different. You must be fooling yourself . . . or teasing me."

"If I wanted to be with a female version of myself I would have married long ago and probably died from boredom. I chose to find you. I choose to follow you. And, I challenge you to tell me that you do not want me to stay. Go ahead. Tell me to leave right this minute if this is what you truly want."

"No, not this minute. We have food ready to cook. It will spoil if we do not eat it."

This time they both laughed. "Oh Mikos, I love to hear you laugh. It tangles me up but it also makes me feel better. I want us to be happy together."

Mikos touched her hair. "I know we will find a way, we just have to have patience."

"How can you be so sure?"

"Do you want me to stay?"

"Yes, I do."

"Are you sure?"

"Most of the time. Right now I am. But it is difficult for me to be with someone every moment when I am so used to being alone. I do not think you understand how much I need silence in order to find my stories."

"What matters is that we want to be together, 'most of the time,'" he teased. Then he became serious. "Being with you is interesting, always a challenge. I like this. I like never knowing what is going to happen, even if you think you see the end clearly."

"Do you think I know what is going to happen?"

"No, but I believe you think you ought to know what is going to happen so you can be prepared." He smiled and whistled as he mimicked her walking, worrying, and wondering.

Ninan laughingly protested, "That is not the way I am."

"If this is not the way you walk, how do you know I am copying you?"

"Oh you . . ." Ninan poked him in a ticklish place. Mikos laughed, trying to find a place where she was ticklish but she kept squirming out of his reach. Grabbing her, he picked her up and spun her around his shoulder. Ninan tried to make him release her but he held her tightly.

"Do you give up?" he asked.

"No!" He kept whirling her around but she kept saying, "No." She would rather die than give up, especially in a competition with Mikos. Still, the playfulness between them was a relief.

"If you do not put me down, my breakfast will soon be all over your face." She kept struggling but Mikos held her tightly and she could not free herself.

"Say you give up!" he laughingly growled, beginning to feel dizzy.

"No," she vowed, "I will never give up." As stubborn as Ninan, Mikos might have had to spin her forever, to avoid giving in, but he stepped on a small stone and lost his balance. They fell to the ground, rolling down a small hill neither of them had noticed while tussling. Catching their breath, they lay exhausted and exhilarated. "Mikos, what made you fall?"

"I think I tripped on a stone."

"Had it not been for that stone we would still be spinning. Perhaps we need to make sure there are always a few stones wherever we are, to give us a way out of our stubbornness." She stood up, brushed herself off, and then held out her hand to him to help him up.

As he took it and stood up he said, "You may be more right than you know. After all, we met when you tripped on the only stone in the road for as far as I could see." He paused and then pronounced, "I have just decided, not only do I love you, I love stones." He began studying the ground as he slowly walked back up the hill, his eyes carefully scanning the earth.

"What are you looking for?" she asked.

"I am looking for our stone." She put her hand in his as they both looked for it.

When they reached the top of the hill Ninan said, "It does not matter that we did not find it. What matters is the idea."

"Now that gives me an idea," said Mikos. He put his hands on Ninan's face and gently kissed her. They held each other for a long time. The argument was over. Something else was beginning. Mikos led Ninan to a small clearing where they sat down on the soft earth. He held her close, caressing her body, murmuring words that filled her with happiness. For the moment, all their arguments were silenced as their bodies spoke what was in their hearts. For the moment all was well. Ninan could not imagine greater happiness. Mikos felt the heaviness inside him dissolve.

During the days that followed, they explored ways of being together, often stopping to enjoy being close. Ninan felt herself relax and enjoy the company Mikos provided, finding it easier to share tasks, to follow as well as lead. Mikos stopped pressuring her to meet people or tell stories. Although part of her worried about feeling empty of stories, she tried to take comfort from what so many people had told her. If she was going to be a storyteller she had to do it in her own way, and for her, it seemed stories had to come from within, through choice, when they were ready to be told. So Ninan waited and listened and walked, keeping her worries to herself. She had told stories while she was with Taya and her family, maybe she could find a way to tell them while traveling with Mikos. She was pleased that he had stopped asking questions about her way of telling stories.

He was pleased at her newly discovered softness and her capacity to laugh.

Habitually, when she was upset she chose the most difficult paths and roads to walk on, hoping that successfully negotiating arduous terrain would help ease her inner turmoil. Often, she followed a stream or rock wall, wishing the outer struggle would relieve the pressure of her inner conflict. At times she would have welcomed a complaint by Mikos to distract her, but he kept up with her pace and she remained silent but she could feel pressure building. The pleasure of being with Mikos and the pain of not having a story inside her began to tear her apart though she knew there was nothing she could do to force the birth of a story. She began to think her parents were right: to be a storyteller, one had to live alone.

After walking for several weeks, he decided to work on a barn that was being constructed close to where they camped. The farmer, eager to finish it before the first frost, welcomed the unexpected help provided by Mikos. Ninan watched him leave in the morning and arrive back late at night. Unused to adjusting her rhythms to his, she found herself becoming resentful; she wanted and needed to keep walking.

To pass time she tried to remember stories from her grandfather's book but fragments were all that came to mind. She told these bits and pieces to birds and insects that crossed her path, but she could not remember a whole story. She was tempted to leave, to return to Mima, to get her book and shawl, yet she was unwilling to leave Mikos. She enjoyed the smell and feel of him. She passed some of the time making an evening meal, pleased that she could prepare something she knew he liked. Greeting him with a hug, she offered him a plate of food, but he refused. "I have eaten. The farmer fed us so we could work until it was too dark to see."

Ninan tasted a mouthful before she realized she was no longer hungry.

Mikos was in a good mood. "I need a swim. Come with me."

"I have already been to the river; I am going to bed." She cleaned the dishes, banked the fire, and lay, staring at the stars, wide-awake, determined not to speak. When Mikos returned, he saw that she was pretending to be asleep and said nothing.

The next night, Mikos returned to find no fire and no food cooking. Tired, dirty, and frustrated, he scolded Ninan. "Why is there no fire to boil water? Why have you not cooked our food? I have been working hard all day. Surely you could do these simple chores. I would do as much for you. What have you had to do all day? Nothing but sit and be lazy."

"I am not your wife. I am not here to wait on you. What I choose to do when I am alone is not your concern. If you choose to work from dawn to dusk that is your affair, not mine. Cook your own food. I am not hungry. I have work to do and I do it as I please. It is not your place to complain about what I do or compare your work to mine!"

"What work?" yelled Mikos. "You have done nothing since we left the market. You call yourself a storyteller? How can you be a storyteller when you tell no stories? You make me laugh!" But Mikos was not laughing.

Ninan glared at him and then slowly and deliberately separated her things from his. "I am sorry you do not like my way of living but it does not surprise me. I hope you find a woman who will please you, who wants to serve you as your needs require." She gathered her things.

Mikos looked at her in disbelief. "Are you leaving just because I am hungry? Because I am cross? Because you had all day to prepare and yet you cooked no food?"

"I have been here, waiting for you while you worked, many days longer than you said you would, with never a word of thanks for my patience or my willingness when I did prepare meals. I do not like the way I feel and I cannot continue this way. You are happy when you work with other people, repairing and building, but I need to travel. I think we have been fooling ourselves thinking we could make a life together. I see no way to do this. Our ways are too different."

"So, you are giving up because I was angry at you for not preparing dinner?"

"I am not giving up. I am leaving because I see no way for us to make a life together that is good for both of us." She packed her things, hoping he would hug

her and ask her to stay. He made no move and said no word. She left with a terse, "Goodbye."

Mikos wanted to call out to her, to apologize for his harsh words, but he was too angry. Ninan kept walking, too proud to admit she wanted to turn around and seek comfort in his arms. Mikos watched her leave, slowly growing smaller until she disappeared. No longer hungry, he made a fire, boiled water for tea, and stared at the flames, already missing Ninan intensely. He tried to console himself but found no words of comfort. Though he yearned for the relief of sleep, he remained awake, thinking of her. Wondering. Wishing.

Ninan walked slowly, wishing that Mikos would stop her and apologize, but he did not break his stony silence. Tears blinded her as she walked away from him, remembering the gentleness of his touch, the joy of his laughter. She walked despite increasing darkness, with not even a slip of a moon to guide her way, not caring about the howls of animals prowling in the night. When she stopped, too exhausted to walk any further, she slept in her clothes by the side of the road, astonished and distressed that life could change so quickly from one moment to the next with no warning or hint or clue.

THIRTEEN
THE CENTER OF KNOWING

*I*n the morning when Ninan woke up, she reached to touch Mikos before remembering their quarrel. Her heart ached. We had so many good days together, she thought. Perhaps I should have stayed. Perhaps we could have talked when we were not so angry. She missed the warmth of his body, the way he made her laugh. "Yes," she said to a passing bird, "I will retrace my path. He might still be there, working for the farmer." She had walked only a few steps, her heart a little less heavy, when a disheveled and upset young man ran out of the cottage near where she had fallen asleep. "My wife is in labor with our first child. I must fetch the midwife. She is afraid to be alone. She wants a woman with her. We have no neighbors. I am desperate. Stay with my wife. I will return as soon as I can."

Ninan kept walking. She needed to find Mikos. "I cannot. I must keep going. There is someone I need to meet."

The man blocked her way. "I am desperate. My wife needs a woman. Please."

Ninan kept walking. "Find someone else. If I stay I will . . ."

"If you leave, my wife will die."

Ninan stopped. She looked at the man. There was no mistaking his misery. Perhaps Mikos had already left. Perhaps he was happy she had gone. "I am dirty from my journey. I must wash before I sit with your wife." The man showed her to the water, mumbling his thanks. Ninan shrugged off his words of gratitude. "I will do what I can. I have never helped a woman in labor."

As she entered the cottage, she heard the woman moaning in pain. What can I do, she wondered. She had never even seen the birth of a baby. Ninan smelled the

woman's fear as she neared the bed where the woman lay writhing in agony. Not
knowing what else to do, she stroked the woman's forehead until the pain subsided.
She placed the woman's hand in hers and told her to squeeze her hand when the
pains were bad. In between contractions, Ninan washed the woman's face and body
with cool water to soothe her and lessen the smells of sweat and struggle. When the
worst of a pain had eased, the young woman asked, "Who are you? Where did you
come from?"

"Your husband bade me stay with you until he returned with the midwife."
A new contraction engulfed the young woman, making it impossible for her to
speak. Ninan was terrified. She had never seen anyone in such pain. If I have no
husband, I will have no children. Maybe, she thought to herself, maybe not having
a husband is a good thing.

The woman screamed as the pain wracked her body. Ninan tried to
comfort her but all she could do was to wipe the sweat from the woman's body. In
desperation, she said, "Would you like to hear a story? Perhaps it will help to take
your mind off your pain for a moment."

When the woman was able to speak she said, "Tell me my favorite story,
about the pink flower. My mother used to tell it to me when I was a little girl."

Ninan had no idea what story the woman had heard as a child. "There are
many stories about pink flowers. I will tell you the one I know, about a flower that
grew in the crack of a large rock." Not hearing any protests from the woman, Ninan
began her story, hoping the idea of a pink flower would be sufficient inspiration.

here was a land filled with boulders, so huge, no one could see
over them. Here the wind blew fierce and the sun shone hot.
There was seldom enough rain to fill the streams. Life in this
country was harsh and difficult. Few creatures lived in such
an unforgiving climate. The winters were long and cold, the
summers short and sweltering. Spring came and went almost
without notice. The trees that managed to grow were stubby and stunted, as if
nature conspired to keep all living things small and weak and short, except for the
rocks that flourished, strewn about the landscape.

The woman stopped crying. She was listening intently, breathing through her pain. "Please go on. I want to hear about the pink flower." Ninan wondered how she would find a pink flower in such a bleak place. Where did the beginning come from? The woman was hurting; she did not need to hear about a harsh landscape. But, this was the picture that formed in her mind and she could not change it, though she tried. She wished, once again, she had her grandfather's book so she could read a story. She kept hoping that some day she would be able to tell the stories in his book. For now, she could only tell the story wanting to be told.

"Why have you stopped? The story is not finished. I want to hear about the pink flower," pleaded the young woman. Ninan had no choice; she continued . . .

There were three families living in a small flat area near a stream, which moved slowly when there was rain enough to fill it. They had come long ago, running away from soldiers who had threatened their village. The men chipped bits of colored stones out of the rocks that the women shaped and polished. When a cart was filled, the families took them to a town, three weeks' journey from where they lived. With the money they earned, they bought supplies for the many months of bad weather when they could not travel. Although their life was difficult, they felt safe here, and each was doing what their ancestors had done. The town, where life was easier, was too noisy, too dirty, too crowded, and too busy for them. And, if the soldiers came again, the families would still be safe.

Life might have continued without change had not one of the children noticed the tall patch of pink flowers standing next to the mill where they had stopped to water the horses and buy flour. "Look," she cried. "Look at those…" She did not know the name of the flower. Jumping down from the cart, she ran over to them. Taller than she was, the flowers had bright pink petals with a darker, rosy center on thick deep green stalks. The child smelled their fragrance, staring at their beauty, unable to stop touching and sniffing. "Could I plant some at home?" she asked although there was no one to hear her. There were no flowers where she lived but these blossoms seemed so strong. Perhaps if she were careful and lucky, they might grow.

She knew nothing about seeds or bulbs or even who to ask for information. She had no money nor did she think to ask for any. What little money there was her people used to buy supplies. While the horses were drinking water, she ran to the mill, hoping to learn more about the beautiful flowers.

Shyly, the girl entered and waited until the miller's wife was by herself. She slowly made her way to the busy woman who was covered with white dust, but the girl could not make herself speak. The miller's wife was a kind woman, with many children of her own. She had seen the child staring at her flowers and knew the power of their beauty. The girl twisted her hands, desperate to speak, knowing it would soon be time to leave. The miller's wife smiled, "I have seen you looking at my flowers. I think they are very beautiful. Do you?" The child nodded.

The woman screamed and writhed with a pain so large it seemed her body could not contain it. Her legs kicked the covers off the bed. She squeezed Ninan's hand so hard Ninan yelped. The woman cursed and cried. Ninan had never seen such agony. She hated feeling so helpless. Looking around the room, she noticed a small jug. She pulled off the stopper and smelled a sharp pungent smell. Anxious to do something, she poured some liquid into the woman's mouth. It seemed to help. Not knowing what else to do, she continued the story, as much for herself as for the woman.

The miller's wife said, "I have time before we grind more flour, let us visit the flowers." She held the child's hand and they walked to where the flowers grew tall and graceful in the late afternoon sun.

"Do you have flowers like these where you live?" The girl shook her head. "Would you like me to cut some of them, for you to take home?" The child's eyes opened wide; she could not believe her good fortune. She nodded, incredulous. The woman cut a few flowers and wrapped them in moist earth that she covered with a flour sack. Then she cut off one of the flower heads. Inside were hundreds of seeds.

She showed them to the child and said, "If you plant these seeds in the ground before the first frost, and you water them every day in the spring, the seedlings will be strong enough to survive by themselves."

The child thought about the long cold winter and the burning hot summer. The lack of water . . . She wondered how the flowers would ever be strong enough to grow and bloom. She sighed so deeply and looked so unhappy the miller's wife asked, "Do you think caring for the seeds will be too much

work for you?" The child shook her head. She wished she knew how to make her herself speak. Looking helplessly at the miller's wife, she wished the woman could read her thoughts.

The woman's pain worsened and her screams filled the cottage. Ninan wondered how much longer it would be before the husband returned with the midwife. Helplessly she asked, "I wish I could help. Is there anything I can do for you?"

The woman moaned, "I think the baby is coming."

Ninan tried not to sound as frightened as she felt. "What shall I do?"

"Boil the water in the pot in front of the fireplace. Put the sheets that are on the chest underneath me to protect the baby's head when it comes."

"Surely your husband will bring the midwife . . ."

"Babies come when they want. You will have to catch the baby." A loud cry from the woman shook Ninan. She felt dizzy and faint. The woman groaned a deep sound that seemed to come from the center of her being. Then, a long, loud scream filled the room. Ninan held her hands to her ears, ashamed of her panic. The woman yelled. "The baby is coming. Use the cloth to catch the head. Hurry!"

Ninan did as she was told, fighting back her terror. When the head appeared, she cradled it carefully; trying not to squeeze too hard as she eased the tiny baby girl out of the mother, into the world. Fascinated, she stood absolutely still, looking at the new life in her hands, ignoring the blood that splattered, amazed at the power of the infant's cry that filled the room. Birth was a miracle she had never thought she would see. Instinctively she wiped away the thick mucous covering the baby's eyes and ears. She looked around for something to wrap the baby in, fearing it would be cold.

In a weak voice the woman instructed, "Put the baby on my stomach and get the knife on the table. Put it in the boiling water and slowly count to ten before you remove it. Do not burn yourself or touch the blade," she said, caressing her daughter.

Ninan could barely remember one instruction before the woman gave another. "Let me do as you have asked before you tell me what I must do next." She was afraid to use the knife and prayed the husband would come. The woman urged her to hurry.

When Ninan came to the woman's bedside, gingerly holding the knife, the woman was stroking her daughter's face, wiping away the last bit of slime from the baby's face. "Cut the cord. And then take the afterbirth and bury it in the yard." Upset by the blood and the look of the placenta, Ninan forced herself to do as she was told. When she had washed and dried the baby and wrapped her in a soft blanket, she put the child on her mother's breast. Exhausted, Ninan watched the mother and child, filled with awe at the sight of the infant, now a person, eating and then sleeping on her mother's chest.

A few hours later, when the mother had eaten and was feeding her daughter, she said, "We could both do with a cup of tea." Ninan nodded, still in a daze, and walked to the fire where the water was boiling. Her hands shook and half the cup spilled before she reached the woman who drank greedily, asking for cup after cup until her thirst was quenched.

"I am sorry to be so clumsy," apologized Ninan, "but your daughter is my first child." Hearing her words, she corrected herself. "I mean she is the first child I have ever delivered."

The woman laughed. "She is our first child. We have done well. Sit beside me. I am tired but I would like to hear the end of the story."

Ninan almost asked, "What story?" Delivering the baby had been so exciting she had little memory of the story and was more tired than she could ever remember being, using her last burst of energy to make the tea. She was filled with gratitude that she had done no harm.

"Did the flowers grow?"

Ninan saw the picture of the miller's wife carefully wrapping the head of seeds.

The child took the seeds. The miller's wife did not understand why the girl was at first so pleased and then so unhappy. It was only when she remembered herself as a child, when she had been given seeds and despite her care, nothing grew, that she guessed this might be the problem. She said to the child, "Nature knows not every seed will flourish. Look at all the seeds in the head of this flower, more than we can count. Perhaps only one or two will survive, but this is enough to make more seeds for more flowers. And, if the worst should happen, that no

flowers grow, I will give you more seeds, from next year's flowers." Relieved, the child carried the seeds to the wagon where the others had already gathered, waiting for her to return.

'So, you have a package from the miller's wife?" teased her father. Her brother rushed up and tried to snatch the bundle, but the child howled in outrage. Turning, to protect the seeds, she tripped and the package broke. Seeds tumbled out. Her brother ate what he could find. The child shrieked in anger and despair, ready to kill her brother. Her father knelt down and began to pick up the seeds. "I think it best for you to return these seeds to the Miller's wife. It is too hot and dry in the summer. There is no sense to wasting good seed. I will go with you to explain why you are returning her gift."

The child ignored his words, picking up the seeds, putting them into a corner of her skirt. She held on to them tightly and refused to move from her place in the wagon where she sat, stone-faced. This time she found her voice. "No. I will not return the seeds. They were a gift from her to me."

After several attempts to convince her failed, the others in the wagon grew impatient. "Let her keep the seeds. She will find out soon enough that wanting is not everything," said her mother. "It is time to leave. I do not want to travel after dark. It is not safe."

"Very well," agreed the father, but he turned to his daughter and said, "Keep your seeds if you must, but do not cry when they refuse to grow." His daughter cradled the seeds and vowed to herself she would make them grow.

Closing her eyes, she saw the whole countryside filled with beautiful pink flowers growing in and around the rocks.

All winter the child kept the seeds warm and dry. Each day she looked at them, to make sure they were still there, ready to be planted. Winter seemed to last forever. When the ice disappeared she planted the seeds. At first, the melting snow provided moisture, but as the days grew warmer, she had to dig deeper to find water. Still, she refused to give up. The memory of the pink flowers gave her courage and energy.

Finding moisture for her plants took up all her spare time so she stopped playing with the other children. Some of the seeds never sprouted, others died soon after the first tender shoots appeared. The child grew fearful that her father's words would prove true. She worked harder to find water and built tiny haystacks around the seedlings to shield the young plants from the scorching sun.

When the last of the seedlings died, the child felt all life drain from her. She walked in a daze, eating when she was fed, sleeping when told to go to bed. Her dream of growing flowers was dead. Nothing mattered to her anymore.

Ninan looked at the new mother who seemed to be sleeping. She felt peculiar, as if the new life had taken something from her. She did not want the seedlings in the story to die yet the words had come out of her mouth. The seedlings were dead and that was the way it was. There were no miracles to save them. Memories of Mikos overwhelmed her. The young mother opened her eyes, wondering why Ninan had stopped talking and saw her crying. "Do not cry. Not all the seedlings died. You will see this is true if you finish the story."

Bewildered, Ninan looked at the new mother. "But the story is finished. All the seedlings died. Nothing could grow in that climate and certainly not pink flowers."

"No," said the woman, "this is not true. Listen to me, I will tell you what happened. You see the child did not plant all the seeds. Some of them were blown about by the wind. And, one day, when the child had given up all hope, she took a walk among the largest of the rocks. There, in that place, protected by the wind and the sun, grew a few pink flowers. Not as tall as those in front of the mill, but bright, lovely pink flowers, all the same. And the child touched them and smelled them. Happiness filled her as she sat watching them."

"How do you know what happened in my story?"

"You told me you would tell me the story of the pink flower which grew in the crack of a large rock. That is how I know the ending. It is a good story; I will tell it to my daughter just as you have told it to me."

"But I did not finish it this way, you did. It is your story, not mine."

"It is our story. You helped me give birth to my daughter and I helped you finish your story. A good exchange in my opinion."

Ninan could not help herself. "In my story, all the seedlings died. If I told you about flowers which grew, I was thinking I could make this happen in the story, but I could not. The seeds died. There was too much sun and not enough water for them to survive. I cannot tell my story your way." Just as I cannot make my way back to Mikos, she thought.

"You are too harsh. Miracles happen. Look how you appeared just when we needed help. What about this?"

Ninan did not know what to say. She only knew that in her story she could not make the seeds grow. The seedlings were dead. They died from lack of water and too much sun. She could see the dead seedlings in her mind. "I will not tell you a seed survived because the seeds died, yet the child had an indelible memory of the beautiful flowers. When the wind howled and dark days seemed unremitting, the thought of pink petals with dark rose centers reminded her that winter does not last forever."

"You are stubborn, but at least now there is some hope. Please stay with me until my husband returns. I am not ready to be alone with my baby daughter." Ninan was too tired to leave and readily agreed.

When the husband returned with the midwife, he found Ninan and his wife asleep. Only his baby daughter was wide-awake, waiting for him. When he knelt down to touch her tiny face, her fingers touched his cheek, then her eyes closed and she too fell asleep.

When Ninan awoke, hearing the child crying, she sat up, dazed and anxious, stiff from sleeping in the chair, shocked to see the father looking at her, wondering if the birth had been real or a dream. The sight of the mother feeding her baby brought everything into focus. She rubbed her head, trying to ease the ache behind her left eye.

"My wife told me how you helped her. We are grateful you were here. The midwife says you did well; there was no further need for her so she left to attend another birth."

The man watched the baby suck greedily. His wife looked at her husband with such love Ninan was stunned by a powerful pang of jealousy. As calmly as she could she said, "All is well. There is no need for me to stay." Although both urged her to remain with them, at least for a few days, Ninan knew it was time to leave.

"Before you go, please tell me your name," said the woman. "In all this time we have not called each other by name."

"I am Ninan. And you?"

"I am Elena and my husband is Seth." She smiled shyly, meeting her husband's eyes, coming to an agreement that Ninan saw but could not understand until the woman spoke. "And we have decided, we will name our daughter, Ninan. She will keep our memory of you alive. We thank you for your help. Without you my pain would have been many times worse."

Ninan shook her head, unable to imagine such a thing. "You do me too great an honor. I am not worthy," but no matter how she protested, the couple remained firm. Their daughter's name would be Ninan.

"Her name will remind us that miracles can happen, just as you passed by when we were desperate."

Ninan wished she could find a way to miraculously make Mikos appear, knowing this was not the only miracle she would need, even if they were to meet again.

Before leaving, she bent down and stroked the tendrils of hair on the baby's head, astonished at the soft, fine strands. Kissing her cheek, she whispered, "Goodbye, sweet Ninan. May your life be blessed with pink flowers growing in the cracks of large rocks."

FOURTEEN
TRAVELING IN SPIRALS

Memories besieged Ninan. Singing songs with Taya's two oldest children before splashing each other in the river. Laughing with Mikos as they set up camp for a night and then holding each other close. Loving looks exchanged by Elena and Seth. Was it was too late to retrace her path to find Mikos? She picked up a stone and threw it with all her strength, wishing there had been a stone to trip over before she left Mikos. Returning to Mima and her family might make her feel better but Ninan knew she if she returned now it would be because she missed Mikos and that felt like the wrong reason. She wondered how she would know the right time to return to the book of her grandfather and the shawl of her grandmother.

She thought about the last argument with Mikos and wondered if what he said was right. Was she being lazy when she spent time thinking and playing with ideas for stories? Was her need to empty herself before telling a new story just a way of avoiding people? Could she force herself to tell a story whenever people were around? Could she stand to be surrounded by people all the time? The more she wondered, the more questions she had. She wished her grandfather were alive so she could ask him if he too had felt the need for the solitude and quiet she often craved. She had never met a person who lived life as she did, not even one who considered living as she did. Was something wrong with her?

When night came, despite fatigue, she followed a worn path, not caring where it led. Her relentlessly accusing thoughts pushed her to keep walking. When the sun rose, as she watched the darkness give way to light, the cool of night to the warmth of day, she reminded herself that nothing ever stays the same. Not days nor seasons nor people. She found a grassy place just off the road and boiled water, hoping the light of day would ease the darkness in her heart. Each time she remembered the way Seth and Elena looked at each other, she felt a piercing pain in her heart. How long would it take her to stop missing Mikos? How could she miss him so much when being with him was so difficult? And, she was the one who had left!

For the next few weeks she resorted to her old ways, walking by night, sleeping by day. Although she pushed herself to cover distance quickly, Mikos kept intruding into her thoughts; she felt lonelier than she had since the death of her parents. Occasionally she considered looking for him, but did nothing to find him. Instead, she wandered, walking, sleeping, and eating with no particular place in mind until the day came when she was ready to find a village.

A story was building inside her. Perhaps all the days and weeks of walking had been a time of preparation, not simply aimless meandering. "I am not lazy, Mikos," she said out loud. "I have my own way of working and it is not wrong because it is different from yours."

Exhilarated by this thought, she began to run, and it came to her that perhaps she was running toward something, though she did not know what it might be. For the first time since she and Mikos quarreled and parted she began to feel better about leaving him, choosing to live the life she felt was right for her.

By early afternoon she came to a tiny village where there were few signs of people but she was content to wait and learn whether she would find a place of welcome before evening. Refilling her water bag, she sat by a large tree in the middle of a green common surrounded by small cottages. Before long, a group of children gathered around her, eager to meet the stranger who called herself a storyteller. Ninan told of places she had been and people she had met. Time passed pleasantly. Soon two of the children ran off, quickly returning to invite her to share supper with their family. Ninan happily accepted their invitation, feeling her old dark thoughts lighten. That evening she told stories far into the night until her voice grew tired. Sharing a bed with two small girls, feeling their warmth and adoration, lessened the doubts of the past. She fell asleep nestled between the two tiny bodies.

The next morning, as Ninan was preparing to leave, one of the children asked, "Will you return to our village? Will we hear your stories again?"

"Probably." Ninan smiled, impressed by their easy affection.

"When?" asked the oldest of the sisters.

"I cannot tell you exactly when since I do not travel in a straight line. Mostly I move in spirals but what begins can find its way back to where it started. She hugged them and asked, formally, "Would you do me the very great honor of accompanying me to the edge of your village where I must sadly take my leave of you?" Delighted by her tone, the children danced and sang as they made their way to the place of parting.

Ninan kept the image of the dancing children waving goodbye to her in her mind for many hours, smiling at the thought of how much bigger they would be when she next saw them. She noticed this thought did not cause her pain. Seeing herself as a traveler who moved in spirals, sometimes returning, sometimes not, made her feel better. She would see old friends again, she just could not say when.

Since leaving Taya and Kurro, Ninan had been unable to work on the basket Taya had given her. Now, finding a pleasant place in which to sit, she took out the unfinished basket and thought, this too is a kind of spiral. What Taya started, I will finish—her basket, my story. We will see each other again. She wove slowly, with awkward fingers, yet this did not displease her. She had no need to finish quickly; a little each day was good enough. In time, her fingers would become more knowing. When her hands grew tired, she put the basket down, ran to a nearby hill, and rolled down the grassy slope. Reaching the bottom, she lay still for a few minutes. She remembered how she and Mikos had rolled down a hill but the memory hurt less than it had a few days before. Climbing up to the top, she spread her arms in the air to catch the warm rays of the sun.

Although she passed through a few villages as she walked, she did not linger. With no story clearly in mind, she called out friendly greetings that did not invite conversation. After observing herself for a few days, she realized she wanted to tell stories. Pleased at the thought, she hummed a song she remembered Mima singing to her and Amina, sensing she would know when it was time to return to them. She smiled, thinking of the pleasure she would have reading the stories of her grandfather once more, feeling the shawl of her grandmother against her body.

When she grew tired of walking, she rested and wove some reeds on Taya's

basket. She noticed her fingers were less clumsy. Working on it brought back
cherished memories of the times they had spent together. She wondered what
Taya was doing at this moment, wishing she could ask, "What were you doing the
afternoon I began to work on your basket?" Her determination to make the basket
perfect meant more ripping than weaving at first, yet while working on it she felt
connected to Taya, remembering with awe how she had defied her father's wishes,
defeating his plans for her, despite his wealth and power. Their stories were different
yet there was something in Taya's struggle that eluded Ninan. She spoke her
thoughts out loud, trying to understand "Her father decided he knew what was best
for her but she disagreed and fought to live life in her own way. My parents told me
how I must live my life and I agreed, yet I still struggle. Taya had a man she loved,
but if she had not, would she have done what her father wanted her to do? If I had
a man I loved, would I have done what my parents wanted me to do?"

    She thought of the traveling she had done since her parents' death, the
people she had met. It did not seem that many people even thought about finding
their own way, particularly at the expense of someone else's needs or wishes. Ninan
felt close to Taya because they had both struggled to choose their own way, despite
the obstacles each had had to overcome. She chose to honor her parents' choice for
her because of her love for them. Taya chose to defy her father because of her love
for Kurro. The idea that love could give you courage to do something you didn't
think you could do was a new thought.

    When it grew too dark to weave, she made a fire and sat in front of it,
allowing herself to think about Mikos, the love they had shared, the love she still
felt for him. Would she ever see him again? A voice inside her reminded her that she
could look for him as he had looked for her; she knew the village where he lived.
She answered the voice, "Yes, but for what purpose, except more misery. We are too
different to live together. I cannot be the woman he needs me to be, no matter what
he says." Thinking about him rekindled her unhappiness and made her wish their
parting had not been so unexpected and bitter. She fell asleep looking at the stars.

    When the first rays of the sun woke her up, Ninan began working on the
basket. Although her fingers were sore from the day before, she did not want to
leave until it was finished. Her mind was crowded with questions about how the
next story would begin, where she would tell it, and who would hear it. Though she
had no answers, she wove and felt content. For most of the day, Ninan ripped and

rewove all the messy places until she felt pleasure with her work. Lovingly, she put her blue shawl into it and walked slowly, not with the high energy of previous days, but with quiet wonder and a budding sense of anticipation as she followed a well-traveled road knowing it would lead to a village.

Two days of walking passed before she saw the first sign of people. A lone cottage and grazing animals indicated she was at the outskirts of a community. As she walked, she noticed more cottages, closer to each other, with fences to keep animals contained. She found a well and stopped to refill her water bag. When she entered a village, she always refilled her supply of water because it gave her a sense of being part of village life and provided her with a graceful opportunity to meet new people. As a stranger, she was usually noticed by children, who often waited only a few minutes before the boldest gathered the courage to blurt out, "Who are you?" The others would then gather round, confirming the importance of the question.

This time, the first child was a boy about ten, accompanied by a little girl who turned out to be his sister. "Who are you?" he asked. A second boy added, "Why are you here?" They stood between her and the village, as if guarding its entrance.

"I am a storyteller," said Ninan, amused by the intensity of their questions.

"What is your name?" asked the girl.

"Ninan. What is yours?"

"Yara. My brother's name is Yorum, and his name," she said, pointing to the second boy, "is Ethan. Who do you tell stories to?"

"Anyone who wants to hear them. A storyteller cannot be a storyteller unless people want to listen to the stories she tells."

Yorum asked, "How many people do you need to listen to you before you tell a story?"

"No particular number. What matters is that people want to hear my story and are willing to stay until it is finished."

Yara asked shyly, "In this village, when people want things they trade what they have for what they need. But you are a stranger, do you trade or do you ask for money?"

Ninan smiled at the girl's cleverness, pleased that her daring impressed the boys. "I charge what I need. Sometimes I ask for food, at times a place to sleep, occasionally I ask for money. Once in a while I tell a story just to make myself feel better. There are many ways to repay a storyteller, just as there are many reasons to tell stories."

The three children talked among themselves. Yorum spoke for the three. "We want to hear a story. What will you charge us?"

"That depends. What do you have to offer in exchange for a story?" The children looked questioningly at each other. None of them had money. Ninan waited patiently, impressed by the seriousness of their negotiations.

Yara made her decision first. "I will give you the pretty white stone I found last week." She unrolled the hem of her sleeve, revealing a tiny, perfectly round white stone that she held in her outstretched hand, her offering for the storyteller. Ninan's heart ached when she saw it. A stone. Another stone. Was this an omen?

The child noticed her hesitation and worried, "Is my stone not good enough?"

Ninan shook her head. "It is beautiful. I accept it in full payment."

Yorum, encouraged by the stone's reception, offered what he had to give. "I will show you baby kittens that were born this morning. Nobody has seen them but me."

"That would be lovely," said Ninan, her eyes sparkling.

Ethan, wrapped in desperate silence, could think of nothing to give. Although the other two made suggestions, he shook his head. "If I am to give a gift, it must be my idea." His ragged clothes and pinched face gave testimony to his family's poverty. Ninan was about to suggest that two gifts were good enough when he sighed. "I could show you my favorite place. It is on the top of a mountain. From there you can see forever. I always go there . . . I mean I go there whenever I can." Mistaking her silence for disapproval he added, "It is a special place. No one knows about it but me. I could take you there before you tell us the story so you will know how wonderful it is . . . Is this good enough to be a gift?"

His offer made Ninan's heart lurch. "I would be pleased to see your special place on the mountain. I am sure the view will be payment enough for the story."

"I must leave soon, to do my chores. Perhaps I could take you up the mountain now and you could tell your story later. Perhaps you would not mind if my family heard the story?" He frowned. "Would they need to pay you for the story?"

"No," said Ninan, "what you are offering is payment enough for everyone."

"Could we come with you?" asked Yara. "I would like to see your special place, too. I could try to find a pretty stone for you."

"Let us all go," said Yorum. "Then we can take her to see the kittens. I am sure my mother and father will invite her to share our evening meal. They will also want to hear the story."

Ethan looked worried. Ninan asked, "Do you like this plan?"

"How will my family hear the story?" he asked.

Yara and Yorum found this no problem. "We will invite everyone to come to the commons to listen to Ninan's story. It is only fair."

"I agree," said Ninan. "Your gifts are payment enough. I will tell my story to anyone who wants to hear it. There is no need to worry."

Ethan smiled for the first time. With him in the lead, Ninan following, and the brother and sister right behind, they made their way up a narrow trail, mostly overgrown. It was obviously not a path many people had walked on. The steep ascent made walking difficult. Ninan wondered how Ethan knew his way when there was no visible sign of a path, pushing back brambles and bending branches with alacrity. Although Ninan, Yara, and Yorum were sweating as they struggled to climb over ruts, fallen trees, and large rocks. Ethan moved lightly, almost dancing up the path.

As they moved toward the top, the trees grew smaller yet the undergrowth remained thick and dense. Suddenly, Ethan turned, pulled Ninan's arm, and said, "Look!" Ninan gasped. There, appearing as if out of nowhere, was a spectacular view of mountain after mountain, a vast space with no end in sight. Ninan and the two children stared in silence at the power and grandeur that greeted them. Ethan was pleased but quickly warned them, "Do not take another step. We have come to the end of the path. I do not want you to fall off the cliff." Ninan peered through the bushes. Right in front of him, not more than five steps away, the earth stopped. They were at the edge of the world.

They huddled together, transfixed. It was only when Ninan felt chilly that she realized how long they had been staring. "The sun is going down. I think it best we leave while we have light to see where we are going." Ethan took the lead and the three followed him, marveling at his certainty. Wondering how he knew where to go when there was no clear way to be seen.

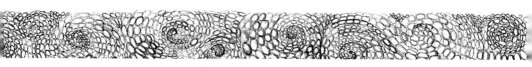

Just before parting, Ethan said, "I must leave now. May I see the kittens tomorrow?" Yara and Yorum nodded, still awed by the view. "You will promise to keep my special place a secret?" They readily agreed, not sure they could find it again even if they wanted to. Satisfied, Ethan left while the three stared at where they had just been. They could see no path nor were there signs anyone had walked there.

Yorum led Yara and Ninan to the kittens, much to mama cat's displeasure. Filled with delight, Ninan watched the tiny, squirming, bodies and spoke to the mother cat in a grave tone of voice. "Thank you for allowing me to see your babies, Mama Cat. I know they are in good hands with you." She watched the babies struggle to suck and marveled at how the mother cat kept them in line, making sure each had enough time to drink from her teats.

Yara nodded. "Mama says life is a miracle."

She and her brother exchanged knowing looks, and then Yorum told Ninan, "Papa is always telling us, 'All life is sacred.' He will not kill anything unless he needs it for food or clothing or tools. Before he kills he always asks permission and then asks the animal to forgive him. I have no idea why he thinks the animal gives its approval. I would not like to die to be food or clothing."

"Thank you for showing me the kittens." Ninan remembered the awe she felt helping to bring Elena's baby into the world. What would it be like, having a child?

Yara pulled Ninan's arm. "Come, I want to tell our family about the storytelling."

After dinner, Ninan sat watching the fire at the center of the commons and felt the smooth, round, white, stone in her pocket. She told Yara, "I must think about my story. When I see the coals of the fire, I will know it is time to come." She had a powerful urge to welcome the story inside herself. For the first time this was not upsetting. She felt excited.

FIFTEEN
A WAY OF TELLING

Many families sat near the roaring fire as word spread about the presence of a storyteller in the village. From a distance, Ninan gazed at the flames, sparks from the fire dancing to kiss the sparkle of the stars. Only when the flames were barely visible did she walk to meet those gathered. She noticed she was not worrying about her story even though she could barely see a clear beginning. She felt powerful and fine, ready to speak.

"Would you like to hear the story now?" People nodded their heads and made themselves comfortable. With the sound of the stream behind her and tiny flames growing out of white-hot coals to provide heat and light, Ninan spoke.

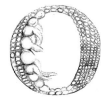

Once upon a time, in a place like your village, in a time long ago, two brothers and two sisters lived with their parents in a small cottage half way up a high mountain. In winter, when heavy snows covered the countryside, the children guided travelers through the woods, up to the top of the mountain and down the other side, to a small village nestled at the bottom. The four knew the mountain so well they could almost lead people with their eyes closed. Although their parents often worried about them, the four never lost their way, nor did they fail to help travelers arrive safely at their destinations. When the children went their separate ways, they developed sounds that resembled bird and animal calls, each with a special meaning. Some warned of dangers such as falling rocks or ice, others told where they were, and some were just for the fun of calling to each other. The four spent so much time in the mountains that one night, as they sat around the fire, their father felt compelled to warn them, "If you are not careful you will turn into Wood-widgers."

"Wood-widgers?" asked the children. "What are they?"

"They are creatures who live in the mountains"

"How did they get there?" asked Noli, the eldest. "I have never heard of them."

"No, I am sure you have not. Those who know about Wood-widgers never speak a word of what they know."

"How did you learn of Wood-widgers?" asked Sele, the youngest.

"One of them once saved my life," replied their father.

"When? How?" asked the twins, Andreas and Andrea, at the same time. "Tell us what happened. Why have you never told us of these creatures before?"

Their father said solemnly, "It is necessary to wait until the proper time to talk of secrets. You are now of an age where you can listen to my story and take its meaning for your own."

"Are you trying to scare us?" asked Sele.

"Perhaps, and perhaps not. Listen and decide for yourselves." Their father prepared his pipe, inhaling a few times until the bowl glowed brightly. The children nestled against each other, intent on their father's words.

"It happened a long time ago, when I was a boy, no older than you are," he said, pointing at his oldest son. "I was cutting wood for my father to sell and I worked so hard and so long that before I noticed, darkness had fallen. I was surrounded by darkness. I did not know where to walk to find my home and I did not want to leave my wood for someone else to take and sell. It was freezing cold and I had on a light jacket because I thought I would be home before the day turned to cold night."

Their father paused, lost in thought, remembering how it was. His children urged him to continue, wanting to know what happened, but he remained silent, puffing on his pipe, almost unaware of their presence. Finally he said, "I was foolish to bring this matter up. I can hardly remember what happened. Anyway, I returned home safely and it is time for you all to go to bed."

No matter how they pleaded, their father remained silent, refusing to say more about the episode. A curious pall hung over the room as if a warning spirit had entered. The children left the room, quietly, confused by the sudden change

of atmosphere.

Discomforted by their father's sudden loss of memory, they said nothing among themselves until they were in bed, whispering so no one could hear their voices. Each wanted to know the same thing. "Do you really think he forgot? Why does he start a story and then stop so suddenly? What are Wood-widgers? How is it we spend so much time in the woods and have never heard of them?"

That night, each of the children dreamed the same dream, about a group of loggers who wanted to find a growth of trees that had never been cut. Each logger was sure that cutting this wood would make his fortune and none of them wanted to share the money with their fellow loggers so each went out separately, giving his mates an excuse about why he had to work alone for the next few days. Although no man knew where the primeval trees stood, each knew the story that had been told for generations which ended with the warning, 'No one who goes in ever comes out alive.' Yet each of the loggers felt sure he would be the one to find the huge trees and live to enjoy the fortune to be earned by selling the logs. And so it was that each man went in to the forest and no man returned. When their bodies were discovered, in a swampy patch, far from any forest, each man was holding a tiny blue feather between the thumb and forefinger of his lifeless right hand.

When the children woke up, each felt odd, and instead of teasing and laughing, as was their wont, they were thoughtful and quiet. The unusual silence only increased each child's discomfort, especially when, Noli, a girl of fourteen, finally blurted out, "I had a very strange dream last night. I cannot stop thinking about it." The others admitted that they too had dreamed strangely. Their fears greatly increased when the youngest, Sele, only ten years old, told his dream and they learned each of them had dreamed the same dream.

Sele asked the twins, "What do you think this means? Have you ever had the same dream before?"

The twelve-year-old twins admitted that close as they were, they had never before dreamed the exact same dream. The four children looked at each other and asked, "What shall we do? Should we tell anyone? What do you think this means?"

"I know one thing," said Noli, "we better keep this to ourselves. If Father would not tell us how the Wood-widger saved his life, who knows what he will do

if we tell him about our dream." They agreed to say nothing to anyone about the strange coincidence. Although both their father and mother noticed the unusual quiet, neither asked any questions, which in itself was strange. The children were afraid to imagine what might be happening.

The first snows of winter had long since covered the ground when the blizzard hit. For days everyone was snowbound as the swirling snows blanketed the earth, hiding bushes and covering rocks. No matter how people struggled to shovel paths to their animals, by morning, there were none. When the snow finally stopped, people were unable to leave their homes. Snow pressed tightly against doors. Paths and roads could not be seen. Travel was impossible.

The four children sensed they were needed on the mountain road so they bundled themselves up and dug their way out through a high window, tying themselves together with Andreas's rope so they would not lose each other. The work was exhausting and when they were too tired to continue, they lay back onto the snow waiting for their parents to come help. It took the whole family working together, to shovel a passage to the place where they usually went up and down the mountain but they were too tired to make more than a narrow path for a short part of the way. Further clearing would have to wait until morning.

"Do you not think it more than a little curious, that right after we first hear about the Wood-widgers we have the same dream, and then we have the worst storm we have ever seen?" asked Andrea. The four were resting while just ahead their parents stomped snow to widen the path.

Sele shivered, but not from the cold. Whispering, he said to his sisters and brother, "I have to tell you something but promise you will not laugh at me." The others were in no mood to laugh. They felt too strange and uneasy.

"What is it?" asked Noli. As she moved closer to Sele she noticed heavy snowfall and looked up to see a giant snowball careening down toward the place where Sele was standing. Noli rushed to Sele, pushing him out of the way, just in time to protect him from the avalanche of snow falling from a tree above them. She wondered why there was such a large ball of snow just in the branches above them and why it chose to fall at that moment.

Sele was so busy watching Noli he never saw the snowball but when he looked at the mass of snow he had narrowly escaped, his anxiety increased. More than ever he needed to find a private place to speak with Noli. He looked around

to make sure what he had to say would be private. "I keep hearing a sound. It is very faint, and when I think I am imagining it, the sound increases. It is almost like a cry for help but I hear no words. I do not know who is making the sound and I cannot tell if it is a bird or an animal or . . ." He stopped, not knowing what more to say about the sound that was making him feel so anxious.

Andreas asked, "Where do you think the sound is coming from?" The others huddled close to hear him whisper his answer.

Sele looked toward the top of the mountain. "From there," he pointed. "I think it is coming from the high place just beyond the trees." He looked at the other three. "Do you hear it?" They strained to hear what he heard.

Noli put her arms around him. "No, but I feel as if something is pulling me. I keep thinking I am imagining this, just as you said, but when I look, I am facing the top of the mountain, not the path to our cottage."

Andreas spoke quietly. "We have something to say as well. Andrea and I keep thinking we see a tiny blue object. It looks as if it is beckoning us to come toward it but it is so tiny, it is impossible to say what it is. Perhaps it is a very small blue bird that . . ."

Andrea interrupted, "I do not think it is a bird but what else could it be? There are no blue flowers in the woods in winter and no flower I have ever seen moves from place to place."

Sele asked, "Do you think it is a Wood-widger? And what about the blue feathers in the right hands of the dead men in our dream?" The children stared at each other in fear and wonder. Each felt something was wrong. The four peered at the top of the mountain, hoping to find a simple explanation for the peculiar occurrences taking place all around them.

Noli stood up and walked away from the other three and closed her eyes, moving her arms gently up and down, imitating the flapping of a bird's wing. She flapped four times then rested her arms, silently, slowly opening her eyes. She opened her mouth, as if to scream, yet the children heard no sound. The three watched with fascination and awe and dread as her mouth opened and closed.

Although they felt like moving toward her, something kept them rooted in their place. How long she would have stood there will never be known because at that moment, the children's parents came up to them. As if a spell had been broken, Noli greeted her mother and father with no sign of what had just happened.

"It is time to return home, children. We do not want to leave you alone in the forest with all this snow," said their mother.

"It is much too dangerous to remain here by yourselves, even for you who know the woods so well," advised their father.

The children, recovering from their fright, protested. As the oldest, Noli spoke for the others, "Look, the sun is beginning to shine through the clouds and the birds are singing. We have been inside for so many days. Let us stay. I promise you we shall be careful. We will surely be home before dark."

The parents looked at each other, uneasy yet unable to insist. What Noli said sounded reasonable. Taking advantage of their silence, Noli hugged her mother and said, pretending to be cheerful, "Do not worry. We four know how to take care of each other. We will return home safely." She poked Sele and laughed, "Race you to that far tree."

Andreas followed her example. The four children took off, clumsily making their way in the deep snow, laughing, happy to be free of the watchful eyes of their parents and, for the moment, of the strange events which none of them understood.

When they could no longer see their parents, Noli stopped moving. Standing quietly she listened, looking up at the top of the mountain.

"What do you hear?" asked Andreas.

"A kind of stirring," she answered. "I think we must go to the top of the mountain if we want to find what is waiting for us."

Andrea said, "It will take us much longer than usual to climb to the top of the mountain with all the paths blocked by snow. If we try to make it to the top now, we will never be back before dark. We will be late for supper."

"You are right," agreed Noli, "but I think someone or something keeps trying to get our attention. I say we must help."

Sele asked, "How do you know? What makes you so sure?"

Noli stared at the top of the mountain. "I do not know how I know but I am sure I am right. And I need all of you to come with me. We must go together."

Andrea gasped, "Do you think we would let you go by yourself?"

Andreas grew impatient. "Enough talk. If we are to go to the top of the mountain, we have no time to waste. The sun sets early these days. If we do not

return before dark, we will never find our way home."

The four started to walk, Noli in the lead, looking for windblown paths where the snow was not so deep. It was exhausting and Sele began to lag behind. When Sele fell, Noli called out to him. "Are you hurt?"

"No, but I am so tired I can hardly move. Go on without me. I will wait for you here." He sank down into the snow and closed his eyes.

Noli thought this strange and unlike Sele who usually scampered in front, bounding about as if he were a creature of the forest. She said to the others, "Rest here. I will go to help Sele." She walked back to her brother who was almost in tears, struggling to move, acting as if an invisible force was holding him down.

"Something is wrong, Noli. I can barely move. It feels as if there is a spell on me but this is silly. Tell me I am being foolish."

Noli looked around, trying to comfort Sele, holding him so he could not see her anxious searching. "I think you are just a little tired. After a short rest you will be waiting for us to catch up to you." Her eyes sought out evidence of unusual occurrence yet she noticed nothing extraordinary. Not satisfied, she said to him, "Rest here, I will be right back." She walked backwards in Sele's footsteps, looking intensely for an unknown sign. It was almost under her foot, protected by a stray leaf in the snow, when she saw the tiny tip of a blue feather. Carefully, she picked it up, almost dropping it when a current of energy surged through her body. "Oh!" she yelped, trying to catch her breath.

The blue feather lay lightly in her hand yet it took all her strength to hold it. Beads of perspiration covered her forehead and she felt dizzy, fighting to keep her balance. Something told her she must not fall so she willed herself to remain upright, fighting an unseen force with fierce and steadfast determination.

Sele struggled to his feet and forced himself to walk to Noli. "What is it?" he asked. He had never seen his sister look so pale. She did not have the strength to answer. "Andreas, Andrea, come quickly." Horrified, they stared at the blue feather, unable to look away.

With her brothers and sister close to her, Noli recovered some energy. "Whatever needs our help is here, but it is not alone. There is something else. Huge. Dangerous. It wants us to leave immediately. I think we will be safe as long as we do not lie down, no matter how sleepy or tired we are. We must remain standing, no matter what. We must also stay together, within touching distance.

Whatever it is cannot hurt us as easily if we are four rather than one." They huddled together, trying to decide what to do.

Andreas looked around and saw no evidence of anything sinister. "What do you think it is?"

Before Noli could answer, seemingly from nowhere, a huge matted beast came toward them, unlike any creature they had ever seen before, frothing at the mouth. A foul smell emanated from its stained mouth filled with jagged black and red teeth, blood and pus dripping from its nose and mouth. Noli screamed. "Do not be afraid. Hold onto me. It will not hurt us if we do not run. It wants the feather and we will not give it up."

The beast roared and charged but the children held their ground, standing together, hugging each other in fear and love. It belched out a stream of scalding bloody saliva at them but Noli yelled, "Stay still. The beast cannot hurt us if we keep together." Suddenly, for no apparent reason, the creature ran away.

"Why does it want the feather?" asked Sele, still holding tightly to his brother and sisters. Noli, Andreas, and Andrea shook their heads, mystified. No one questioned that the beast wanted the blue feather and wanted it badly.

Andrea, her voice quivering with excitement, blurted out, "It reminds me of an old story mother used to tell us, about a prince who was captured by fairies. His lady had to hold him tight while he was changed into all manner of fearful creatures. As long as she held him the changes could not hurt her, nor could he be transformed into a fairy for all time. Remember, at the end, he turned into a naked man and his lady covered him with her cloak and even though the fairies cursed and yelled they disappeared into the night without him because they knew they could not keep him with them any more?"

"I remember," admitted Sele, "but what does that story have to do with us? Everyone knows there are no such things as fairies these days. Maybe there never were fairies. Probably, people made them up to scare children."

"Hush!" admonished Noli. "There is a strange wind beginning to blow. Hold tight to me. No matter what happens, do not let go."

The wind grew stronger, coming in bursts and gusts, toppling trees that crashed all around them but the children held on to each other and the wind could not separate them. The blue feather remained safely protected in Noli's hand. And then, the wind disappeared leaving in its wake an eerie calm.

"I do not trust this silence," warned Noli. "Do not let . . ." Before she could finish what she was about to say, the air was filled with dreadful deafening screams and cries. Noli hugged the three, mouthing words for her sisters and brothers to read, knowing they could not be heard. "Do not let go of me to hold your ears. Sing! The sounds will pass." She sang a song they had learned as small children. The louder the sounds, the harder they sang and when the sounds gave way to a terrible smell which made them gag, and cough, and retch, Noli sputtered out the words, "Throw up if you must but do not let go! We are safe only if we hold on to each other." The four huddled so close they could not tell where one left off and the next began.

Andrea spoke in a strangled voice. "I am sure what is happening is like the story. Whatever is making these sounds and smells wants us to let go. It wants to destroy us. The tighter we hold on to each other, the sooner the scourges will stop. It wants the blue feather and we will not give it to whatever is causing these things to happen. If we do, I am sure that something terrible will happen."

Each of them wondered what would come after the odors that grew so unbearable they were not sure how much longer they could endure them.

Andreas suggested, "Think of the smells of spring flowers or the roses that grow next to our front door. Pay no attention to the smell." This made them all laugh though none thought it was funny.

Sele was about to say that this was easier to say than to do, but much to his amazement, imagining he smelled his favorite flowers eased the worst of the foul scent. He was about to tell the others when Noli whispered, "Look! The feather is fluttering." They watched, astonished, as the feather began to wriggle and twist in Noli's hand. Cupping their hands together to give it more room to move safely, the feather transformed into a tiny bird, hopping from hand to hand. As it grew stronger, it chirped tiny trills, testing its wings, ready to fly. Noli relaxed her hands to make spaces between her fingers and the others followed her motion.

The bird flew from hand to hand, soon growing strong enough to fly out of their hands on to a low branch of a fallen tree. The children followed the bird and when they reached it, the bird flew to another branch, and another branch, always towards the top of the mountain.

Noli warned, "Follow the bird but remember, do not let go. We must hold

on to each other if we want to be safe." They scrambled to follow the bird with awkward maneuvering in the deep snow. Despite huge drifts and fallen trees, they made progress. When they could not see the bird, they followed its urgent chirps.

Their way grew steeper but the pressure of the bird's cries goaded them to keep moving. Remembering the power of the strange forces kept them close together, finding comfort in each other's presence. Suddenly, the bird swooped up to the top of a large fir tree and chirped loudly, flew to another tree and cried shrilly, flying to a third and a fourth tree. The children watched, unsure what to do. The bird flew down to them and began flying in small circles that gradually grew larger until it rested on a misshapen, gnarled, old tree. When the children reached the tree the bird flew to the top of the mountain and soon was out of sight. The children felt abandoned.

Sele finally spoke. "Andrea, if you are right about the story, I think the bird has woven us some kind of protection so we can go to the top of the mountain safely. Perhaps the bird means for us to hurry. The trees and drifts grow smaller as we climb. We can make our way more easily."

Andrea took up his suggestion. "If this is so, we must be even more careful to remain connected. Whatever tried to stop us before will now try harder to keep us from finding whatever it does not want us to find."

Andreas said, "I still have the rope. Let us tie ourselves to each other. This way, if we have to let go of our hands, we will still be touching." They worked quickly, each feeling a growing sense of urgency to hurry to the top of the mountain. As they twined the rope around them, the temperature fell precipitously and the air grew frigid. They looked at each other, knowing whatever it was, was hard at work, desperately trying to destroy them.

Noli said, "Think of the sun roasting us on a summer day. Remember how good it feels to loll about in a hot bath. How nice it is to drink steaming lemonade after we have been skating." While they made their way to the top of the mountain, shivering, they reminded each other of time spent near the heat of a large fire, sipping scalding soup. Their memories and words lessened their shivering.

They were beginning to move more quickly when Andrea noticed it was getting warmer, despite the snow. By now they understood what to do and ignored the sweltering heat by talking about being cold, freezing in bath water

that had stood too long, shivering as bits of snow unexpectedly melted down their necks, and swimming in an icy river.

The warmth gave way to delicious smells of food, which appeared to be emanating from a place just behind them. The children grew hungry at the scent of cookies and cakes freshly baked, still warm from the oven but Noli reminded them, "This too is a trick. We must keep going, we must stay tied together." The rope connected them and gave them a sense of security as they continued to climb. Using hands to find places for their feet, boosting each other over craggy crevices, and pulling and pushing each other, they finally reached the top of the mountain.

They stood, staring into empty space. All was silent. The new snow sparkled in the brilliant sunlight. The four found it difficult to keep their eyes open. Suspecting this too was a trick they huddled together, shading their eyes. Although they heard and saw nothing, they felt as if a fearful battle was waging all around them. Noli said, "Think about the bird. Concentrate on the way the blue feather transformed in our hands."

Andrea whispered, "I think we must stand even closer."

Sele suggested, "Maybe we should sing our song" As Andreas tightened the rope, they sang for a time that seemed long yet passed quickly. They serenaded each other, gently, urgently, and lovingly, until they were so tired they sang off key, the song changing, ebbing and flowing as if it had a life of its own. Then, without prior agreement, all four stopped singing at the same time. Andreas loosened the rope, and the children noticed they could look without strain. Still, they saw and heard nothing. Tired as they were, they dared not sit. They waited, hardly able to breathe.

It was Sele who saw the woman walking toward them, holding a small child in her arms. He pointed to the two, helping the others to see. The four watched in silence, wondering what to do. The woman walked as if she had been many nights without sleep. The child was dressed in blue woolen garments, exactly the color of the small blue feather. When the woman reached them she stopped. "I thank you for your courage and your faith. You saved my child."

"How did we do this?" asked Sele.

The woman answered slowly, too tired to say much. "There are creatures that live in the forest called Wood-widgers but no one ever sees them for they use

many disguises. Often, they take the shape of a blue feather. They help those who
need help and punish those who transgress or destroy. But sometimes, the forces
of evil are so great, even the Wood-widgers must have help. Only people who are
willing to see and hear what is not easily seen or heard are able to be of service,
yet even then, not everyone will endure the trials or accept the necessary risks.
Had you not followed the feather, my child would have been lost to me forever.
He would have died as my punishment for standing up to the forces of evil. I
revealed their presence. I defied their will."

She caressed the child, gathering the energy she needed. "Now I must
warn you! Never speak of what has happened. Never mention Wood-widgers.
If you do, you will bring harm to those you love most dearly. Never forget my
words!"

The children nodded, silently promising the woman and each other,
remembering how their father had abruptly stopped talking. "I know you are
tired, as I am, but we must find our way down the mountain immediately. It is
not safe to remain here. If we are not down before dark, we will never find our
way home. The sun will soon be setting so we must hurry. I will assist you and
we will have help if you do exactly what I tell you to do. Tighten your rope and
put the end of it around my child and me. Follow my footsteps and do not look
down. If you heed my words, all will be well. You may hear sounds or see visions
but pay no attention. Look only at the person in front of you. Do not turn away
for any reason. I repeat——do not turn in any direction, for any reason."

Andreas tied the rope as the woman instructed and they started down,
following the path they had made as they climbed up the mountain. The way was
steeper than they remembered. Flashes of bright colors, sweet smells, and peculiar
sounds assailed them yet they kept their word and looked only at the back of
the head of the person in front of them. The closer they got to the bottom, the
more tempting the sounds and scents and sights became, but the children did not
respond.

When at last they reached the bottom, close to the short path to their
cottage, the woman spoke. "Untie the rope and run home as quickly as you can.
Run faster than you imagine possible. Do not stop for any reason. If you are
inside before the sun sets, all will be well."

She took out a small knife, cut part of the rope, and firmly tied her child

to her body.

The children's questions poured out. "What about you? Where will you go? Do you have . . .?"

The woman put her finger to her lips and smiled. "If you are inside before dark, I will be safe and you will know this."

"How?" they asked.

"You will know, I promise you. Now hurry, do not squander the little time that is left."

The children ran as she instructed and arrived inside their front door just as the last rays of sun disappeared behind the top of the mountain. The four stood waiting, feeling a terrible inner tightness, each of them gasping for breath. Then, Andrea started to laugh and the others followed, laughing so hard tears ran down their cheeks.

Their mother came into the room, relieved to see them safely home. "Did you have such a good time?" Their continued laughter puzzled her. "Tell me, what is so funny?"

When the last of their laughter finally subsided, Noli made up a story. "Well . . .Sele jumped into a snowdrift and rolled in the snow until he looked like a snowman that had drunk too much ale. You should have seen him, Mother, trying to stand up, falling down . . . He looked so funny we cannot stop laughing just thinking about it." Their mother looked at the four children, not believing what she heard as each added on to the story.

"Yes, mother, we had a fine afternoon," said Sele, giving his mother a hug, hoping she would not ask more questions. Flopping about in the snow made me hungry. Is supper ready? I could eat a mountain of food."

The next morning, each child awoke holding a tiny blue feather.

Ninan sat quietly, still seeing the image of blue feathers resting in each child's hand, her reverie shattered by questions. A man asked, "How did the woman get on the top of the mountain?" Before she could answer, several more people spoke at the same time.

"What does a Wood-widger look like?"

"What happened when the children woke up and found the blue feathers?"

Others looked as if they too had questions.

Ninan put her hands up in front of her face to shield herself from their queries. "What I have told you is all I know to tell."

The townspeople nodded, thanked her, and left slowly, still absorbed by the story. The children stayed by the fire.

Yorum offered his own challenge. "You are the storyteller, you must know the answers to our questions."

Ninan sighed. "There are parts of a story that are known by the storyteller, but in every story there is mystery. Listeners imagine what happened or how people look, and this is why the same story is different for each person who hears it. Then new stories arise to answer questions about the old story. To me, this is a kind of magic."

Ethan asked, "But I still want to know why was the woman being punished?"

Ninan laughed. "You tell me."

The children sat for a time, and then Ethan spoke, his eyes still closed. "The woman was standing with her child in the market and saw a man steal money from another man. When she called him a thief, he called her a liar. He was really an evil magician disguised as a peasant and was angry that the woman saw him. He created a blizzard and hurled the woman and her child on to the top of the mountain to teach her a lesson. But she was a good woman so the Wood-widgers tried to help her."

The three children opened their eyes and looked at Ninan who grinned again. "That is one story. What about the two of you?" she asked Yara and Yorum.

Yara said, "My story is very different."

"Tell us," encouraged her brother.

"There was an ugly old man who saw the beautiful young woman and wanted to marry her but she said no. She already had a fine husband and a small child. So the ugly old man killed her husband and forced her to climb the mountain with her child. Then he took the child and put him in a cave so the woman couldn't find him when it started to snow." Yara sighed. "What was your story, Yorum?"

"Well, there was a war and the woman's husband was killed. The soldiers burned down her house and she escaped with her child. They followed her to the top of the mountain and would have caught her except the Wood-widgers created

a blizzard so the soldiers couldn't find the woman who was searching for her child. They lost each other in the storm."

"There, you see what I mean? You all heard that the woman was on the mountain but you each have different stories as to how she got there. I think this is magic." The three children looked at each other, wonder in their eyes. Ninan added, "I may never have children of my own but I am giving birth to storytellers."

Ethan said, "We are too little to be storytellers."

Ninan shook her head. "No one is too little to be a storyteller."

Yorum asked, "When did you first tell stories?"

"I remember when I was a small girl, helping my mother. I would be mending clothing or chopping vegetables or washing dishes and feel a strange tightness in my throat and chest and stomach that seemed to come from nowhere. My mother would ask if something was wrong and I would not know how to answer her. But soon, I would find myself telling her a story. Sometimes it would start with something that had happened that day. Or with a dream. Or an image I saw in my mind. Sometimes it was something I felt, like someone else's story wanting to be told. I never planned what to say, the words just came out of my mouth. Perhaps my parents were right. Perhaps I have been a storyteller for a long time and did not know it."

"Will you tell us another story tomorrow evening?"

Ninan shook her head. "I need to leave."

Yara reminded her, "But you said you would tell stories as long as there was someone to listen to them. We want to hear your stories. Please stay . . ."

"In truth, I did not know that I would be leaving tomorrow morning before I told the story," said Ninan, brushing a lock of hair from the girl's eyes.

"I do not understand," Ethan sighed, "but I liked your story very much. I wish you would stay with us, at least for a few more days."

Ninan felt the children's sadness yet she knew it was time to say goodbye. She saw how reluctant the three children were to leave and tried to help them. "I have learned that it is only difficult to leave when you think you will never see the person ever again. But I travel in spirals and circles. We will see each other again. You have my word."

Yara ran to the edge of the commons and picked Ninan a bouquet of wild flowers. Her brother reached into his pocket and gave her a stone that had been

sharpened on one edge. "You can use this to cut branches for your fire."

Ethan said, "I have nothing to give you but I will remember your story. And our stories. I think I would like to tell stories." He grinned. "I will have a story for you when you return."

"I look forward to hearing it," said Ninan, enjoying the sparkle in his eyes.

"I too will have a story to tell you," countered Yara.

"Me too," added Yorum.

"Then we shall be very busy when I return," laughed Ninan.

Reluctantly, the children left, waving to her as they looked back. She watched and waved until they disappeared. Ninan went to her campsite and made herself a comfortable place to sleep, delighting in the sound of the gurgling stream.

SIXTEEN
A WOMAN WALKING

he next morning, Ninan saw Yara's flowers, still fresh and beautiful. She decided to weave them into the basket Taya had started. As she wove the bouquet into the reeds, she thought about the story. Like Noli, the twins, and Sele, she had had her own demons to deal with, and yet she had stayed true to herself and her stories. She had no doubt there would always be demons, testing her convictions, but for the moment all was well. She basked in the joy of having told a powerful story, well received by those who had listened attentively.

After bathing in the stream, she packed up her belongings and left, feeling content rather than upset. Although she still found it difficult to say goodbye to people after telling them a story, she believed what she told the children: she would return. Rather than worrying about when or how she might see them again, she found herself looking forward to hearing their new stories. She walked at a brisk pace, invigorated by the cool morning air and the feeling that she really was a storyteller.

Intrigued by the chirping of a bird overhead, Ninan tripped, feeling a sharp pain in her foot. "Ouch!" She sat down and took a large stone out of her sandal. Holding the stone in her hand, she felt an ache in her heart. "I will not think about Mikos," she told the bird settled on a branch overhead. "He is not like Kurro. He says one thing and does another." The bird sang merrily and Ninan laughed. "You are right. I will think about how many stories Komas will want to hear in exchange for making me a new pair of shoes. Maybe I will think about how big baby Ninan will be when I next see her. Perhaps she will have a brother or sister. Or, I will think about seeing Mima and Amina, holding my shawl and grandfather's book, and looking at them with new eyes."

Ninan understood that even if she could not tell the stories in her
grandfather's book they had nourished her and helped her find a way into her own
stories. She took out a large piece of bread and watched the bird swoop down and
gobble a crumb off the ground. "Are you hungry? Would you like some more?"
She put bits of crushed bread in the palm of her hand and held it out, waiting,
wondering if the bird would dare to come so close. The bird chirped and swooped,
swooped and chirped. Ninan held her hand steady. The bird came closer. "You can
do it," she urged. The bird came nearer still. "Three more steps, little one. A feast
is waiting." The bird looked at Ninan who nodded imperceptibly, hoping that the
bird had the courage to keep moving. Slowly, the bird walked up to her hand, on
to her fingers and then, with a wild swoop, grabbed a piece of bread and flew off.
"Well done, little bird. Enjoy your bravery."

Ninan stopped for lunch in a place shaded from the sun by tall trees and
took pleasure in resting on the soft pine-needled ground, lulled by the sound of
a roiling stream. She thought about the way she had left her village, the anguish,
resentment, fear, and anxiety she had felt, the difficulties she had experienced as she
found the way to be her own kind of storyteller. She remembered the certainty and
confidence of her parents when they told her she was a storyteller, the gravity with
which they had given her the shawl and her grandfather's book of stories. She felt an
urge to tell her parents they were right, that she had become what they had known
she was, a storyteller. As she walked she began telling a story for her parents, her
brothers, her grandparents—and herself.

nce upon a time there lived a young girl who wanted nothing
more than to grow up like all the other girls in the village,
marry a handsome young man, have children, and live the life
her parents had lived. She could not imagine any other life for
this was all she knew.

But her parents, who were older than most, had buried
many children and known times of war and devastation, drought and famine.
They wanted more for their daughter than she wanted for herself. Unbeknownst
to the girl, her parents had been keeping a secret from her until they were
absolutely sure that she was ready to learn it.

One night, during a ferocious storm, when it seemed as if the wind and

the rain and the thunder and lightning would never stop, the mother lit many
candles to brighten the room. The father made a fire, larger than usual, to warm
the room. The daughter was puzzled. This was the time they always went to bed.
The mother brought out a freshly baked cake on the silver tray she had inherited
from her mother. The father poured wine into three glasses he had inherited from
his mother. "Come, daughter, sit by the fire," said her mother."

"We have something to tell you," said her father.

More bewildered than ever, the girl did as she was told. After they had
eaten the cake and sipped the wine, her father spoke, warmed by the loving looks
from his wife. "You are the granddaughter of a famous storyteller. He traveled
far and wide, telling the stories of our people, giving them hope and courage,
knowledge, and wisdom from the ages. He had a gift for listening, hearing what
people could not speak. He gave voice to their stories."

Her mother continued. "Ever since you were a little girl, you would tell us
what you had seen and heard and done. Sometimes you would tell a story that
you said came from nowhere, from a place you could not name."

"Yes," said her father. "That was what you thought. But we knew better.
The stories came from the spirit of your grandfather. He knew that you were
born a storyteller just as he had been."

"I am a storyteller?" questioned the girl. "I think you are mistaken. Stories
are about important people like the mayor. What I tell, if they are stories, are
about the life I see around me."

Her parents spoke more sharply than was their wont. "Everyone is
important," said her mother.

"Everyone's stories matter," added her father.

The girl felt bewildered. Her parents had never spoken to her so harshly
yet it was as if neither noticed their changed tone of voice.

The mother cut each of them another slice of the cake. The father poured
more wine into their glasses. They listened to the crackle and sizzle of the fire,
watching the flames dance. The parents were comforted by the sense of peace
inside the house while the storm raged outside. The girl paced the small room,
wishing she could run to her special place high up on the mountain where she did
her best thinking, where she felt most herself.

"Sit, down, my dear," said her mother.

"We have something to show you," said her father.

The girl did as she was told, troubled by an unfamiliar sense of danger and excitement. She watched her father open a locked chest that was covered with a blanket woven by her mother. He gave her a book and a shawl unlike any she had ever seen. It was made of coarse wool, dyed blue, with fringes. He gently draped it over her shoulders then he put the book in her hand. "These belonged to your grandparents. We have kept them for you until you were ready to receive them."

The girl brushed the shawl with her fingers, feeling them tingle. She caressed the old book, wondering what was inside. "Why are you giving them to me?" she asked.

"Because they belong to you. Just as your mother inherited the silver tray and I inherited the wine glasses, you have inherited this book and shawl and the storytelling spirit of your grandfather. When you are lonely or troubled or joyful, think of your grandparents, your parents, and your brothers. We are always with you in spirit. This is the way it was, is, and always shall be."

Although the girl was filled with doubts and questions, she did not know what to say or ask. Perhaps her parents knew her better than she knew herself. The next morning her mother gave her a basket filled with food. Her father gave her a warm coat made from the sheep he raised. After breakfast, with tears in their eyes, they walked her to the edge of town.

"It is time for you to leave, daughter," said her mother.

"It is time for you to find your way, storyteller," said her father.

And so the girl started walking on the path that led out of the village, carrying with her the blessings of her parents, their love and hopes, into the beginning of her new life, telling the stories of her people.

Mima's voice came to her, so loud and clear she turned around, even though she knew she was alone. "Well done, dear one, enjoy your gift."

The voices have changed, thought Ninan, amazed by the discovery.

With a smile on her face, warmed by the sun, she began walking. Although Ninan was still not sure which path to take, she was sure that whichever one she chose would be the right one. She was a woman walking.

ACKNOWLEDGMENTS

Years ago, David Hart told me that when I felt a certain kind of pressure in my head, something wanted to come out. He said that when this happened I needed to go to my desk and start writing. Although I initially resisted, he was right. His certainty and encouragement continue to be gifts beyond measure.

I thank friends in England, Sweden, and the United States for reading chapters and convincing me that I was writing a novel.

I wish to thank Maureen Burdock, Cinny Green, and Doug Bullis for their talent and support in transforming the manuscript into a book.

Claudia Reder, Diana Wolff, Anita Grunbaum, Karin Gustafsson, and Maria Thaddeus play a special role in my life. They know what it is.

Nancy King, PhD, Union Institute and University, has told stories and conducted storymaking workshops throughout the USA, Scandinavia, the UK, Canada, Mexico, and Hungary. Her latest books include: *Dancing With Wonder: Self-Discovery Through Stories* and a novel, *Morning Light*. An active member of PEN USA, she writes, weaves, and lives in Santa Fe, NM. Please visit: www.nancykingstories.com for further information.

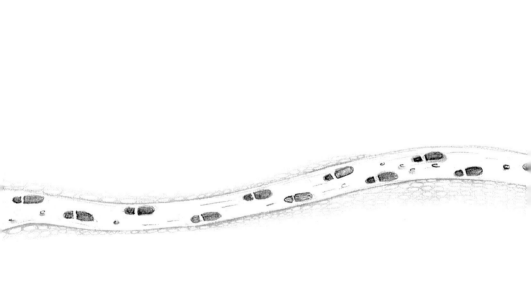

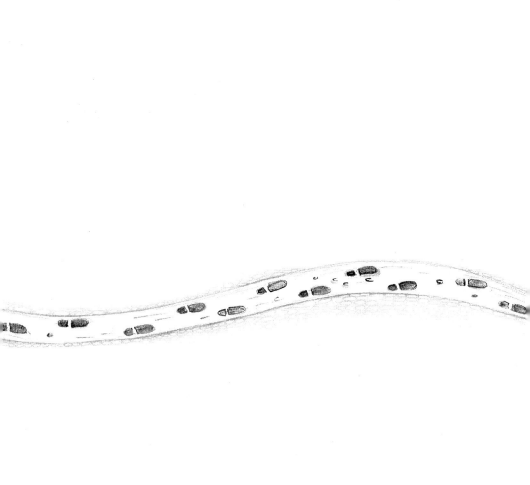

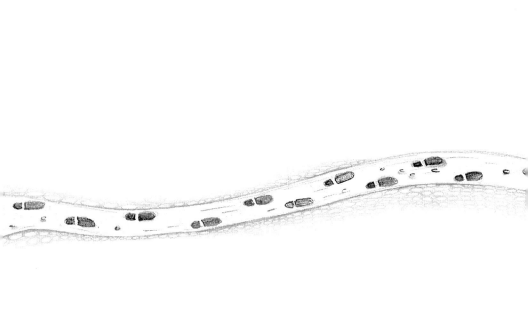

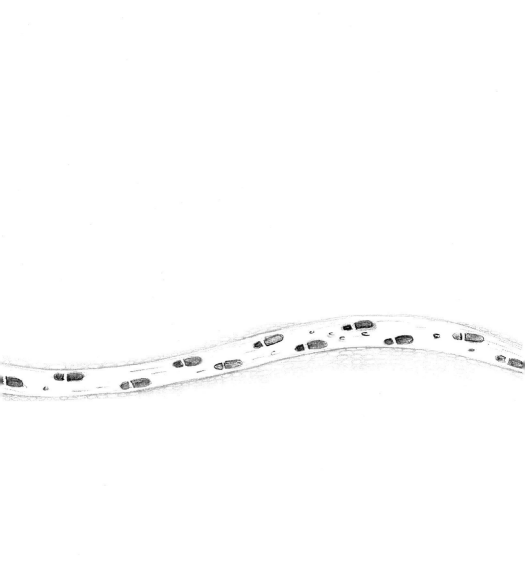

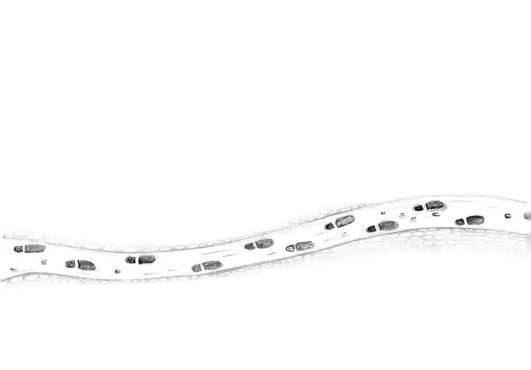